CW00517995

CHRISTMAS WITH THE LORDS

HANNAH LANGDON

Storm
PUBLISHING

This is a work of fiction. Names, characters, business, events and incidents are the products of the author's imagination. Any resemblance to actual persons, living or dead, or actual events is purely coincidental.

Copyright © Hannah Langdon, 2023

The moral right of the author has been asserted.

All rights reserved. No part of this book may be reproduced or used in any manner without the prior written permission of the copyright owner.

To request permissions, contact the publisher at rights@stormpublishing.co

Ebook ISBN: 978-1-80508-279-8
Paperback ISBN: 978-1-80508-281-1

Cover design: Eileen Carey
Cover images: iStock, Shutterstock

Published by Storm Publishing.
For further information, visit:
www.stormpublishing.co

For John and Rose
'To every thing there is a season'

ONE

When I stepped off the train, a wave of Christmas cheer washed over me despite feeling worried about the way I'd decided to spend the next few weeks. It was much colder here in Dorset than it had been in London, and in the weak afternoon sunlight frost sparkled on the bushes and my breath puffed out in smoky clouds. I piled my suitcases into the waiting taxi and pressed my nose against the cold glass as we drove through pretty villages, their decorations up and festooned trees standing in every window. As we paused at traffic lights outside a church, I saw a group of carol singers, muffled up against the cold in scarves and hats, and quickly wound my window down so that I could hear a snatch of their music before we drove on. It was one of my favourites, and I joined in softly as they sang:

'*O little town of Bethlehem, how still we see thee lie.*

Above thy deep and dreamless sleep, the silent stars go by...'

'Looking forward to Christmas, are you?' enquired my driver.

'Oh yes, I love it. Do you think we'll get snow down here?'

She shrugged.

'We often do, so you might be in luck. Staying with the Lords, are you? Up at the house?'

'I'm working for Bunny – helping to look after her twins.'

'Ah, of course, they'll be up for Christmas as usual. Well, you'll certainly be busy.'

I didn't want to gossip about my new employers, but I couldn't help asking: 'Are they... nice?'

She laughed.

'You'll have a memorable time with them, that's all I'll say.'

I didn't have time to ask her what she meant, because we were pulling up on a sweeping gravel driveway outside an enormous house, disturbing three or four large crows who cawed loudly as they flew to perch in the branches of a grand oak tree, stripped now of its leaves. Frost iced the holly trees that grew to one side of the drive, their red berries glowing through the sprinkling of wintry glitter. Opposite them a rather overgrown yew hedge, also dusted with white, ran alongside a small stream, still bravely flowing despite the cold day. A pair of mallards snuggled together beside it on a mossy stone ledge, their feathers fluffed up, and – alighting from the taxi – I rummaged in my bag for some leftover oat biscuits to share with them. A rustling drew my attention away from the ducks, and I turned slowly to see the russet face and bright, black eyes of a fox watching me from a gap in the hedge.

'Hello, Fox,' I said softly. It retreated a step or two but didn't run away. 'Are you hungry too? Let me see what else I've got.' I looked again and found half a cheese sandwich, which I threw in its direction. The fox sniffed it suspiciously, then picked it up delicately, glanced at me and turned, disappearing into the dense woodland behind. I wondered what other animals I would see if I waited long enough – a hare, maybe – but turned my attention back to the house.

I stared up at its imposing stone chimneys and asymmetric gabled roofs, silhouetted against the pale sky and jewelled with icicles, and wondered how many bedrooms it had. Eight at least, surely? Lights shone warmly in two of the windows and someone had strung fairy lights in another. They twinkled gently into the chilly day, invitingly festive. An extravagant wreath hung from the front door, made from the evergreens growing around the house and finished off with an enormous red velvet bow and – I peered a little closer – yes, a couple of plastic Bluey figurines placed incongruously amongst the foliage, surely the work of the twins I was going to look after. It couldn't be any more different from my neat, two-bedroomed newbuild with its astroturfed postage stamp of a front lawn and white uPVC porch. The elegance of the house was only slightly marred by a giant inflatable chimney next to the door, out of which a wheezing, blow-up Father Christmas emerged arthritically every minute or so. He wobbled, lopsided, for a few moments before descending again with what looked to me distinctly like relief. I could relate to that. All I wanted to do was crawl under my duvet away from all society with some high-sugar, high-carb snacks and try to numb the pain not only of Timothy's desertion, but of a wasted decade, waiting for something that would never happen. But here I was, so I had better get on with it.

Until now, I had led a sensible life and I never made rash decisions. But when Timothy ended things, I found myself with three of them under my belt in as many days. Hard-working and well-behaved, I had made my way through school and a teaching degree without causing many ripples in my own life or anyone else's. I wore sensible clothes, ate sensible food and read sensible books. Now and again, I explored sensible hobbies such as quilting and fell-walking. I had been in my sensible teaching job for fifteen years and lived in a sensible house in a sensible town at a sensible distance from London. I had a sensible relationship with Timothy, who was a sensible man. Or so I had thought. Timothy and I had been together for ten long, sensible years. We had, very sensibly, delayed marriage and children until everything was just so. I kept an eye on my age with increasing panic but, even at nearly thirty-eight, didn't pressurise Timothy. Everyone knows that is not a sensible thing to do. Then one day, nevertheless, Timothy sat me down and told me he was leaving me. He was, he said, very sensibly doing this before December 1st, as everyone knows that December is proposal month, and he didn't want me to get my hopes up... again. When Timothy left, taking the only items of his own he had ever left at my house – his second-best toothbrush and a cheap coffee machine – I contemplated the empty spaces in the bathroom, on the kitchen worktop, on the fourth finger of my left hand and in my womb. Then I realised that the empty space in my heart was no bigger for Timothy's desertion. I reflected that this was, on balance, a good thing. I knew, now, that he had led me on – not for a month or two but for ten years. And I had let him. And that is when I decided to stop being sensible.

Decision Number One: I will never get involved with a man, ever again.

This was not a sensible decision for a woman who longed for love and for babies, particularly a woman careering towards forty at breakneck speed. But how could I? How could I trust myself, let alone a man? My ability to judge them was clearly woefully inadequate. I had wasted ten years of my precious life waiting for a man, and I wasn't going to waste a second more. The ache for love would wane. Given time. Wouldn't it?

Decision Number Two: I will hand in my notice after Christmas and move to India.

I loved my job. Correction: I loved the children I taught, but the job itself? Meh. The only reason I had stayed so long was because I thought – believed – that Timothy would propose at any moment and soon I would be knee-deep in white tulle, swiftly followed by nappies. Now *that* wasn't happening, I didn't want to stay a moment longer. I certainly didn't want my colleagues' prurient sympathy, and the best way to avoid that was to give them something else to talk about. So, I decided that I would move to India and get a teaching job there, starting at the beginning of the school year there: May. This was not as reckless as it sounds. My parents had moved there six months previously, and I missed them. At their leaving party, my mother, prescient as ever, had looked askew at Timothy, who she thought was boring, and suggested I look at the 'International Jobs' section of the *Times* Educational Supplement.

Decision Number Three: I will spend Christmas living with and working for people I have never met in a place I have never visited.

This opportunity came about by luck, when a friend posted about a family she knew in dire need of a 'mother's help' over the Christmas break – all of the three weeks holiday I got. I would, naturally, normally have scrolled past, but that day I leapt on it with a haste fuelled by panic that someone else had got there first. This was what I needed to keep me busy and my mind off Timothy. Well, off the subject of my own craven stupidity in staying with him, which I beat myself up about throughout each day. I could be useful, earn some money and spend my spare time composing my resignation letter, to be handed in on the first day of the spring term.

As soon as I had seen the Facebook post, I messaged my friend and said I was interested in the job. Not usually that bothered by social media, I refreshed the app obsessively for the next twenty minutes, until a message pinged back with the phone number for the Lords. I rang immediately.

'Hello?'

'Hello, may I speak to Mrs Lord please?' There was a loud crash. 'Um... hello? Hello?'

All I could hear now was someone shrieking 'put it down, put it down!' and some muffled swearing. And then a breathless voice:

'Hello, sorry about that. Don't ever have twins. Yes, I'm Mrs Lord, although that makes me sound like a particularly devoted Sunday school teacher. Call me Bunny, everyone does.'

'Er, all right, hello Bunny. Joanne said that you were looking for some help over Christmas?'

'And you have been sent from Heaven to save us! Oops, touch of the Sunday school teacher there again. Yes, I am desperately in need of help. Lovely Joanne said that you would call, she said you were the *perfect* solution – wonderful with children and so *calm*. You used to work together?'

'Yes, that's right, we were teachers at the same school until a year or so ago. I can send you references and my DBS. I can cook a bit as well—'

Bunny interrupted me with a shriek of joy.

'Splendid! Yes, send all that and then can you come on Monday 13th December? Everyone breaks up on the Friday, so we'll travel down over the weekend sometime.'

'Sorry, travel down?'

'Yes, didn't Joanne mention it? I suppose she didn't know, come to think of it. Anyway, we spend Christmas with my husband's brother down in Dorset, that's why we need the help. He's a frightful bore, won't leave his bloody studio to come to London, so he invites everyone down, then gets cross when we make a noise.'

I felt slightly faint.

'Everyone? Joanne just said about the twins. They're four years old, aren't they?'

'That's right, although it feels like they've been around forever. In a *good* way, of course. And half the family rolls up usually. I'm not sure who it is this year, but there'll be simply piles of us and of course William – Ben and Lando's father – lives there too. Don't worry, you'll have your own room and bathroom, and you won't have to deal with any of them. Oh, do say you'll come, please!'

We spent a few minutes discussing exactly what the job would entail – mainly childcare, as I had expected, with ad hoc 'helping me with other bits and pieces when I'm absolutely *frantic*' as Bunny put it – and the pay, which seemed generous, especially considering I would also get full bed and board. Despite these rather good terms, between the hundreds of relatives, the wild-sounding twins, and the tyrannical brother-in-law, it didn't sound like a remotely sensible situation to walk into over Christmas.

'Yes, of course I'll come. Let me know the address, and if you're happy with my references and so on, I'll come down on the 13th.'

'Oh, thank you, thank you. Oh! What's your name?'

I hesitated. The children at school call me Miss Windlesham, but that clearly wasn't going to be the scene in Bunny's family.

'Well, my name is Penelope, but everyone calls me Penny.'

'Lovely! See you on the 13th then, Penny.'

With a touch of Maria von Trapp about me, I hummed 'I Have Confidence' as I stepped up to the door and lifted the heavy knocker. The resulting bang could be heard reverberating through the hall beyond, but there was no answering patter of feet, and the door remained firmly shut. I knocked again, but still no one appeared. Then a scrabbling sound on the gravel made me turn; running towards me grinning and with lolling tongues, their breath puffing clouds into the cold air, were two dogs. One, a small smooth-haired dachshund with an absurdly friendly face and the other a larger dog of indeterminate breed, which skidded to a halt next to me and immediately shoved its cold, wet nose into my hand. I crouched down and stroked the dogs, who responded as ecstatically as if they had won the doggy lottery. I was encouraged by this display of approval.

'Hello lovely dogs, what are your names then?' No answer was forthcoming. 'Ah, tags, let me have a look.' I checked the dachshund first. 'Garbo, that's a great name! And how about you?' I ruffled the bigger dog's fur as I read its name: Hepburn. 'And is your master or mistress around anywhere?' Again, the dogs offered no response other than to roll over and nudge my hands insistently, oblivious to anything other than their own pleasure. Quite right, but I really felt I should find someone and announce myself, so I fussed over them for a few more minutes, then stood up.

'Come on, you two, maybe you can help me?'

They bounded off around the side of the house and out of sight, so I decided I might as well follow. Leaving my bags at the side of the door, I crunched off over the gravel, resisting the urge to peep in through the stone-mullioned windows with their tiny diamond-shaped panes of glass. When I turned the corner, I was met with a glorious view, even in the fading daylight: huge lawned gardens dotted with gnarled trees, currently without any leaves, spread in front of me. To my left, there was a walled garden with its gate open. Telling myself I might find someone there, but really just consumed with curiosity, I went over and peered through. Within the walls were more lawns, paths and artfully arranged box trees, all leading to an oval swimming pool, covered now of course but nonetheless impressive. Sadly, this place, too, was deserted, so I turned and noticed, across the lawn, a red brick outbuilding with steam pouring from the boiler outlet. This was more promising, and I hoped I would find Bunny there, although I did feel some trepidation. After all, I had come all the way to Dorset, to the house of complete strangers, and now the place appeared deserted with no one even to open the door, let alone welcome me. I hoped I hadn't made a huge mistake: what had felt like a daring adventure could easily turn out to be a foolhardy flop. I pulled out my phone to comfort myself with a timetable of trains back to London, just so that I knew I could turn tail if I needed to, but there was no reception. I put it back in my pocket with a sigh. There was nothing for it but to square my shoulders and keep going, although my earlier feelings of confidence were rapidly ebbing away.

I trotted across the cold grass, my shoes leaving prints in its pristine frosting, and pushed open the door of the little building. It opened into a single, large room, lined with shelves which groaned under their burden of lumps of wood, books and a cornucopia of tools. There was more wood everywhere you looked: stumps, planks and what appeared to be half a tree, which stood next to an unmade double bed and had a mug balanced on top of it. The floor was liberally sprinkled with shavings, and I could see the motes of dust floating around in the pale sunlight that streamed in through the enormous windows which had all but replaced the wall at the far end of the building. A wide workbench stood in front of the windows, and I could see carved figures in various stages of completion. There was a comforting smell of freshly cut timber, and the room was warm and cosy. I was beginning to entertain thoughts of a gentle, Geppetto-like fellow living and working here, at one with his craft, when a door I hadn't noticed at the far end of the room flung open and a man appeared. Geppetto he wasn't. Tall and extremely good-looking, with ruffled dark hair, he stopped dead when he saw me, and glared.

'Who are you?'

'Hi, I'm Penny. I'm Bunny's mother's help?'

I stumbled forward, trying not to skid on the wood shavings, and offered my hand. He took it briefly in his, which felt dusty and was covered in scars and marks old and new; from the wood carving tools, I supposed.

'Oh yes, she said she was expecting you. Well, where on earth is she?'

I wasn't sure if he was expecting an answer, but just then the door was pushed open and in bounded the dogs.

'Garbo! Hepburn! Good to see you again.' I crouched down, thankful for this distraction, and scratched and patted their delighted, wriggling bodies.

'How do you know my dogs' names?'

I looked up, up the long, jeaned legs and slim torso in its worn work shirt until my eyes reached that gorgeous face, which seemed fractionally less annoyed than before.

'Oh, they have tags, and, well... they're the only ones who have greeted me so far. They're lovely dogs. But I did want to ask – Audrey or Katharine?'

A flicker of confusion touched his face before being replaced by a microscopic upturn of the lips.

'Katharine. No contest.'

I returned to the dogs. The dachshund, Garbo, had now clambered up onto my shoulders and seemed to be attempting to fashion herself as a living stole. I tried to steady her, worried she would topple off, when a pair of strong hands scooped her up.

'Sorry, she can be rather overfamiliar.' The man draped her over his shoulders where she settled contentedly, giving his ear the odd lick, and went to sit at his workbench. Hepburn followed and curled up in a basket near his feet.

'Look, I need to get back to work. There should be someone at the house; why don't you try again, and if you really have no luck, then I suppose I can come and let you in?'

What a rude man, I thought, and mentally patted myself on the back for my decision not to get romantically involved with anyone again. Handsome he may be, but that was obviously the beginning and the end of his charms.

'Right. Well, thanks. I'll do that.'

I turned to go when the door flew open and in blew a woman. She was tall and very slim with wavy, honey-coloured hair that must have cost a fortune to maintain. She was dressed in neutral tones – tailored caramel trousers, conker-shiny pointed boots, and a chunky yet close-fitting ivory sweater. A waft of Chanel reached my nose as she flung her arms out towards me.

'Oh! Are you Penny?'

I nodded and she hugged me warmly.

'Oh, how marvellous to see you, thank you *so* much for coming, what utter bliss. I'm Bunny. It's all completely hopeless; I'm trying to work, Ben is still up in London, Pilar had to go shopping, William is spending *far* more time than I would have thought was necessary down at the grotto and now my dreadful children have vanished.'

I had no idea who any of the people were that she was talking about, but it was the final comment that caught my attention.

'Children? Vanished?'

'Yes, my twins. Seraphina and Caspian. I can't find them anywhere – I did hope they might be in here. You haven't seen them, have you, Lando darling?'

The man at the workbench shook his head.

'No, I'm sorry, Bunny, they've not been in here. They won't have gone far. Didn't you find them raiding Dad's Christmas sherry last time?'

'I did! It was hilarious, Penny. Two tiddly twins!'

Lando raised an eyebrow. 'Let's at least hope they're sober this time, with nothing missing.'

Bunny waved an airy hand. 'Yes, well, the fingertip has nearly grown back. Isn't nature wonderful?'

'Well, I'm sure that Penny will help you look. Now, I have to get on with my work.'

He picked up a chisel and turned his back on us. I stood there awkwardly, feeling both piqued at this summary dismissal but also a gnawing anxiety. Did I really want to spend Christmas like this? I was, after all, essentially their servant for the season, and maybe they were the type of family that would expect me to 'know my place'. I was used to being in charge of my own classroom; I suddenly wasn't so sure that this had been a wise idea. Bunny's voice broke through my thoughts.

'Come on, darling Penny, we won't get anything else out of Lando for a while, we'll just have to forge on alone.'

I was still reeling from my worries and from the image of drunken children with severed body parts when she tucked her arm through mine and swept me out of the studio and back into the cold garden.

'It's so lovely to meet you,' continued Bunny. 'You arrived at the *perfect* moment. I *do* hope that you'll feel at home here.' I was starting to nod my slightly shaky acquiescence when she let out a cry, making me jump. 'Oh! I've thought of the *ideal* way to make you feel like one of the family straight away. A nickname!' She clapped her hands with joy at this idea and carried on before I had a chance to speak. 'But what could it *be*? I suppose Penny is short for Penelope already, and it's very nice, but what about something more *fun*? I've always liked 'Bunny', much better than the sensible name I was given when I was born.'

'What was it?' I asked.

'Belinda. All right, I suppose, but my parents started the whole Bunny thing and it stuck. We called my brother Xander Newt for years, but that eventually wore off.'

I giggled, despite myself. 'Maybe you should pick it up again?'

She let out a peal of laughter.

'Maybe I should. Oh, I know!' I looked at her apprehensively. 'How about Pixie? Oh yes, it's adorable, the children will love it and it does rather suit you. Oh, may I call you Pixie?'

I was stunned by this excited outpouring but also undeniably flattered. It *did* make me feel included and, what's more, it wouldn't be remotely sensible to go around being called Pixie, which fit in beautifully with the Grand Plan. Timothy would have a heart attack if he were here.

'Pixie,' I said, trying it out. 'Pixie... I love it!'

'I'm so glad! Now, we must find those children. Of course, the problem is that this house and the grounds are so massive, it's easy for them to lose themselves. Where to start?'

Time to prove my sensible credentials, however shaky they currently felt.

'Okay, well, where did you last see them?'

I was doubtful any four-year-old would have remained in the same place for this long, but it was a start.

'I was trying to get some work done in the little office downstairs – I design greetings cards and personalised wall art so you can imagine how frightfully busy I am at the moment putting the finishing touches to Christmas commissions – and they were playing in the passage outside. I suddenly realised it had gone quiet, but I don't know how long that had been. I do get very absorbed, you see.'

'Let's start there.'

We strode back to the house, calling the twins' names, and Bunny led me in through a back door to a tiled boot room. It was about the size of my living room, lined with shelves and cabinets which were only sparsely populated with a few coats and items of footwear.

'Lando hardly uses this, such a shame, but he's always holed up in that studio, whittling away.'

'This is his house?'

'Yes, oh dear, didn't he introduce himself? I don't know why I'm surprised, he can be tricky, especially when he's working. Yes, that's my brother-in-law. It's his house, but you'd hardly know it. He only really sleeps and eats here, such a waste. Oh well, I suppose it won't be for much longer.'

With no further explanation, she led the way out of the room into a thickly carpeted passageway with a couple of closed doors, which we passed by. Turning a corner, the corridor ended with a narrow, twisting staircase to the left and an open door in front, which I supposed led into Bunny's workspace, as the floor outside was strewn with Lego.

'This was their last sighting,' she announced. 'Oh, I do hope they're all right.'

We stood helplessly by the colourful bricks, and I gazed up and down the corridor, hopeful that they might have left some sort of breadcrumb trail of bright plastic. No such luck. I was just about to suggest we tried their bedroom when I thought I heard something. Probably just the central heating, but there was a chance my luck was in.

'Bunny, did you hear that?'

We listened again and were rewarded by the sound of a little giggle, coming from the staircase.

TWO

'Oh Pixie, you are clever, they hadn't gone very far at all.' Bunny clapped her hands in delight. 'Phina! Caspy! We're coming to *find* you.'

I let out the breath I didn't even realise I'd been holding. Not remotely clever, whatever Bunny said, but I wasn't about to argue.

More giggles answered her singsong call, and we started up the little wooden staircase, finding the twins sitting on the small return, surrounded by a sea of colourful tin foil. Seraphina was the image of her mother, with her tumble of messy blonde hair, wide-eyed gaze and ready smile. Caspian was, I supposed, more like his father – Lando's brother. He had brown hair, a sweet snub nose and a generous smattering of freckles. Both were liberally smeared in chocolate. Bunny let out a peal of laughter.

'Oh, just *look* at the two of you. How *did* you find those tree decorations? I thought I'd hidden them brilliantly this year, but you're *too*, too clever.'

Seraphina broke into a matching grin.

'Mummy, you hid them in your wardrobe, of *course* we found them.'

'Of course you did, my darling. Next year I'll have to be even more cunning, won't I?'

Seraphina jumped up to hug her mother, who grabbed her at arm's length before the chocolate could be transferred from the sticky hands and face to her pristine knitwear.

'Cuddles later, gorgeous girl, let's get you both cleaned up first. Oh! And I must introduce you. This is Pixie – she's come to help us out while we get everything ready for Christmas and I finish my work.'

'Hello,' I said. 'It's lovely to meet you both. Do you always have chocolate for lunch? Maybe I should try it?'

Seraphina giggled, but Caspian regarded me solemnly.

'It's not a good idea to have it for lunch *every* day, you know.'

I matched his seriousness and nodded.

'No, you're right. Perhaps I will save it for special occasions.' I glanced at Bunny, unsure if I should take charge with her there. She smiled benevolently back at me and took another step away from her daughter's sticky hands. I decided to risk it. 'Come on, shall we tidy up these wrappers, then wash those mucky faces and hands?'

To my immense relief, no one seemed to mind my teacherly tones. We scooped up the foil and Bunny led the way downstairs and back along the corridor, through one of the doors, which led into a small, light-filled hallway. The carpet was a muted sage green and the walls painted in the palest yellow and crowded with framed vintage-style prints of the local area. A delicate console table stood against the wall bearing a huge arrangement of winter stems: spruce, bright red winterberries, eucalyptus and ivy. A glass door led out to the gardens and there was another staircase, which we went up. At the top, Bunny pushed open a door into a bathroom. As we started to usher the twins in, Caspian began crying. *Uh oh.* A sudden meltdown after a tummyful of chocolate means, in my experience, one thing. I felt a rush of panic as I tried to steer, rather than shove, the sobbing child into the bathroom.

'Quickly, Caspian, quickly, in you go—'

I was too late. He leant forward and vomited lavishly, all down himself and across that beautiful carpet. There was a moment's silence, of respect, perhaps, for the expensive décor, which may never be the same again. Then the sobbing started in earnest. Caspian started and Seraphina soon joined in, wailing as if her heart was breaking. Bunny was at a loss, staring between the brown pool on the floor and her distraught children in horror and confusion. I did wonder if she might also begin crying.

'Oh, Pixie! Oh God, what do we do, what do we *do*?'

For a moment I, too, felt completely overwhelmed. The chocolatey puke was gently soaking into the carpet and would be almost impossible to remove. I was used to scraping sick off the vinyl floor of the classroom, but this was completely different. I also feared it was only a matter of time before Caspian was sick again, or Seraphina started. Bunny looked horribly pale, and I wasn't entirely confident that she wouldn't join in – the smell can have that effect. Then I realised that they were all looking at me to sort things out, and I knew it was time to start doing the work I had been employed for or giving it my best shot at any rate.

'Okay, nothing to worry about. Come on, into the bathroom, and let's peel off these sicky things and get you both clean.'

The children allowed me to steer them into the bathroom, a stunning affair in cream marble with thick forest green towels, recessed lighting and the delicate scent of lily-of-the-valley in the air. Pulling the soft, heavy bathmat onto the floor, I jammed in the plug and started the water running. I spotted a bottle of something that was probably very expensive and wasted on four-year-olds, but grabbed it and dolloped in a generous measure, knowing the magical effect that bubbles can have. I hoped no one would mind too much. Bunny didn't even seem to notice; she was still wringing her hands and patting the twins ineffectually as they cried, clearly worried about soiling her beautiful clothes. I didn't hugely want to get vomit on my clothes either, but my drip-dry high street bargains had been bought with small children in mind, so now I held my breath, swiftly stripped each child, then plopped them into the steamy, bubbly water. The foam was extravagant, probably about thirty quid's worth, and instantly they were enchanted. Within seconds, Seraphina had fashioned herself a frothy beard and was cackling with laughter at her reflection in the overflow cover and Caspian, whose colour had returned from a greenish grey to a healthier pinkish hue, was blowing holes in the foam to make skull faces. Bunny sank down onto the lid of the loo and looked rather pale herself.

'Well done, Pixie darling, you are marvellously efficient, I'm so happy you're here. But what about the carpet?'

'Yes, the carpet doesn't look good, does it? Would it be all right for you to stay with the twins while I try and sort it out?'

She nodded weakly.

'Great. Where can I find some cleaning stuff?'

She gave me directions to the kitchen, and I set off, back down the stairs, round the corner, through a large but cosy living room and into the front hall of the house, which was galleried and wood-panelled, with the same lovely green carpet that seemed to flow through the whole house like a gentle brook. Other than the bit upstairs now, of course. I crossed the hall and pushed open a door at the back which led, as Bunny had said, into a large kitchen. It looked as if it had been recently kitted out at great expense, yet it retained a cosy, countryside feel as the heart of the home. A small woman with short, dark hair was standing by the Aga and turned as I came in.

'Hello?' she said in a heavy accent. 'Who are you?'

For the second time that day, I identified myself rather breathlessly.

'Hi, I'm Penny, I've come to help with the children? The thing is, Caspian has been dreadfully sick all over the carpet and it needs to be cleaned as soon as possible.' I didn't add that I felt I had no hope whatsoever of doing anything of the sort.

The woman sighed theatrically and started putting lids on pans and adjusting dials.

'*Vale*, I suppose this can wait, but Bunny! *Dios mío*, always the help she needs so much. I am supposed only to cook, clean a little, you know, but every day something extra.'

'Oh! No, no, I didn't come to ask *you* to do it. If you would be kind enough to show me where a few things are, I'll try to fix it.'

Hopefully. I dreaded to think what Lando would say if I couldn't get the chocolate stains out of his immaculate carpet. He was obviously extremely houseproud, judging by the luxurious interior design, although looking at his messy studio, you would never have guessed it.

'*Muy bien*, what do you need? Oh, and I am Pilar. I am *very* happy to meet you, Penny.'

She shook my hand firmly.

'So am I. Er, I'm not really sure what I need. It's mostly chocolate, you see, and on a pale carpet – oh God, it's probably wool, isn't it? I'll *never* get it out.'

'Penny, did you vomit on it yourself?'

I looked up at her in surprise.

'No, of course not.'

'Then do not worry so much. You will do your best, yes, and that will have to be good enough. Mrs Lord, she should not have left them stuffing themselves with so much chocolate. Come, let me find you some things.'

I staggered back through the house under the weight of buckets – one filled with hot water, one empty – a spatula, a fat roll of kitchen paper, washing-up liquid, vinegar, a giant tub of bicarb and a cordless stick vacuum cleaner. Mrs Mop, eat your heart out; I looked like some kind of crazy cleaning one-man-band. All I needed were some cymbals tied to my knees to complete the outfit. I reached the back hallway again and shuf-fled through awkwardly, sideways, trying not to splash water or knock over the flower arrangement with the hoover when the back door opened and in walked Lando. He regarded me with a mix of curiosity, irritation and maybe, just maybe, a smidgen of humour on his handsome face.

'What on earth is going on? Where are you going with all those things?'

What did he think I was doing, robbing the place? I gathered as much dignity as I could muster.

'There has been a slight... incident with the twins. Every-one's fine, but I need to clean up.'

'At least you found them. Was there much blood?'

I smiled hesitantly. 'No blood at all. That must be consid-ered a win?'

'With those two, definitely. Dare I ask what happened?'

'I think it's best you don't. I'll do my best to rescue your beautiful carpet, though.'

He shrugged.

'It's only carpet. Don't worry too much, as long as the chil-dren are okay. See you later then.'

He strode off through the house, and I wasted no more time in clanking up the stairs to start scraping up the sick. Once I had got the worst of it into the empty bucket and dumped on plenty of bicarb, I put my head around the bathroom door to see how the party was going in there. It sounded riotous from outside the door and, indeed, proved to be so inside. The scented foam was now spread around much of the bathroom and the twins had started remodelling their hair into rather limp spikes. Bunny had sunk her head into her hands, but looked up when I came in.

'Oh, Pixie, there you are. How are you getting on?'

'All right, I think. Pilar was wonderful, she helped me find everything I need.'

'Pilar did?'

'Yes, she was really kind.'

'Darling, how on earth do you do it? I find Pilar absolutely *terrifying*. I barely dare ask her for the time, let alone anything else. She fixes me with such a stare and I simply quail. I'm sure the bulls never stood a chance.'

'Bulls?'

'Oh yes, she's Spanish.'

I wasn't quite sure how to respond to this; did Bunny think there were enormous bulls roaming the streets of Spain, which needed to be regularly quelled by the residents? Or maybe Pilar had an exciting past as a matador? Today, nothing would surprise me. I might have asked more, but Bunny looked too drawn and tired to be questioned about such things, so I returned to the landing to inspect my soggy efforts. I was about to wield the spatula when Pilar arrived.

'How are you doing? Is it coming off?'

'Phase one has been successful, and I'm about to start removing the bicarb. It doesn't look as bad as it did, so I'm hopeful.'

'Can I help?'

I lowered my voice.

'Not with this, but if you've got a few moments, Bunny looks exhausted. Maybe you could sit with Phina and Caspy while I carry on out here? I won't be much longer.'

'Sí.'

She went into the bathroom and, within seconds, Bunny had emerged, smiled gratefully and disappeared for a lie-down. The squawks of excitement from the twins stopped abruptly and, peeping in, I could see them being removed from the bath and wrapped in towels. For all Pilar's sternness, she was smiling, and gave each child a hug as she dried them off.

'*Bien*, now run to your room and find your pyjamas. I am following you.'

They scampered past me shouting, 'Look at us, Pixie, we're naked!' as I sponged a mixture of detergent and vinegar into the stain. Pilar followed at a more stately pace.

'Thank you so much,' I said. 'I shouldn't be much longer here and then I'll come and take over.'

'*Ningún problema*. We will be in the kitchen having tea.'

It was there that I found them twenty minutes later, glued to Paw Patrol on a tablet propped up against a jar of jam and eating baked potatoes and beans. It never fails to amaze me how quickly children recover; I wouldn't be gobbling down supper so soon after being violently sick. They looked adorable in their pyjamas: Phina's were orange and scattered with glow-in-the-dark insect pictures and Caspy's green with various hedgehogs and squirrels gambolling across them. I put down my cleaning paraphernalia and went to give them both a squeeze around the shoulders.

'Are you feeling better, Caspian?'

'Yes thanks, much.' He paused. 'Can I ask you something?'

'Of course you can.'

'Is your name really Pixie?'

Seraphina looked at him in disgust.

'Of *course* it is, that's what she said, isn't it? I think it's a lovely name, I wish I was called Pixie. Or Robert,' she added contemplatively.

I was distracted.

'Robert? Why Robert?'

'It's the postman's name,' explained Caspian, as Phina was

now transfixed by the cartoon again. 'He's one of her favourite people.'

'Oh, right. Actually, my name isn't really Pixie, although that is what some people call me.' Well, it was true as of today, anyway. 'My name's Penelope, or Penny, so you can call me that if you prefer?'

Caspian nodded solemnly. 'I do like Penny.'

He resumed his potato. I was just going to put the kettle on when the doorbell rang.

'I'll go,' I said to Pilar, who was elbow-deep in the sink.

I opened the door rather apprehensively, as the possibilities of who might turn up on the Lords' doorstep felt infinite but was delighted to see that it was the courier I had arranged before I arrived. She handed me a large box that I knew to be filled with all manner of Christmassy craft materials, games and little toys that would keep the children busy until the New Year. I signed on the dotted line and staggered back to the kitchen with it.

'Ooh, Pixie, what *is* it?' squealed Seraphina. 'Is it presents?'

I grinned.

'Of a sort, I suppose, but nothing that I'm opening tonight.' They both groaned theatrically, and I relented. 'Okay then, and *only* because it's nearly Christmas...' I peeled the box open, being careful not to let them peek inside, and pulled out a clockwork Santa and snowman. 'You can race these guys up and down the table, but you have to keep munching. Deal?'

They agreed enthusiastically and with them happy and occupied, I went over to Pilar, who was alternately studying a recipe and gathering together the ingredients.

'Can I help?'

'*Claro qué sí.* You are okay to chop?'

I nodded and she pushed a bunch of carrots, a board, peeler and a wicked-looking knife towards me. I started my task and glanced over towards her. The recipe was stuck into an old exercise book, fat with clippings and covered in scribbled notes.

'Is that recipes you've collected?'

'Yes, and it was my mother's also. My best recipes are saved here, and some in my head.'

'You should write them all down. Do you have children who might want them?'

'Ah, yes. My daughter, Marisol, is waiting for me to die so that she gets this book.'

She cackled with laughter, clearly not planning to pass it on any time soon.

'My parents are awful cooks, that's why I had to learn, otherwise I would have starved – or lived on toast. I'd love to learn some of your recipes, my stuff is all fairly basic.'

'Basic is good, it is your ingredients that matter.'

We chatted for a while about food and Spanish cuisine, about which I knew very little, then the conversation took a more personal turn.

'So, tell me, *Penélope*...'

I loved the way she pronounced it, with the emphasis on the middle 'e' and wondered if I should start telling people that *this* was my name: not Penny, or Pen, not even Pixie.

'Do you have a boyfriend?'

I quickly peeled an onion, hoping that I would be able to blame it for the annoying tears that had sprung to my eyes.

'Erm, no, no, I don't. Not anymore.'

'There was someone?'

I hacked into the innocent onion. 'Yes, until quite recently. Timothy.'

'He left you?'

I was taken aback by her directness but didn't want to be rude. 'Yes, that's right. We had been together ten years.'

I could hear the edge of bitterness in my voice and hoped that Pilar had not.

'You are angry with him. *Yes*. Did he go to another woman?'

'No, I don't think so. He just didn't want to be with me anymore. If you don't mind, Pilar, I'd rather not get into it.'

She shrugged.

'Is okay. Don't worry about it, Penélope. He wasn't for you. You will be fine, you will find love.'

A tear, not onion-induced, dripped down my cheek.

'No. I'm getting too old, my time is running out. I have to find something else to do with my life.'

'Nonsense! You are still young enough. Well, only just, but don't give up yet. In a year or two, maybe.'

Her honesty pulled me out of my self-pity, and I managed a smile. 'We'll see.'

'Is true. You're quite pretty, not too thin, you're kind and helpful. Maybe you are also intelligent?'

I half nodded and half shrugged, hoping this appraisal was reaching an end.

'You are also a girl with a very good soul, that I can tell.'

I brightened.

'So, this is what matters. Your soul is ageless, not like your face. Yours is good and it will stay good. You'll find someone.' She calmly tipped my onions into the pot. *'Todo a su tiempo, mi hija*. All in good time.'

I would have reached out to hug her, so grateful was I for her calm wisdom, when a movement outside the window caught my eye.

'What was that?'

'I didn't see anything...'

'A man just ran past, but he was only half dressed, I'm sure of it.'

A crash outside in the hall sent us both dashing out, past the tired twins who were still posting beans in their mouths and captivated by their cartoon puppies, the clockwork toys forgotten. A man stood at the bottom of the stairs. At my best guess he

was in his seventies, and he was gathering together a collection
of umbrellas and sticks that had fallen from a large brass urn he
must have knocked over. But the most striking thing about him
was that he was only wearing a Father Christmas hat, a vest and
a pair of boxer shorts, festooned with cheerful, red-nosed reindeer in a variety of gymnastic poses. He looked up guiltily as we
skidded to a halt.

'Señor Lord, what *are* you doing?'

A chill ran through me at the tone of Pilar's voice, and I
began to see what Bunny had meant.

'Oh, good evening, ladies.' He turned to me. 'I don't think
we've met. I'm William – Lando's father. Terribly sorry for
my state of *déshabillé*, there's a perfectly reasonable
explanation.'

I grinned.

'I'm sure. I'm Penny, I've come to help Bunny out over the
holidays.'

'Delighted, delighted.'

He shook my hand firmly and smiled back. I could see how
dashing he must have been as a younger man – well, he was still
pretty dashing now actually, with his warm brown eyes and
ready smile. It was easy to see where Lando had got his stunning looks.

'Señor Lord, you cannot stand around here chit-chatting in
your underwear.'

A giggle came from behind us, and we turned to see
Seraphina and Caspian standing in the doorway of the kitchen,
clutching each other in glee at the sight of their grandfather in
his pants.

'Oh yes, rather, very sorry, I'll go and put something on and
be right down.'

He scuttled off upstairs, and we returned to the kitchen to
find the twins some pudding. He came back a few minutes later
wearing a ludicrous turquoise silk dressing gown with black

piping, in which he looked absolutely marvellous, and carrying some soggy bundled up clothes.

'My sincere apologies to both of you. Penny, I hope you won't let that dreadful first impression colour your opinion of me going forward.'

'Er, no, not at all. Quite all right.'

Every first impression so far in this house had made me wonder if I'd be better off safely back in London, but William's state of undress was on the lower end on the alarming scale. At least – I assumed – I wasn't here to look after him as well.

'You're very kind. If you will allow me to explain. Once the Christmas grotto closed for the day – I work as Father Christmas at the department store – the elves and I decided to have a few refreshments. It can be quite a long and tiring day even for the jolliest of us. I mean, the children are mostly adorable, of course, and so excited, but...'

'I quite understand,' I said with sympathy in my voice. 'I'm a primary school teacher.'

A smile of relief broke across his worried face.

'Oh *yes*, you *will* understand, perfectly. It's the *questions*, Penny, endless *questions*. Some little tinker asked me today what we do when a reindeer dies, and no amount of demurring on my part would put him off. In the end, I found an emergency candy cane which bought me sufficient time to say my bit, produce a present and shove him back in the direction of his doting mother. Anyway, so we were having a drink, just to relax the nerves, and unfortunately Snowflake, one of the elves – *she's actually called Deirdre and is married to a bank manager,*' he added *sotto voce*, with a quick glance in the twins' direction. 'Snowflake knocked her second bottle of red wine all over my outfit. We tried to rinse it out immediately, but then of course I couldn't put it on again. I got a lift home and thought I might make it upstairs without being seen, but alas, you heard my clumsy crashing and here we are.'

I almost gave him a round of applause for this wonderful speech but was too busy mulling over the fact that he felt he should conceal Snowflake's true identity from the twins but not her drinking habits. I had a lot to learn about the Lord family.

'Okay, Señor Lord, give me those wet things, they drip on the floor.'

'Dear Pilar, are you sure? I can wash them...'

He trailed off pathetically, a master of his art.

'Give them to me.'

She snatched the bundle and bore it off to the washing machine, grumbling the whole time but clearly as happy as a clam. William beamed at me.

'Order is restored. Now, Penny, why don't you get those two off to bed and we'll open some more wine, and you can tell me all about yourself and how you came to be spending Christmas with us?'

As I steered the twins upstairs, grabbing my bags on the way, which were still sitting forlornly outside the front door, I thought that this Christmas was going to be anything but sensible. What remained to be seen was whether or not that was a good thing.

THREE

I woke early the next morning; it was still dark. My mind racing, and knowing I had no hope of getting back to sleep, I switched on the lamp beside my bed and thought about all that had happened the day before. Bunny had surfaced, briefly, to kiss Seraphina and Caspian goodnight and show me my bedroom, but then returned to her room and not even come down for supper. She had looked drained, very different from the woman who had breezed into Lando's studio earlier in the day, and I wondered if she was unwell. Maybe it was just life taking its toll. It can't have been easy trying to look after two lively children at the same time as finishing her Christmas commissions. I had seen some of her work, and it was astounding: delicate, whimsical watercolours that conjured up images of Christmases past and were appealingly sentimental. Cards for the printer to make up multiple packs had, of course, been finished weeks ago; the pieces she was doing now were one-offs for wealthy clients and, it seemed to me, some particularly entitled friends.

I had gone back downstairs to find William in the kitchen with, as promised, a bottle of wine open and a glass waiting for me. He even persuaded Pilar into having a drop as she put the finishing touches to supper, and when no one else appeared, we ate together around the kitchen table, one of the nicest meals I have ever had. It wasn't only the food, but the company – light, friendly and comfortable. I thought back to dinners I had had with Timothy's parents and felt very glad that Christmas would be spent at the Lords' table and not theirs. Timothy could be ponderous and had a tendency to lecture rather than converse; his father was the same. His mother, who looked permanently panicked, and I had all but given up trying to join in and would sit in near silence as they mansplained politics, economics, social theory and even education without ever asking for our input or opinion. As William chattered away, asking me all about myself, checking up with Pilar about her infirm sister and wondering what we thought was the best way to teach children classic literature, I wondered why I had put up with Timothy all those years. I suppose I had thought that was 'the way it was', that you got together with a man and then spent the next fifty years slightly dissatisfied, which was the path that many of my friends had embarked on. I certainly couldn't blame my parents, who had a wonderful relationship, always laughing together and never moaning at each other about socks on the floor or stacking the dishwasher wrong. Maybe because they seemed to be the exception, I thought that such ease was unrealistic to aim for and that I should be grateful for Timothy.

I pulled myself up to sitting and looked around the lovely room I had been given, as a way to distract myself. It was too early in the morning to be ruminating over Timothy, or any man, I thought, remembering my resolution. I was lying in a large double bed with a cosy, rustling duvet and cloudlike pillows. Before I got in last night, I had had to remove six cushions of varying sizes, all in different shades of pink ranging from softest rose to a rich magenta. I wondered who had selected them and whether it could possibly have been Lando, but given his indifference to the sicky carpet, it seemed unlikely. The rest of the room was pink and cream, which makes it sound like the bedroom of an eight-year-old, whereas it was, in fact, extremely sophisticated. A sunburst mirror glowed above the velvety padded headboard and botanical paintings of roses adorned the other walls. The window looked out over the lawns, concealed now by floor-length damask curtains, and a door led to an immaculate en-suite bathroom, in swirly pink and cream marble. I had never stayed anywhere so beautiful; just the room itself felt like an adventure.

Picking up my phone, I took a few photos and WhatsApped them to my parents. They had been pleased to hear that I was having a change of scene over Christmas, and although this room wasn't remotely their style, I knew they'd find it fun to see what luxury I'd landed in. Glancing at the clock, I realised I had whiled away nearly three quarters of an hour, and although it was still very early, I slid out of bed and padded quietly down the corridor to see if the children were awake. They were both sleeping peacefully, and the house was in silence, so I returned to my room and waded through the deep carpet for a little luxury: a morning bath. This certainly didn't feel like work, but as I lay in the warm, fragrant water, I found it hard to relax. Kind though Bunny and William undoubtedly were, and the twins undeniably sweet, I wondered if they would end up being too high maintenance for me. I had been so determined to get away from home and all the painful memories that I hadn't asked enough about what the job really entailed. I had believed Bunny when she had told me about the job, but *everyone* here seemed to be in need of looking after, and I wasn't sure if I was up to the job.

Maybe I should have stayed at home and put a note on my front door like Winnie the Pooh, saying I was out, busy and back soon, none of which would have been true. Then I could have holed up with a dozen Christmas films and an enormous chocolate panettone and passed the festive season in peaceful solitude. But even as these thoughts passed through my head, I knew that it would only have made me more miserable to be alone; at least here I would be kept busy, there was little doubt of that. I would simply focus my attentions on the children, avoid Lando and have friendly relationships with everyone else. With this pep talk spurring me on, I dried off and got dressed.

It was about seven o'clock when I left the room and went to peer around the twins' bedroom door. They were both still fast asleep under their Paddington duvets, as they clutched their essential night-time items: not teddies for these two, of course. Seraphina had some horrendously expensive nightgown of her mother's, oyster-coloured silk with soft lace edging, and Caspian was snuggled up to an inflatable parrot that he had been given to attend a 'Talk Like a Pirate' day at school. Smiling at the eccentric pair, I closed the door softly and went downstairs, where I found Pilar busy in the kitchen.

'Good morning.'

'Ah, *buenos días, Penélope.* How are you?'

'Very well, thank you. You?'

'Sure, I am fine. What would you like for breakfast? Go through to the living room, I bring it for you.'

I find it difficult to be waited on, and I hesitated, not sure whether or not it would be rude to demur. Pilar didn't give me time.

'Come along,' she said firmly. 'You need a good breakfast to run after those children all day. What will you have? I have everything.'

I could well believe it, so I meekly requested porridge and tea, which was my favourite, anyway, and went into the living room, which was solely occupied by William, in the same dressing gown as last night but with some colourful paisley pyjamas showing at the ankles and cuffs. He put down the enormous broadsheet he was reading, raised himself slightly out of his chair and greeted me warmly.

'Penny! Good morning. You slept well, I trust? You look marvellous.'

'Oh, thank you. Yes, I slept very well. And you?'

'Ah, plagued as ever by dreams of what could be in this life, but fine, fine. Now, it looks as if no one has yet explained breakfast to you.'

'Er, no. No one has said anything—'

'Well, breakfast here is a very relaxed, one might almost say louche, affair. Lando always hated table breakfasts as a child, making idle chit-chat over the marmalade when all one really wants to do is eat porridge in peace and read the paper. So, his house, his rules, we have breakfast in pyjamas, and all do our own thing, always in the living room and never the dining room. Feels a bit odd at first, but you get used to it quickly.'

I looked down at my jeans and jumper.

'I didn't realise. Should I go and get changed?'

'No, no, find something to read, sit down and enjoy your food.'

He waved his hand towards a table groaning with magazines and newspapers. I had been thinking that I would have to go back upstairs and retrieve my book, but there was no need. I went over and rifled through everything until I found a copy of *Good Housekeeping*. I like to think I'm still too young to read it, but it's so full of interesting articles and easy recipes that I can never resist. The only parts I skip are the fashion, which always strikes me as very complicated, lots of scarves and buckles and things that need ironing, and articles about the menopause. It wouldn't be long before I'd be reading them, I knew, but why upset myself when there was still a glimmer of fecundity left? As I sat down and started reading about what to do with any unwanted Christmas presents, Pilar came in and handed me a steaming bowl of porridge topped with dried fruits, and a large mug of tea. *I could get used to this*, I thought, as I snuggled deeper into the plump armchair and turned a page. Next to drift in was Bunny, in a long, peach silk dressing gown worn over bright orange silk pyjamas covered in pictures of zebras wearing purple trilbies. My own sleepwear – white and red plaid – was going to look rather dull tomorrow morning.

'Hello, William, hello, Pixie darling.'

'Hello, Bunny, you look well this morning.'

It was true. The colour had returned to her cheeks and her energy was back.

'Thank you, I am. I can't tell you how wonderful it was to have you to sort everything out yesterday. I just *knew* you would be worth your weight in gold, you heavenly creature.'

I beamed. I had never been so rapturously appreciated, and it felt good.

'I'm so glad I can help, and Phina and Caspy are gorgeous. But I'm not surprised you're exhausted, with the pressures of work too. How are the paintings going?'

'Oh fine, fine.' She selected a *Vogue* from the table and curled up in the corner of a sofa, looking tiny. 'I say every year that I won't carry on with private commissions, but they are worth it in the end. The picture I'm working on today is going to auction for a children's hospice near us in London, so it's extra special. Poor William, you must get fed up with having an extra artist in the house at Christmas. Lando is stressed enough for all of us.'

'Not at all, I appreciate the artistic temperament, although I was surprised when Lando took it up. Suits him, though,' he mused, peeling a banana.

I waited to see if there was going to be any more information forthcoming about the handsome lord of the manor, when the door opened and in he walked, Hepburn and Garbo alongside him. It felt intimate to see him in nightwear and gave me something of a jolt, particularly as he managed to look gorgeous even in his pale blue pyjamas and soft navy dressing gown. He muttered a general 'good morning', then came over to me.

'Hi there, look, I'm sorry for being rude yesterday. I'm trying to finish a commission for the church, and it has to be done by Christmas Eve, so I'm under pressure. And I'm not good with that. I'm glad you've come. It's a great help to Bunny.'

With this, he departed abruptly and picked up a newspaper, behind which he promptly disappeared. Bunny raised her eyebrows at me.

'Wonders will never cease,' she said in a loud stage whisper. 'Lando apologising! Maybe Santa *will* drop down the chimney this year, after all.'

Without moving his paper, Lando lobbed a cushion at her, and caught her neatly on the shoulder. She shrieked, then laughed and returned to her magazine, as did I. My awkwardness was wearing off, and I was beginning to think that Lando had got the breakfast thing right. My parents would certainly approve – they spent half their time in pyjamas, being comfortable, but always looked stylish. I wondered if I had become a bit inflexible after all those years with Timothy, worrying too much about being seen to do the right thing, rather than simply being at ease. I stared unseeingly at some pictures of winter borders I knew I would never plant and remembered the times I had been to stay with Timothy's parents.

They lived in a small, modern, semi-detached house in Luton (although he never mentioned the name of the town if people asked where he was from, merely said 'Bedfordshire' and hoped not to be probed) which was as neat as a pin. Everything was immaculate and much of it brand-new as things were replaced as soon as they were even slightly worn or faded. The cushions were plumped and karate-chopped to within an inch of their lives, matching mugs stood in serried ranks on the spotless glass shelves and even the flowers in the pots on the patio outside were fake so that they could never brown and let the side down. His parents were cautiously welcoming, but I always felt uncomfortable there, worried I might inadvertently shock them by using the wrong knife or putting the loo roll on the holder the common way round.

The Lords couldn't have given a hoot about knives, and although the house had been beautifully decorated, it had an air of comfort about it, as if no one could care less about the cushions; in fact, Garbo had now curled up on the watered silk one Lando had thrown at Bunny, which still lay where it had fallen, and all anyone had done was to give her an affectionate glance. It was all a vast improvement on the faux elegant performance of Timothy's parents, which was nerve-wracking and exhausting.

Pilar came in to bring Bunny and Lando their breakfast. He had a hearty plate: buttered toast and scrambled eggs as well as a bowl of porridge piled with fruit. Bunny, however, restricted herself to a dry brioche roll and some herbal tea. I barely knew her, but I was concerned, both about her exhaustion and now, this meagre diet. She must have caught the look on my face.

'Pixie, are you upset about something?'

Embarrassed, I wasn't sure what to say. I didn't want to look nosy, or as if I was checking up on her, both of which I suppose were true.

'Oh, no, Bunny, not at all. I just hope you're feeling okay.'

'You're very sweet to be concerned about me. I really am fine, but I don't fancy much for breakfast. I want to settle my stomach. I'll graze my way through the day, don't worry.'

I smiled.

'Sorry, I didn't mean to interfere.'

'Not at all, darling, you're kind, that's all.'

I would have returned to my magazine, but at that moment, the twins came bursting through the door, full of vim and joy despite the early hour.

'Mummy, Grandpa, Uncle Lando, Pilar, Pixie... Penny!'

They greeted us breathlessly, running from one to the next showing us the cuddly toys that were in favour that morning and Caspy trying to describe a dream that was slipping away from him as he spoke:

'There was a funny man in the kitchen, sort of hiding, then the wallpaper peeled off, and then the man – the one who was hiding – he... oh wait, there was a kitten as well...'

'It sounds marvellous, sweetie,' Bunny enthused. 'Dreams are so *odd*, aren't they? I once dreamt that I was eating cucumber sandwiches in the jungle and a hippo walked by and asked me to put my hat away properly next time. I wonder what it meant?'

The twins shrieked with laughter.

'Did you really, Mummy? Did you really dream that?'

Bunny nodded solemnly. 'It was most peculiar. Now, what are you two going to do over breakfast?'

Used to the routine, they sloped off to the corner of the room and put on the TV, plucking out the correct remote control from a selection of four and finding their preferred channel with an ease I suppose comes naturally to children these days. I got up to go and get their breakfast, but Pilar stopped me in my tracks.

'Sit down, Penélope, I get the breakfast, please.'

'I really don't mind, I'm here to help look after the twins...'

I trailed off when I saw the darkening look on her face.

'I do the breakfast. You have a long day ahead. *Gracias, pero no.*'

I got the message and slunk back gratefully to my comfortable chair, my magazine and the new steaming cup of coffee which had appeared next to me.

After about forty minutes, I could see that the twins were beginning to get restless, no longer paying attention to their programme. With a deep sense of gratitude for the relaxed start to the day, I closed the magazine, tucked it under my arm, picked up my breakfast things and went to stand up. It was at this point I realised my mistake. I had sunk so far into the cushiony depths of the armchair that my bottom now seemed to be lower than my knees. Getting up with two free hands would have been inelegant enough, but with my hands full and one arm clamping the magazine to my side, it was nigh on impossible. An experimental wriggle, which I hoped might push me up a little, succeeded only in working me deeper into the chair – so deep, in fact, that I now couldn't reach the side table to put anything down. Every time I breathed, the cup wobbled on its delicate saucer, threatening to fly off and shatter. I watched enviously as Bunny raised herself effortlessly from sitting to swap over her magazine, swiftly followed by William. How did they do it? They seemed to sort of *float* out of their seats. It must be years of practice, I mused, still stranded, of extricating themselves from feathery upholstery, whereas I had only ever tackled the helpful spring back of IKEA foam. Finishing schools probably did special classes in it for those who hadn't learnt at their mother's knee. I looked around furtively to see if I could make another attempt at escape, but only succeeded in meeting Lando's eye, then going beetroot with embarrassment. *Please look away*, I thought desperately, *just pretend you haven't seen.* No such luck. He came over, took my crockery from me and then offered me a hand, which I took, mortified but grateful. Then – and I'm afraid there is no other word for it – he hoisted me out of the chair, so I landed on my feet.

'Thanks,' I muttered, busying myself with the magazine.

'No problem,' he replied. 'The springs have gone in that chair, we've all been stuck in it at some point. I should probably get it mended, but it's ridiculously comfortable.'

The shame ebbed away in the face of this kindness, and I smiled at him.

'Yes, I could easily have stayed there all day, but I think it's time I got these two moving.'

I went over to the children.

'Right, come on, I think it's time the TV went off.'

There were some token complaints and moaning, but Bunny stayed determinedly buried in her magazine, and I stood firm.

'If you turn it off, we can talk about what you want to do today. I'm new around here, so I don't have any plans of my own – it's all up to you.'

This caught their attention, and Phina soon found the remote and switched off the TV.

'Ooh, Pixie, we want to go into the village, don't we, Cas?'

'Yes, yes, they've got some tree things in the shop, and we really want them.'

I looked over at Bunny for confirmation that this was a suitable activity, although, to be honest, I think she would have approved anything that gave her a break to work and rest.

'Yes, that's a super idea, we saw them the other day, didn't we? It's a shop called 'Present Box', they've got animals which are sort of knitted – or are they crocheted?' She shrugged, clearly unsure if there was much difference or whether it mattered. 'Maybe even woven? Anyway, you'll see them. Very sweet, they'll help our tree look gorgeous, my darlings.'

The children had completely forgotten the TV now, their butterfly minds utterly fixated on this new venture.

'Come *on*, Pixie, let's go and get dressed, hurry up.'

They pulled at my hands, and I laughed.

'Okay, okay, let's go! I'm sure the shop isn't going anywhere.'

'It doesn't even open till ten, so there's no rush.' This from Lando, emerging from behind his newspaper. 'Actually, I've got a few things to do in the village myself, so I'll walk down with you, if that's all right?'

To my intense annoyance, I felt a blush rising in my cheeks.

I berated myself. *For goodness' sake, Penny, your resolutions can't be worth much if you get so pathetically excited about walking for fifteen minutes with a good-looking man. No wonder you're so easily taken advantage of.* I nodded my assent and was glad that the twins covered my momentary confusion.

'Yay, Uncle Lando! Maybe we can find some wood for whittling.'

'Good idea, you wanted to try a mouse, didn't you, Cas?'

'Yes, please.'

'And I want to do a giraffe,' said Seraphina, then added sternly, 'but I *don't* want to be late for the shop, so can we *please* get moving?'

'Good idea,' I said. 'Shall we see you in the front hall in maybe twenty minutes?'

We both turned to the twins, who were now parading around the room, heads stretched up high, pretending to be giraffes. Lando and I looked at one another.

'Perhaps half an hour?' he said.

'Yup,' I replied, 'half an hour seems safer.'

'See you then,' he said, smiling, and I ushered the twins off upstairs to get ready before I could linger on any creeping unsuitable thoughts about Lando Lord for a second longer.

FOUR

I bundled the twins up in multiple layers, much to their disgust. Caspian had wanted to wear swimming trunks and a Snoopy vest, and Seraphina was keen on a thin, silky Batman costume; judging by their shocked outrage when I said they had to wrap up warm, I suspected that Bunny didn't usually contest such outfit choices. There is something to be said for letting children discover consequences for themselves, but when the consequence was hypothermia, it seemed harsh.

We were only five minutes late downstairs, which I considered a win. For under fives, I usually add the age of each child in minutes to the ETA, so, given the twins were four, we should have been eight minutes late. Lando was waiting for us, wearing a smart, dark grey overcoat, which would have looked more city than country, had it not been for the muddy pawprints decorating it and the light sprinkling of sawdust. He raised an eyebrow as we appeared.

'My goodness, you're all eminently suitably dressed for a walk to the village. Last time I seem to remember rather a lot of sequins and a rainbow cape.'

He scooped up a child in each arm, making them shriek

with laughter, and I opened the front door so that he could sweep them outside, where he proceeded to drop them on the cold gravel, which made them scream with even more delight, especially when Garbo and Hepburn came galloping over and joined the wriggling pile.

'Come on, let's get moving,' I said after a few minutes of this mayhem. 'I want to see this wonderful shop you're so excited about.'

They clambered to their feet, pink-cheeked with the fun of it all and arranged themselves between Lando and me so that we were all holding hands in a chain. We set off down the drive, and I felt a curious mixture of emotions. There was happiness at being a part of this joyful picture as we crunched along, our breath puffing out clouds in the chilly air and the smell of something deliciously spicy being prepared by Pilar drifting along behind us, but there was also a profound melancholy. This seemingly simple tableau was all I had ever wanted – a husband and a couple of kids – but it had proved frustratingly elusive. I tried to conjure up a picture of India in my head, seeing the sunny school I might teach at, a market replete with piles of colourful spices, different and exotic sights and smells, but it made me feel even more pathetic and desperate, like when you put on particularly bright lipstick the morning after a heavy night before and only succeed in looking more haggard and exhausted.

As all this had come to me, I thought I had done a good job in concealing my feelings, swinging Phina's hand and looking up to exclaim at a robin that Caspy excitedly pointed out. But obviously not. As the twins broke away to clamber on a fallen tree trunk that lay near the lane we were now walking down, Lando spoke.

'Hey, Penny, are you okay?'

I arranged my face into what I hoped was an expression of casual calm.

'Yes, yes, I'm fine. Gorgeous day.'

That, at least, was true. The sun had that beautiful golden hue you sometimes get at this time of year, and there were only wispy little clouds to temper it, not that solid iron grey that can dog December. It was very cold, but in that invigorating, flattering way that makes you rosy-cheeked rather than blue and pinched. Lando, however, was not to be drawn into a discussion about the weather.

'Are you sure? You looked a bit forlorn for a while there.'

Forlorn. Well, that just about summed me up. It certainly made me sound pitiable, which was not the look I was going for. I turned away rapidly, before he could see the tears that had sprung to my eyes.

'I'm great, thanks,' I called over my shoulder as I strode towards the twins, and didn't catch his reply if, indeed, he had given one.

We arrived at the little village of Monkton Abbot after about twenty minutes. You could do it faster, but Phina and Caspy stopped every few paces to examine something that interested them: a pinecone, a mossy twig, a colourful dropped sweet wrapper. Given Lando's terseness the previous day, I worried that he would be impatient with them, or even march on ahead to conduct whatever business it was he had in the village, but to my surprise, he was a model of tolerance, greeting their every find with a murmur of interest or approval and asking questions which got them thinking and lent a sense of importance to each piece of treasure. Who do you think could have dropped it? It looks as if it's been nibbled – what animal might have done that? What do you think would happen if you planted it? I was tempted to offer him a job in my classroom; he had a wonderful way about him. So wonderful that I was greatly relieved when the lane developed into a road and buildings started appearing;

arriving in the village meant that we would soon part ways and I could stop feeling so conflicted over this gorgeous, considerate man who was also great with children – but who had already shown a less friendly side and of whom any romantic thoughts were in direct opposition to Decision Number One.

'Is it ten o'clock yet, Pixie, can we go straight to Present Box?'

I looked down at Phina's excited face and drew her into a big hug.

'You're in luck, it's five past ten, so our timing is perfect.'

'Oooh, I'm so, so happy. Come on, let's go!'

I felt a little hand seize each one of mine, and I let myself be dragged off down the road.

'At least say goodbye to your uncle,' I said, and they sang their farewells over their shoulders, their minds set now on the goodies that awaited them. I turned to smile my goodbye, but Lando had already gone, so I set my sights on Present Box and the treasures that surely lay within.

The shop sat snugly between a greengrocer's and a florist's. It had a charming bow window which was strung inside with golden fairy lights and decorated in such a sumptuous, festive way that I could hardly bear to leave it to go inside. A huge central vase held large branches, some spray-painted silver or gold, some frosted, some left natural and some heavy with red berries. These branches were hung with hundreds of Christmas decorations and small gifts; felt Santas bobbed next to glass deer, crystal earrings jostled for attention with sweet, embroidered satin purses, and there was every colour of bauble imaginable, many painted with pretty designs, from mistletoe to Chinoiserie-style birds and flowers. Under the branches teetered piles of presents, some elegantly wrapped with silky bows and vibrant papers and some half-opened, the paper torn as if their recipients hadn't been able to wait till Christmas Day. These displayed beautiful cookery books, artisan soaps, bead necklaces and other tempting treats. Seraphina and Caspian were pointing to a branch bending under the weight of the hanging knitted creatures Bunny had mentioned.

'I'm *definitely* getting the otter, I love it *so much*,' pronounced Seraphina, pointing to where it hung. It was lying on its back and the ribbon was attached to its hands – do you call them hands? – which were folded over a baby otter, nestled on its tummy. It was undeniably sweet.

'Good choice. What about you, Caspy, which one do you like?'

He regarded them seriously.

'When we saw them before I was very keen on the sausage dog, because it looks exactly like Garbo. But now I like the donkey. It's more of a Christmas animal, and it has sad eyes. Maybe it will be happier on our tree.'

I squeezed his shoulder.

'Lovely idea. Come on then, let's go in and get them.'

The bell above the door gave a welcoming 'ting' as we entered, and the woman who had been sitting by the till stood up and came around the counter to greet us. I was immediately reminded of Mrs Tiggywinkle. She was small and very plump, with the twinkliest, most smiling eyes I had ever seen outside a children's picture book. She beamed at each of us and held out her arms to the twins, who immediately ran to her for a cuddle. I rather envied them: the thought of resting my head on her soft shoulder and letting her solve all my problems was almost irresistible.

'Phina, Caspy, how wonderful to see you, darlings. And who is this lovely lady you have brought with you?'

'This is Pixie, she's helping to look after us this Christmas. She's good at cleaning up sick and didn't mind seeing Grandpa in his pants.'

They both fell about laughing at this memory, and I stood

slightly open-mouthed, not knowing quite where to start explaining all this.

'Don't worry, dear, it sounds as if you are settling right in with the Lords. So lovely to have Ben's family back for Christmas. I do miss these two when they're in London, but we see quite a lot of you down here during the year, don't we? I'm Hetty, by the way.' She offered her hand, which I shook. 'Now, what have you come in for? A present for Mummy?'

The twins seemed a bit worried and glanced up at me.

'Not this time.' I smiled. 'This is a special trip for Phina and Caspy to choose one each of the beautiful, knitted tree decorations you have up in the window.'

'Ah, of course.' Hetty looked delighted. 'I make them myself, you know, I'm so glad you like them.'

She reached into the display and deftly plucked out the whole branch so that the children could pore over it and make their choices. Phina stuck firmly with her otter, and while Caspy vacillated more – in love with all of them and not wanting to leave any behind – he did eventually settle on the sad-eyed donkey.

'Pixie, I think we *should* look for something for Mummy. Can we?'

'Well, I think Daddy will want to do that with you, but why don't you get some ideas together and you can come back with him when he's down?'

Mollified by the prospect of at least window, if not actual, shopping, they went off hunting. I hesitated, then unhooked the little dachshund from the branch and took it over to the till. I hadn't thought about presents for the family, and I wasn't sure what the protocol would be, but this dog was so like Garbo I was sure that it would be a nice gesture to offer Lando. Anyway, I could always change my mind. Once everything was paid for, Hetty and I watched the children for a while as they pointed out the different treasures they thought Bunny would like.

'Such dears, aren't they?' said Hetty, beaming fondly at them. 'A very nice family, although Lando hasn't really been the same since...'

She broke off. I knew I shouldn't gossip, but it was irresistible to at least ask.

'Since what?'

'Well, when he used to come down here before, to his house, he was always such a larky lad in his fancy car and that glamorous girl on his arm. Not that I had a lot of time for her.' Hetty sniffed. 'Cold eyes. Anyway, he seemed quite suited to village life, always happy to help move a cow or have a game of darts at the pub. I did wonder how happy he could have been in London, a nice boy like that, but I don't suppose Madam wanted to move down here permanently with us hillbillies. The rest of the London crowd – and there are plenty of them in these parts – come and go all the time but never really *live* here.'

I was intrigued by this. All my friends have just one home, which they stay put in other than for the occasional holiday or weekend away, but I could imagine it was different with the super-wealthy, and I knew there were pockets of Dorset that had huge, expensive houses; not to mention the landed gentry, who presumably needed to work in London to keep paying for the massive country piles. I would have asked Hetty to expand, but she was into her stride now.

'*Any*way, then he...' She paused and I nearly toppled forward in anticipation. 'He... wasn't very well. *She* vanished and suddenly he was down here for good, but not like he had been. We hardly see him now, and when we do, it's a curt nod and a 'hello' if he's feeling friendly. Although he is doing something for the church, so it looks like the vicar has found an in, even if the rest of us haven't.'

When she came to the end of her long speech, I had a hundred questions but had barely drawn breath before the twins approached.

'We've looked, Pixie, Daddy will be able to buy Mummy *loads* of things.'

'Yes, *loads*. Can we go now?'

I could hardly chatter to Hetty about their uncle with them standing there, and maybe that was a good thing.

'Of course. Thank you, Hetty, I'm sure it won't be long before we're back.'

We went out into the sharp cold of the day.

'Shall we head home now?' I asked.

'Oh, Pixie, can't we go to the pub?'

This from Seraphina. I was getting used to the Lords' eccentric ways, but this phrase, coming as casually as it did from the mouth of a four-year-old, made me bark with laughter.

'The pub? Why do you want to go there?'

'They do the most a-*may*-zing hot chocolate,' said Caspian dreamily. 'With marshmallows and cream and sometimes a bit of a Flake or some chocolate buttons.'

'It's yummy,' added his sister. 'Uncle Xander always takes us there when he comes to visit. *Please* can we go?'

I didn't see any reason to rush back to the house, and a scrumptious hot chocolate in the village pub sounded irresistible.

'Sure, why not? Come on, you two, lead the way.'

We didn't have far to go to reach The Curious Badger, a gorgeous stone building smothered in ivy, with a thatched roof and smoke puffing merrily out of the chimneys. We pushed open the low wooden door and stepped inside. The interior was everything you could possibly wish for in a pub at Christmas time. It was dark, but cosy rather than gloomy. Not much light came in through the small windows; most was provided by the flames ablaze in the inglenook fireplace and real candles dotted about the room. The floor was partly beautiful flagstones and partly floorboards, and the furniture a mix of sturdy tables, wooden chairs and squashy sofas that you could happily spend the afternoon sinking into as you worked your way down a good bottle of red. Whoever had been responsible for the Christmas decorations hadn't held back. There were thick swags of tinsel-wrapped greenery looped around the walls and above the windows and the bar, bunches of mistletoe hung everywhere they might conceivably catch out a couple for a kiss, and the tree, which must have been eight feet tall, was almost completely obscured by hundreds of baubles and more tinsel. Amongst the decorations I spotted several of Hetty's knitted creations, which nestled happily cheek by jowl with some exquisitely carved wooden figures of robins and snowflakes. I wondered if these might be Lando's and was about to go over for a closer look when a voice boomed out towards us.

'Welcome, welcome to the Curious Badger. Although I hardly need greet these two regulars.' The twins beamed with pleasure. 'What will it be – your usual?'

'Yes please, Cecil.' They giggled, and ran off to squeeze onto the tiny, padded benches next to the fireplace and be hypnotised by the flames.

Cecil turned to me and put out his hand.

'Good to meet you. Are you helping Bunny out over Christmas?'

'Yes, that's right. I'm Penny, nice to meet you.'

'What can I get you? When Xander's down visiting Bunny and Ben and brings those two in, he has a spiked hot chocolate – or there's our local brew, which the pub's named after.'

'Oh no, thank you, but it's too early for a drink. I'll have the same as the twins, please, a normal hot chocolate.'

He grinned and started gathering tall glasses and long spoons.

'So, how are you finding the Lords? Lively bunch, aren't they?'

'Very! They've been incredibly welcoming and Phina and Caspy are gorgeous.'

'Seen anything of their dad?'

'Ben? No, I haven't met him yet. Bunny said he was snowed under with work in London.'

'Yes, a busy man is Benvolio.'

'Benvolio?'

'That's his full name, although it's really only William who uses it. Lando's short for Orlando: their parents were Shakespeare buffs.'

'I see. I'm not surprised he shortens it to Ben. What's he like?'

'Friendly guy, when we see him, which isn't much. Bunny's down quite often with the children, but he doesn't always join them. High achieving, he is, like his brother used to be.'

He placed three glasses of delicious-smelling hot chocolate in front of me and produced a can of squirty cream, which he proceeded to pile on top of each drink, to about half the height again of the glasses. I couldn't pretend I wasn't looking forward to it. My interest was also piqued by the mention of Lando.

'Used to be?'

Cecil produced a small tray packed with jars of different sprinkles and started selecting them. He started with something called 'Mermaid Christmas', which turned out to be sparkly, sugar flakes of blue, white and pink.

'Yes, that's right. He was a big shot in the city for years, raking in money, until something went wrong. Some sort of breakdown? Then all of a sudden, he was living down here full-time, but we never see him, or hardly ever.' Finished with the sprinkles, he started dotting tiny, coloured chocolate buttons on the cream. 'Not sure he'll stick around either. There's been some talk of a move abroad, but I can't say I know the details. There you go, three hot chocolates done the Badger's way.'

'They look incredible, thank you.'

I called the children to come and sit at a table and carefully carried our drinks over. Seraphina was squeaking with excitement.

'Look, look, he's put the buttons on! We don't always get those and they're the *best*.'

'I'm not quite sure how to tackle it,' I said. 'Any advice?'

Veterans of the Badger's confections, they wasted no time in breaking down exactly how I should approach it, and soon we were lost in sugary, creamy heaven as we spooned and sipped. I had worked my way down about half of my glass and was reading my mum's reply to the photos I'd sent her – showing the children pictures she had sent in response, of a sunset so beautiful it nearly made me cry – when the door opened and Lando walked in. I smiled at him but received only an icy glare in response.

'Bit early for that, isn't it?' he asked, nodding towards my glass. 'And not very professional. I know Xander does it, but once you've met him, you'll realise you really shouldn't be following his example.'

I realised that Lando assumed my hot chocolate was laced with whisky, but before I had a chance to defend myself, he had turned to Cecil.

'I was looking for Sandrine – has she been in?'

'Not today, mate. Have you tried the community centre?'

'Thanks, no, I'll go there next.'

And with that he was out of the door again, without another glance in our direction. I felt like crying. I'd probably be out of a job if he told Bunny that I'd been drinking on duty. I must have looked upset, because Caspy laid a comforting hand on mine.

'Don't worry, Penny,' he said kindly. 'Mummy always tells Xander that he'll need a drink or two when he's looking after us. She won't be cross.'

'That's right,' chimed in Seraphina. 'And Lando is a goody

goody. Mummy says there's nothing so annoying as a formed singer.'

Caspy nodded sagely, but my confusion lifted me out of despondency.

'A formed singer? I don't understand.'

'Mummy says Lando used to be more naughty – and more fun – but now he just tells everyone else off instead.'

I laughed.

'Oh, a reformed sinner! I see what you mean.'

'Mummy used to like a gin and tonic at teatime, too, to help get her through, but she doesn't do that anymore.'

'No, she's too tired now. Poor Mummy, maybe we should be gooder...'

I reached across the table to squeeze their hands and looked into their dear, serious faces.

'You are absolutely perfect as you are. Mummy's tired because she has lots of work to do, and I'm so happy because that means I get to come and look after you. Come on, let's go back up to the house, it's not far off lunchtime.'

As I paid Cecil and started herding the children out of the door and back up the lane, I wondered about what the children had said. I told myself I wasn't being nosy, just... observant. Extreme tiredness and no alcohol *could* be down to work pressures, but could mean something else altogether, and Ben's protracted absence began to look even more worrying.

Our walk home was jolly, with the twins recovered from their brief moment of worry and now happily discussing where on the tree they were going to put their new ornaments. As we drew nearer to the house, we saw a sleek, sporty silver car parked in front of it, which sent the children off into paroxysms of excitement.

'Uncle Xander, Uncle Xander, he's here!'

They dashed off up the driveway, and I broke into a trot after them, now slightly regretting the vast hot chocolate as it sloshed around in my tummy. I caught them up and took their hands as we approached.

'Pixie, maybe you could marry him. He's lovely, isn't he, Cas?'

'Maybe she's already married.'

'No, definitely not, are you?'

I shook my head.

'See. You could definitely marry him, he's fun.'

I was curious to meet this man, although obviously still firm in my nun-like intentions, but as we got up to the car and the twins broke away from me to go and knock on the window, I could see that the man inside was speaking intimately into his phone. I turned away, half laughing, half embarrassed, and saw that Lando was right behind us, and must have heard everything.

'Looks like Xander has arrived then. He is good fun, but if it's a husband you're after, I'd advise looking elsewhere.'

'I most certainly am *not* looking for a husband. Oh, and by the way, I wasn't drinking whisky in the pub. You should stop making assumptions about people.'

We glared at each other until an indolent, amused voice cut in from behind us.

'Merry Christmas, Lando. And you must be Pixie, Bunny mentioned that you'd be here. I'm her brother, Xander. Delighted to meet you.'

We turned to see a man standing by the car, looking slightly rumpled, smiling at us. Xander, several inches shorter than Lando with a slighter build, had dirty blond hair and an even dirtier twinkle in his eye. His obvious good humour made sure his grin stopped short of being a leer. He was good-looking, I supposed, but definitely not my type; far too foxy and knowing. Plenty of my friends, though, I knew, would enjoy a night out –

or in – with Xander. As he stepped forward to hug us hello, I was enveloped not only by his arms but by a cloud of expensive cologne, which lingered on my clothes long after he broke away from me. With this cast of characters, lunch was shaping up to be another interesting experience with the Lords.

FIVE

Everybody was already assembling for lunch when we arrived, so I hustled the twins off to wash their hands and put their purchases away safely for the big tree decorating session later, then returned to the table to take our places. Pilar seemed to be superhuman: she had knocked up a delicious-smelling lunch for eight people that morning and was now calmly placing steaming dishes on the neatly laid table as if she had done no more than make a few cheese sandwiches. She beamed at Xander when she saw him and placed a particularly sumptuous bowl of golden fish stew by him.

'*Cazuela de pescado con azafrán y almendras,*' she announced. 'One of your favourites, Señor Xander.'

He stood up and kissed her on both cheeks.

'*Gracias, Pilar, mi amor,*' he replied in what sounded to me to be perfect Spanish, then turned to the rest of us. 'Fish casserole with saffron and almonds, utterly delectable, particularly with Pilar's magic touch.'

I was just thinking that he was laying it on a bit thick when Bunny tugged at his hand.

'Oh, do sit down and stop showing off,' she said, not

unkindly. She turned to me with a full eyeroll. 'An A-level in Spanish and he thinks he's Antonio Banderas.'

I laughed and, to give him credit, so did he.

'Don't pretend you're not impressed by your brother's language skills,' he said, serving himself a generous amount of the casserole and tearing off a hunk of bread to accompany it.

'Maybe if I hadn't heard it all a billion times before. Now shut up and eat up. You need to find a girl who is less impressed by a smattering of Spanish and more impressed by the beautiful way you treat her.'

Poor Xander looked put out as everyone around the table – even Seraphina and Caspian – agreed enthusiastically.

'I don't know why people keep telling me to treat women well,' he complained. 'As if I'm some kind of cruel Lothario. Or stupid. I am perfectly aware of how wonderful they are, and just as soon as I find one who'll have me, I intend to treat her accordingly. Forever, if she'll let me.'

'Oh darling, is there a wedding on the cards?' said Bunny, looking much brighter. 'Mummy will be delighted, but only once she's coughed up my hundred pounds. I always *said* you'd settle down eventually.'

'You had a bet with our mother over whether I'd ever get married?'

'Oh, don't look so outraged, it was years ago. But I'm going to hold her to it. Can I be a bridesmaid? I suit pastels.'

'No, you can't, and shut up about weddings. I'll propose to someone when I'm good and ready and only *then* can you start bickering over colours and claiming your immoral winnings.'

The lunch continued in this good-humoured vein, and even Lando loosened up. I realised that, as well as being Bunny's brother, Lando knew him from the City – where Xander still worked – and my ears pricked up for any information about the previous life Hetty and Cecil had hinted at. But he batted away any reminiscences that Xander touched on, and only asked after a few people that they had in common.

'You're missed there, you know, Lando, especially at Carter, Mills and Rumsfeld. Rumour had it they were going to make you a partner within a year or two. I'm sure there would still be an opening if you've had enough of the pastoral idyll. Plenty of money still to be made in the Square Mile.'

Xander drained his wine glass and cocked an eyebrow in Lando's direction. For the first time, there was a slightly uncomfortable silence, then Lando spoke.

'I'm not going back. Ever.'

A little tipsy, Xander seemed to miss the note of warning in Lando's voice.

'Ah, come on. I'm sure Zara would welcome you with open arms, and if she doesn't, there are plenty of others who will. You can't play Farmer Lord forever.'

'I'm not going back,' said Lando flatly.

'Drop it, Xander,' said Bunny. 'You heard him.'

Finally reading the atmosphere, Xander shrugged and smoothly moved the conversation back to something more trivial, and before long we were laughing at William's story about a particularly obnoxious child who had come into Santa's grotto the day before. The uncomfortable moment having passed, I glanced over at Lando, who hadn't spoken again, or joined in with the merriment. He looked strained, and I wondered what painful memories had been dredged up for him. He glanced up then and caught my eye. Instinctively, as I do with a worried child, I smiled at him. His gaze darted away immediately, but almost as quickly came back and he gave me a brief smile and a nod before turning to Caspian, who was on his left, and asking him about his visit to the village that morning. *Who is Zara, I thought, and would I ever get to know this intriguing, talented yet possibly damaged man any further beyond his brittle public face?*

. . .

After an incredible pudding of slippery, sweet crème caramel, with a beautifully bitter burnt sugar sauce and kirsch-soaked cherries (I was careful that Seraphina and Caspian got the plain syrup version as I wouldn't have put it past Xander to swap them as a joke), all I really wanted to do was lie down and let my poor stomach get to work on digesting all the rich food that I loved but wasn't used to. But William stood up and tapped his knife against his glass.

'Oyez, everyone, listen up. Flex your festive fingers – especially you two.' He wiggled the knife at the twins who giggled with pleasure. 'This afternoon is the Grand Decoration. No one is exempt, no matter how much wine they've had.' This time the knife wagged in Xander's direction, who stood up with a good-natured smile and took a bow. 'The tree has been hauled into place while we've been eating, the swags are outside and the boxes of decorations old and new brought down ready for the opening. Let no man – or woman – rest until this house is fully Christmasified.'

He produced two crackers with a flourish and held one out to each child. They seized them and pulled, and a cloud of confetti came out, causing them to scream with joy. Unable to wait a moment longer and uncaring of their full tummies, they leapt up and ran into the hallway where their shouts indicated to the rest of us, as we heaved our unwilling bodies out of our chairs, that they had found the tree. We followed them out to a truly impressive sight: a tree that must have been fifteen feet tall and looked magnificent next to the sweeping staircase, nearly touching the ceiling. Lights had already been wound around it and switched on, so all that was left for us to do was to start putting on the decorations. Phina and Caspy were already diving into one of the large cardboard boxes that stood nearby, even they, at their young age, able to reminisce about decorations from previous years.

'Look! Here's the star I made at nursery – I made it out of dough.'

'Here's my reindeer! I called him Deer, but I might call him something else this year.'

I turned to Bunny, who was smiling at the children and taking photos on her phone.

'I always love decorating the tree,' I said. 'This one is amazing. Is there some kind of plan or pattern? How does Lando like it to look?'

'Oh, no, nothing like that,' she replied. 'Just grab whatever you fancy and pop it on. We always think it's much more fun if it's a family effort, rather than too strict.'

Lando, who was standing nearby, turned to us.

'Absolutely. Christmas is not the time for worrying about colour schemes and perfection, not in my house. Not anymore, anyway. Do you remember the year Zara had the tree delivered predecorated?' he asked Bunny. 'Everyone was so disappointed.'

'Oh yes, it was *terrible*,' she said. 'Luckily, the twins were too small to care, or Christmas would have been ruined for them. This way is much more fun. Come on, Pixie darling, let's dig in.'

I needed no further encouragement. Gleefully, I delved into a box, pulling out a flat, brown paper bag. Intrigued, I carefully opened it and then unwrapped the soft white tissue paper inside to find three dainty lace decorations. One was a star with a candle, one an intricate snowflake and the third an angel. I held them up, marvelling at how pretty and delicate they were.

'Ah, you've found the ones my German friend Annike sent me,' said Lando, appearing at my shoulder. 'Lovely, aren't they?'

'They're gorgeous. I've never seen anything like them.'

'Well, get them up on the tree or we won't be finished before Boxing Day.'

He grinned at me, and I saw a glimpse of the charming man the villagers had told me was lost. Perhaps he was still in there somewhere? I started looking for the perfect places to hang each piece of lace, then realised that around me things were happening rather differently, and I was liable to get left behind if I ummed and ahhed for too long. The twins were working their way around the bottom of the tree, seizing anything they could find and hanging it on – now that their precious new decorations had taken pride of place, of course. Bunny was halfway up the stairs, methodically plucking baubles from a bag and hanging them wherever she could reach, which resulted in a not unpleasing swath of red and gold glitter down one side of the tree. William seemed to know where each thing had been stored and was darting about from box to box, winkling out the most beautiful of the pieces and hanging them strategically but swiftly, using an ingenious long rod to reach the awkward middle parts of the tree. Lando was using a long ladder, leant up against the banisters along the landing, to thread in lengths of tinsel. Timothy had never let me put tinsel on our Christmas tree as he thought it was tacky, but I have always loved it. It's so merry, the way it reflects the light, and its particular dusty, metallic smell never fails to remind me of my childhood. Even Pilar appeared and ceremoniously hung up several baubles before protesting that she had too much to do in the kitchen to stay any longer. Anyway, I realised I was going to have to up my game if I wanted to contribute more than three items to the overall effect, so I quickly positioned the German lace and delved in.

When Lando finally slid down from his ladder and stood back to survey our handiwork, I was surprised to look at my watch and see that an hour had passed.

'Okay, everyone,' he said, 'I think it's time for the topper.'

Phina and Caspy squealed in excitement and scurried over. He opened a large box, and from a fat nest of tissue paper produced an enormous, beautiful golden star. It was constructed from intricately woven wire and stuffed with what looked like vintage tinsel, which had short, almost fluffy strands but was nonetheless shiny.

'Ah, look at that,' said William. 'I do love that star. My mother's mother bought it from Harrods in 1924, and it's topped a Lord Christmas tree every year since, even a few when they were out in India.' Everyone nodded solemnly, and I realised that this reminiscing was part of the tradition. 'When I was about seven, I thought it needed jazzing up, so I filled it with tinsel; a travesty, I'm sure, but my mother, God bless her, didn't mind in the least, so there it remains. Now, as you are all aware, the youngest people present have the honour of placing the star, so if you two are ready?'

The twins had handled themselves masterfully throughout this speech, suppressing their excitement, but now it over-flowed, and they shouted together:

'Yes, yes, Grandpa, we're ready.'

He led them up the stairs and helped them fix the star to the very top of the tree, threading through the end of the lights, which had been left loose for this purpose. As they stood back, Lando flicked off the room lights and we all marvelled at the effect. Despite our haphazard approach, the tree was a triumph. The lights twinkled gently, reflecting off the myriad baubles and trailing tinsel. The various knitted, carved and handmade decorations bobbed cheerfully, each taking its place with pride no matter how old or shabby it was, and the exquisite glass and lace creations smiled kindly at them, welcoming their humble-ness as if they were royalty.

'Well done, everyone,' said Lando, as William led the twins back down the stairs. 'I think we've outdone ourselves this year.'

'Yes, another splendid Lord effort,' said William, brushing

what looked suspiciously like a tear from his eye. 'Now, I have to don the red suit, I'm afraid, and go and do the evening shift at the grotto, so I'll see you all later – or tomorrow,' he added, ruffling Caspy's hair. He left with Lando, who said he wanted to put in a couple of hours in his studio before going out later.

'Come on, you two,' I said to the twins, who were going for a sleepover that night with a family they had made friends with on their frequent visits to their uncle's house. 'Time to get over to your friend's house.'

They took my hands as Xander stepped forward.

'Actually, if it's all right with you, Penny, I'd like to run them over – it's been a while since we've had a good chinwag.'

Giggling and waggling their chins with delight at the new word, they kissed Bunny goodbye and went happily with him to collect the overnight bags I had already packed for them, leaving Bunny and me.

'Go and sit down,' I said, noticing how drawn she looked after the effort of the tree. 'Can I get you anything – a drink or something to eat?'

'I'd love a herbal tea, darling, but most of all some company. Won't you get yourself something, too, and come and sit with me for a while? I have to go out later, but I'd love to chat.'

She went through to the living room where, after dodging around all the various occupants of the kitchen to make two cups of turmeric tea, which I had discovered I loved, I found her lying on a sofa and staring at the ceiling. She smiled when I came in and took her tea gratefully.

'Thank you, darling, how yummy, exactly what I needed. Now tell me, how are you enjoying your Christmas holidays with us?'

'It's only been a couple of days, but I absolutely love it,' I answered truthfully. 'Everyone has been very welcoming and Phina and Caspy are just wonderful.'

'Thank you. They really are, but it's a lot to try to look after them when I'm so pushed with work.'

'Oh yes, almost impossible I would have thought.'

There was a silence while we sipped our tea, and I wondered if Bunny was working up to telling me something. To my surprise, it was a question she had.

'Pixie, sweetie, I hope you don't think I'm intruding, but... well, I was wondering if there was anyone you were missing, maybe someone close to you that you wanted to spend Christmas with? There's plenty of room here, you would be welcome to invite someone for a few days. Lando couldn't care less, he sleeps in his studio half the time, anyway, and I do want everyone to be happy.'

What about you being happy? I thought, looking at her pinched expression, but not feeling quite bold enough to probe. Instead, I replied, with some relief:

'Well, my parents are in India, so not them, although I do miss them. There was a special someone until recently, my boyfriend Timothy.'

'Oh God,' she said, her hand flying to her mouth. 'He isn't *dead,* is he?'

For some reason this question, reasonable enough I suppose, struck me as completely absurd, and I started laughing. And once I'd started, I found I couldn't stop, I was shaking and gasping and felt my eyes filling up with tears and then spilling over. And then I didn't know if I was crying with laughter or with misery and the gusts and sobs became confused, but still, I couldn't stop. I felt a gentle hand on my shoulder and realised that Bunny was sitting next to me, patting me and murmuring soothing words. Her kindness allowed the tears to flow more calmly and then I was taking wobbly breaths and scrubbing at my face until finally I shuddered to a stop.

'Sorry,' I muttered, pulling out a scraggy tissue from my

pocket and dabbing at my face. 'Sorry, I'm so sorry, how embarrassing.'

'Embarrassing?' she asked, giving me a squeeze and then heading over to the drinks' cabinet. 'Darling, crying isn't remotely embarrassing, I make a point of doing it at least once a day, it's very cathartic. Seems to me that you haven't been doing nearly enough of it, so promise me you'll try harder in future.'

I nodded and summoned up a watery smile as I watched her pour a frighteningly large gin and tonic, which she then pressed into my hand.

'Nothing nicer than a massive drink after a big cry, you'll feel like a new woman. Now, tell me what happened to Timothy, if not dead.'

I giggled again and took a bracing sip of my drink.

'No, not dead, but gone all the same. We were together for ten years, and he dumped me so that I didn't get my hopes up – yet again – that he might propose over Christmas. I feel incredibly stupid, like I've wasted all my good time waiting for a bus that was on a completely different route. My mother never liked him; I should have listened to her.'

'You are *not* stupid. He sounds ghastly, what a mean thing to say. At least he could have pretended to have a less patronising reason. Men can be so tedious. And anyway, what do you mean by your 'good' time?'

'I'm thirty-eight, Bunny, a bit late to find a happy ending when you've got to start from scratch.'

She snorted.

'Nonsense! I suppose you mean too late for babies?' I nodded miserably. 'Well, you're not. All my friends are having them at forty and beyond, you'll be positively *à la mode*.'

'Do you really think so?'

'Yes. I mean, look at me. I'm older than you and as well as the twins – well, I'm expecting again.'

'You are? Congratulations!'

So that was it. Thank goodness. I had been quite worried about Bunny, but this explained it.

'Well, I'm not sure congratulations are in order. It wasn't exactly planned and...'

She screwed up her mouth and stared up at the ceiling. Now it was my turn to go and sit by her.

'You're not sure you want another baby?'

'Not entirely. Is that very wicked?'

'Not remotely. What does Ben think?'

'He's hardly said a thing, he's just stayed away more and more... Oh Pixie, he might be gone, too, like Tedious Timothy.'

I hardly knew what to say to her.

'Maybe he simply needs some time to process it?'

'Well, he should be bloody well processing it here with me.'

I couldn't argue with that.

'He should. I wish I could give you a gin and tonic to match mine.'

'Oh, so do I, so do I!'

We laughed.

'How have you found Lando since you've been here?' asked Bunny, changing the subject deftly.

'I haven't seen that much of him, but he's been fine.' I reddened. 'He did think I was drinking whisky at ten o'clock in the morning when I was looking after the twins, but I promise I wasn't. It was plain hot chocolate.'

Bunny let out a scream of laughter.

'He is *awful*. He used to be dreadfully louche himself, he would have thought nothing of a whisky stiffener with break-fast, if the occasion called for it. Nothing like a reformed sinner.'

I grinned.

'That's exactly what the twins said you'd say. Was he... is he... an alcoholic?'

I shouldn't be asking such personal questions about my employer's brother-in-law, but, talking of alcohol, the few sips I had taken of the gigantic gin and tonic had already loosened me up. Bunny shook her head.

'It never went that far, but working in the City in those high-pressured, vastly overpaid jobs – well, it carries a certain lifestyle with it, expectations, and one of those is to be twenty-four-hour *fun*, making it look as though you're effortlessly slipping your flawless and lucrative work in around the partying. He ended up having a bad time of it, but hopefully it will work out for the best in the end. Zara walking out was certainly a good thing, *I* think.'

I was dying to ask why, but I didn't want to distract her. Despite myself, I wanted to know more about Lando Lord. She continued.

'It's a shame he's become so grumpy and puritanical, it's not really him. He needs to bounce back to a sort of middle ground. Maybe being around Xander will help; he's calmed down a bit in the last eighteen months or so, but he's not lost any of his spark. What Lando really needs is a lovely wife and a couple of children. That would cheer him up, I'm sure of it.' I could see her giving me a sideways look, but I stared resolutely into my glass and stayed quiet, although my heart beat a trifle faster. 'Anyway, he's decided he's going to set himself up as some sort of monk or hermit, dedicated to his art. For now, anyway.'

I nodded and muttered something anodyne about people having to find their path in life. Bunny nodded, drained her tea and looked at her watch. 'Oh no, is that the time? I'd better go and get ready to go out. I am sorry you're not coming this evening, Pixie. It seems very odd going out without you – you're one of the family already.'

'I don't mind at all, it was all arranged long before I came on the scene, and I'll enjoy a quiet night in. I hope you have a good time.'

She stood up wearily.

'I'll do my best. These bashes are bad enough at the best of times, never mind when you're at the most exhausting stage of pregnancy and can't tell anyone yet. You'd think the social scene would be quieter down here, but it's worse than London, if anything, and all the same people, just in holiday mode.' She suddenly seized my hand. 'I'm so glad I could tell you about being pregnant, dear Pixie. Thank you for your sympathy. I need a mother's help more than the children do.'

I squeezed her hand back.

'It's my pleasure. I'm here for you all.'

She left to go upstairs and about twenty minutes later they all went out – Lando, Bunny and Xander – to the party at a neighbour's house, calling their goodbyes as they went. I was still nursing my drink and staring into the fire when Pilar popped her head round the door.

'All good here, Penélope? I go now if that's okay – I have left you some supper in the kitchen.'

The house fell into a friendly silence around me, and I thought fuzzily how happy I was here and what good friends I seemed to be making. My thoughts drifted towards Lando then, but as they started to settle dreamily on what it would be like living permanently in this house, married to that handsome, complicated, intriguing man, I turned my attention firmly to supper, some light TV and maybe even an early night. As if that was ever going to happen when I was living with the Lords.

SIX

About half an hour later, I was sitting happily on the sofa, my feet tucked up underneath me, eating a simple but delicious supper of baked cheese on toast with some creamy, garlicky sauce I could happily have had at every meal as it was so scrumptious. I was watching one of my favourite cosy murder series, making no effort whatsoever to try to guess who had smothered the vicar with his own chasuble and left him prostrate across the Nativity scene, when I heard the front door bang open. I didn't have time to put down my plate before the living room door also flew open and in stormed Lando.

'Oh, *you're* in here,' he growled, as he stamped across the floor to collect this morning's newspaper, which promptly fell apart, leaving him furiously gathering up pages and stuffing them together so roughly that I feared there would be nothing readable left. I chanced a question.

'Are you all right? I thought you had gone to the party.'

'I had.' He shook the sheets of paper with a sharp snap, and they finally succumbed to being folded into something manageable. 'I couldn't bear to stay a moment longer – bloody Xander trying to pour alcohol down my throat because he thinks I'm more fun when I'm drunk, and the local do-gooding bloody council member or whatever she is thrusting her poor daughter, who was in agonies of embarrassment, under my nose because she thinks we'll make a good match. I happen to know that the daughter is in love with the greengrocer, who returns her feelings, thank God, and they're trying to find the right time to tell Mummy. Hell isn't freezing over any time soon, so they'd be better off selling spuds in Gretna Green.'

'*Are* you more fun when you're drunk?'

He glared at me. 'Probably. Too much fun. Anyway, I don't want to get drunk, I want to go and work.'

What a shame he's leaving, I thought. He was even more attractive in this cross mood, spilling out his feelings and frustrations. I shoved down my urge to ask more and had another mouthful of my supper.

'You have sauce on your chin,' said Lando. I wiped at it quickly, mortified, but he hadn't finished with me yet. He looked over at the TV screen, which I had paused when he came in. The plump, homely detective was holding up the vicar's limp arm with a determinedly quizzical look on his face.

'Do you like this kind of thing?' asked Lando.

Now it was my turn to glare at him.

'It's relaxing,' I said, and picked up the remote control. 'Very relaxing *on my night off.*'

'All right, point taken, I'll leave you in peace. I'll be in my studio.'

I wouldn't be unkind enough to say that he flounced out of the room, but there was a definite huff about him. Maybe he secretly liked home counties homicide, too, and really wanted to stay? Some chance. Timothy had insisted that his favourite programmes – if he *had* to watch the television (he always used the full word, with a trace of disgust, never the friendlier 'TV' or 'telly') – were dry documentaries about global warming. But I once found him happily devouring something about burly

Australians in the outback hunting gold for a living, and his protests about my tastes didn't hold much water after that.

As Lando stomped off down the corridor, I thought back to my earlier musings – flights of fancy – about marrying him and living here, and the hot burn of shame crept up my cheeks. How ridiculous I was. Having finally woken up to Timothy – and made the very sensible decision to stay away from men from now on – five minutes later, I was fantasising about being with another awful man who didn't want me in the least. *He's not only rude but boring*, I thought, as I resumed my programme and finished off my cheesy, garlicky feast. The gorgeous, talented parts would definitely wear off. Who cared if the sauce dripped down my chin, and who cared if Lando saw it? I knew I did, really, and feeling messy just added to my humiliation. Tears threatened to fill my eyes, and I scrubbed at them with my napkin. What an idiot I was, letting myself be sucked into some *Country Living* fantasy by a few nice cushions and a view. I paused the TV again, took my plate through to the kitchen and went up to grab my laptop from my room. Before I opened it up, I decided that what I required to salve my bruised ego was some of Pilar's chocolate mousse that 'needed finishing'. Heavily laced with Cointreau, it was absolutely delicious and went beautifully with a decaf coffee I managed to coax from the spaceship controls of the coffee machine. I had stopped short of licking the bowl clean and was about to set up my computer to draft my resignation letter to the school and maybe look for some possibilities in India, when I heard the front door open and close. I checked my watch, but it still seemed early for the Lords to be back from their party. The living room door opened, and I was greeted with far more enthusiasm than I had been by the last person to return.

'Penny, Penny, lovely Penny, how glad I am to see you.'

'Hello, William, are you all right?'

'Well...' He eyeballed my laptop. 'I can see you are working away here, and I would *hate* to disturb you...'

I needed no further encouragement and snapped the computer shut.

'Not at all. What's up?'

'I am *lovelorn*, my dear, simply sick with it, but I fear she could *never* care for me.'

'I'm quite sure that couldn't be true – if she's good enough for you, that is. Why do you think that?'

'Because, my dear Penny, simple *because* that – other than my glorious late wife Celeste, Lando and Ben's mother, of course – she is the most divine creature I have *ever* set eyes on. How could she possibly love me?'

'I'm absolutely sure she could. Why don't you sit down and tell me about her?'

'Oh, can I? Thank you. But do let's have a little something while we chat; it makes it cosier, don't you think?'

I knew that a second drink would leave me fuzzy-headed in the morning, but I couldn't resist William's limpid, imploring gaze, and besides, it would be lovely to think about someone else's love life for a change.

'All right then, but a small one please.'

A minute later, I was handed a generous measure of oily, amber liquid, which I sniffed suspiciously. To my surprise, it had a delicious herbal, slightly spicy, scent.

'What is it?' I asked.

'It's called Benedictine, it's the most wonderful liqueur,' said William, swishing his around the glass and then taking a sip and rolling his eyes heavenwards in appreciation. 'Twenty-seven different herbs and spices and positively medicinal. It's made in a wonderful old palace in France – I visited once, many years ago, with darling Celeste...'

He trailed off, looking tragic, so I gave him some encouragement.

'What was it like, the palace?'

'Oh, absolutely *sumptuous*. Paintings and gilding and brocade everywhere, we had a wonderful time. I wonder what poor darling Celeste would think if she could see me now, *moping*.'

'Would she want you to meet somebody new?'

'Oh yes, she was a great lover of life. She would be telling me: "William!" I jumped slightly. "William! You have to *carpe diem*, seize the day, and, what's more, seize this lovely woman! Be brave, be confident!"'

He was warming to his theme, and I took a sip of the liqueur. It had a very unusual, but delicious, flavour, mellow and honeyed.

'She wouldn't recognise me, drooping around, convinced of my failure before I had even tried.'

'So why are you? What is it that's stopping you? I'm sure that... what's her name?'

'Daphne,' he breathed reverently.

'I'm sure that Daphne is as wonderful as you say, but so are you. I don't know you well, of course, but I would have thought she would be thrilled that you like her. And you can't possibly know until you try. How do you know her?'

'She is an elf to my Father Christmas and suits the costume better than I can possibly say. As well as that, she is so kind with the children and keeps us all going with her stories of the theatre... I must be one of a long line of suitors.'

'She sounds great.'

'Penny, it is five years since Celeste died, and there has been no one since her. We grew up together, grew old together, we knew each other so well. I'm seventy-three now and wooing someone... it's not like it was fifty years ago. I'm an old man, I have less to offer.'

I decided to ask the question that had been nagging at the back of my mind.

'Er... how old is Daphne?'

'Oh well, I don't know exactly, of course, and wouldn't dream of asking, but she talks about her theatrical exploits in the 1970s, so she must be of a similar vintage to me.'

I breathed a silent sigh of relief. I thought William was incredibly handsome and eligible, but I might have offered different advice had this Daphne been twenty-five.

'You have everything to offer, William. You're kind and funny and handsome, not to mention fully mobile – what more could she want?'

He laughed, as I had meant him to.

'Yes, I even have all my own teeth, a real catch. Oh, darling Penny, thank you for the pep talk. It's only that when decades have passed since you've done something, you lose confidence. But I suppose as far as she and I are concerned, nothing needs to have changed in the world of dating – we don't have to do it any differently from how we did then. No swiping right or whatever it is you get up to.'

'Exactly. Just ask her out.'

'I admire your rallying cry! I shall! I shall ask her out to dinner.'

'Oh, good for you!'

We threw our arms around one another jubilantly.

'Now, Penny, what do you say to another tiny drop of Benedictine?'

I looked in surprise at my empty glass. That had gone down easily.

'I really shouldn't...'

'You most definitely should. Just a whiff, to celebrate my upcoming date with the lovely Daphne.'

'How could I refuse? I'm glad you're feeling more in the spirit about the whole thing.'

'All down to you, dear Penny, all down to you.' He poured a couple more drinks. 'Now, what about you?'

'Me?'

'Is there a young man? They must be queuing up.'

I snorted. 'Hardly. I wasted years on someone who never truly wanted me and has now gone off to do God knows what, probably meet someone he thinks is more worthy of him.'

'Good riddance! Now it's my turn to encourage you. If he has gone – let him go. Lost years are bitter to remember, but don't let him waste any more of your time or your heart.'

'I'm not hankering after him and I'm not going to have anything to do with men anymore. I'm done. I'm moving to India.'

'Penny, that's the first time I've seen such a stubborn look on your face. You have struck me until this moment as an open, loving person. Forgive me, for I don't know you well, but I don't think this is you. I think you want to find love – but it is understandable that you don't want to be hurt again. The two do not necessarily go hand in hand, and, if they do, sometimes the love is worth it.'

I frowned at him, not understanding.

'The pain when Celeste died was incendiary, so much that one might think I should protect myself against suffering that way again. But no! I am prepared to risk loving, even if it means losing. Just be careful who you choose, so that if loss occurs, you at least have wonderful memories.'

I sat in silence, emotions raging inside me. William had scraped off the thin layer of protection I had laid over my heart, exposing it in its rawness once again. He was right. I wanted to love and be loved more than anything, but I wasn't sure my tender heart could take it. Big tears started rolling down my cheeks, and he seized me once again in his hearty embrace.

'Cry, darling, cry, tears are healing, but then dry them, sleep, and in the morning take one tiny step towards love. Promise me.'

'Oh, William,' I sobbed. 'I promise!'

We hugged for a few more minutes, then, both wiping our eyes, picked up our glasses and beamed at one another with renewed hope. Suddenly, William's finger shot to his mouth, and he was alert.

'I think that's someone on the gravel at the back,' he whispered. 'Yes, there goes the door. It must be Lando. Come on, darling Penny, let's run away before he finds us and tells us off.'

'Do you think he would?' I whispered back.

'Probably. He does it an awful lot these days. Now *there's* someone who needs to find some love in his life. Come on, quickly.'

We drained our glasses, giggling, and scampered upstairs, waving a silent goodbye as we retired to our rooms for a restorative night's sleep.

Before I dropped off, I looked again at the picture of the sunset Mum had sent earlier. It *was* beautiful. I sent her some photos of the tree we had decorated earlier and tapped out a quick message:

> This is what we've been doing today, all good, but the sunset looks gorgeous.

> Can't wait to see it for myself xxx

And I really meant it.

SEVEN

When I woke up the next morning, I felt distinctly unholy; how could monks make something that resulted in such a poisonous hangover? Maybe they didn't mean you to drink so much of it – but then why make it so delicious? I lay for a moment, my head pulsating with pain, my mouth dry and sticky, and wondered how much worse it would be if I moved. I inclined myself fractionally to one side and found out: unbearable. I lay in my new position for a few minutes, gazing pitifully at the smooth, wholesome edge of the pillow next to me and allowed some wistful images of purity and cleanliness to drift through my head: freshly laundered sheets blowing in the wind; cool water sipped by some healthy woman; a large, colourful salad served to a tanned and laughing family. A tear of self-pity slid down my cheek, and I lingered for a while on how polluted I was, how despicable.

This was the normal procedure for a bad hangover, and after a little more gentle involuntary weeping (even that jolted my head), I knew that it was time for the next phase, as I could not stay prone all day, however tempting. Slowly, slowly I raised myself onto one elbow, then wiggled my feet to the side of the bed, eventually inching up to standing. I clutched my head as I shuffled to the bathroom, then turned on the tap and started scooping water into my mouth. It was the only way to start combatting the malaise, I knew that, but took no pleasure in it. Groping for my sponge bag, I located some ibuprofen and swallowed two, knowing that taking them on an empty stomach was not recommended, but would spur me on to my next task: food. Silently thanking Lando for insisting on casual breakfasts, I dragged my dressing gown on over my pyjamas, slid my feet into my slippers and started downstairs, gripping the banister rail so hard for support I feared I might leave nail marks in it. I could only imagine how William was feeling. He had thirty-five years on me and had drunk twice as much. At least I would have someone to commiserate with. I pushed open the living room door.

'Penny! How marvellous to see you. Oh dear, are you all right? Here, let me help you to a chair. Was it something you ate?'

I stared at William in confusion. He was upright, rosy-cheeked and fragrant, his hair brushed back neatly and his attire as dapper as ever. He didn't *appear* to be hosting a trolls' funeral in his mouth, or the afterparty in his head. I let him lead me to a chair and sit me down, fussing over me solicitously, like I was an invalid. The rest of the family did nothing more than glance up and say 'hello', then return to their books, newspapers and devices, so I whispered to William:

'How do you look so... well? I feel awful after all that stuff last night.'

He beamed at me.

'Poor Penny, hangovers are rotten. So I've heard. Don't worry, look – hide behind this copy of *Vogue* and I'll go and brief Pilar, she'll see you right as rain in no time.'

Obediently, I started reading an article on water-based serums, all of which cost about the same as my monthly mortgage but were nonetheless appealing given my current state. Maybe spending hundreds of pounds per gram for one of these tiny, shiny bottles filled with promise would be worth it to quench my parched skin? I wasn't given any more time to think about it, as Pilar appeared, bearing a tray groaning with food. I must have visibly baulked, because she fixed me with a stern eye and said:

'*Vale*, Penélope. You have to eat this, you will feel better. I know you don't want to, but – meh.' She shrugged her shoulders. 'It is good, it will fix you.'

She removed the magazine and placed the tray on my lap, then marched out of the room. Initially, I gazed in horror at the plate of beans, scrambled eggs and toast and the bowl of fruit, but as I picked disconsolately at a fat piece of tangerine, my appetite slowly perked up. A tentative bean went down well, and my confidence grew as I slowly worked my way through it all. Pilar, I decided as I washed it all down with a large cup of tea, had the magic touch.

'Feeling better, Pixie darling?'

I looked up to see Bunny beaming at me from her perch on the sofa.

'Yes, thank you. I'm so sorry, I didn't mean to have a drink at all really...'

'Don't say another word. William is simply *frightful* for pouring alcohol down one's throat and you're having such fun you barely even notice. Then he doesn't even have the decency to feel awful the next day. I have been there, Pixie, and you have my every sympathy.'

I laughed.

'Thank you. I think I'll go and see if Pilar needs any help in the kitchen, before I go and get the twins.'

I stood up carefully, but my head and stomach both held up, so I carried my tray through to the kitchen.

'Thank you so much, Pilar, you're a life saver.'

'You must be careful of that bad *abuelo*, Señor William.'

'It definitely won't happen again,' I agreed fervently. 'I'm not a big drinker normally, so now I've had my warning where he's concerned. Look, can I help you with anything? I'd like to lend a hand.'

'Okay. I am making these Christmas sweets; you can wash up, then watch and learn.'

I peered in interest at the ingredients on the table. There was a bowl full of almonds, a bag of icing sugar and some eggs.

'What kind of sweets are you making?'

'*Figuras de mazapán* – marzipan shapes. They are always eaten in Spain at Christmas.'

I tried to repeat the Spanish words, feeling clumsy and tongue-tied, but Pilar looked delighted.

'Good. Come, I will teach you some more words as we work.'

I washed up as she pulverized the almonds to powder in a food processor, then came to sit at the table. She mixed together the nuts and sugar, then deftly separated the eggs to add the whites, all the while drilling me in Spanish Christmas vocabulary.

'*Navidad* – Christmas.'

I repeated it obediently.

'*Bien. Árbol de Navidad* – Christmas tree. *Regalo* – present.'

After twenty minutes or so, I was feeling quite pleased with myself, especially as Pilar was an extremely encouraging teacher, praising my pronunciation and rewarding me with scraps of delicious marzipan if I remembered a word correctly a few minutes after first learning it. I was trying to get to grips with the Spanish word for 'twins' – *gemelos* – which required a guttural 'g' that made me sound like a cat bringing up a hairball when Xander came in.

'I say, I rather like you speaking Spanish, Penny, very exotic.'

I reddened and returned to my marzipan.

'Please, don't stop on my account, but I wondered if you'd like me to give you a lift to pick up the *gemelos*?'

Of course, *his* pronunciation was as smooth as silk.

'Oh, no, thank you, but—'

'It really would be my pleasure,' he interrupted. 'We could get to know each other better on the journey over; maybe I could help you get your tongue around some more Spanish.'

I glanced up at him and he winked. I was determined not to get flustered by this sudden and not particularly welcome flirtation, but he had taken me by surprise, and I certainly didn't want to be rude to Bunny's brother.

'It's all right, really. The father of the friend they're staying with has offered to pick me up and then drop us home again. Thanks, though.'

'Giles? Oh God, you don't want to get stuck in the car with him, he'll regale you with stories of the latest exciting events in his estate office. Last time I saw him, he cornered me for what felt like about four days with an account of the new pig feed he'd got in. I promise you, lovely Penny, you'll have much more fun with me.'

I looked into his handsome face and for a second was tempted. He was fun, no doubt about it, and couldn't be more different from Timothy; maybe a dalliance with him would be a tonic. But then his grin started to look more like a leer, and I wondered how long it would take for his easy persuasiveness to turn into pushiness. I shook my head and opened my mouth to speak, only for him to interrupt me again.

'Don't say no, Penny darling, come on. I'll ring Giles and sort it out.'

I felt irritated now and was about to speak up when a voice came from behind him.

'I think Penny has made it clear what her plans are. Let it go.'

Xander turned.

'Oh, it's you, Lando, trying to spoil my fun again. Penny was about to say yes, weren't you?'

I spoke quickly this time, before any other man could talk over me.

'No, I wasn't. Thank you, but it's all arranged with Giles. In fact, he'll be here shortly, so I'd better go and get dressed. *Gracias*, Pilar.'

I dusted my hands off and went up to Xander, who only moved fractionally, forcing me to squeeze past him.

'Such a shame,' he whispered in my ear, loud enough for everyone to hear but close enough to feel creepingly intimate. 'Maybe another time.'

I gave a tight smile and passed Lando, who stepped smartly backwards and gave me a curt nod. It was with some relief that I ran upstairs to the sanctuary of my room.

Giles pulled up outside twenty minutes later in a dusty, green, open-backed Land Rover, and I rushed to grab my coat and get out before I had to have any more awkward conversations. No such luck. Here came Lando, a frown on his face. I thought I'd better say something.

'Hi, er, thanks for stepping in earlier.'

'What?'

'With Xander?'

'Oh, right. You didn't seem too pleased at the time. I wasn't trying to be a knight in shining armour, I'm sure you're perfectly capable of looking after yourself. But I know what a nag Xander can be – he doesn't give you the option of saying no.'

I remembered the party the night before.

'You've had a fair amount of practice, turning him down.'

'Exactly.'

'Well, thanks, anyway.'

He grunted and I ran out of the door wondering if maybe I had done the wrong thing in rebuffing the charming Xander.

The ride to the house was short and Giles wasn't in the least bit boring, but his chatter about Christmas preparations and how they clashed with his son Toby's upcoming birthday did nothing to prepare me for arriving at their house. I had thought Lando's place was big, but it was dwarfed by this sprawling edifice with its vast portico and two long wings, each in two sections topped by square towers. We proceeded up a long driveway, flanked by rolling lawns, across which wandered a few deer. I wanted to be coolly unimpressed, as if I turned up at such homes all the time, but it was impossible.

'Is this your house? It's absolutely stunning.'

Giles brought the car to a stop and heaved on the handbrake.

'Yes, yes, this is Markbury Hall, welcome. Been in the family for donkeys' years, roof's a nuisance and most of the rooms are freezing cold, even in August, but we like it.'

I was getting an inkling of why Xander had been so rude about Giles; no amount of city-slickery could ever buy a heritage like this. I wondered if Giles had a title but couldn't think of a way to ask without sounding painfully gauche; I made a mental note, instead, to ask Bunny later. We got out of the car and started up the large staircase towards the front door.

'I bet the children have some amazing games of hide and seek here,' I said. 'I hope we can find them before bedtime.'

But I didn't have to worry, as the door was flung open and out popped Phina, Caspy and another little boy with a shock of dirty blond hair exactly like his father's, who I assumed must be Toby. They were surrounded by various dogs, all leaping and yipping in excitement. A very tall, harassed-looking woman with short, messy brown hair called after them:

'Morning snacks when you hear the stable clock chime the half hour.'

And, with a brief hug and a 'Hello, Pixie, we're off to look for goblin tracks', they were gone.

'Hello, hello!' said the woman, smiling broadly and holding out a nail-bitten hand. 'Lovely to meet you, I'm Lavinia. Won't you come in?'

I felt a little shy about entering the staggering house, as if I should be wearing a ballgown or something rather than jeans and trainers, but the feeling was short-lived. Lavinia was dressed in black cords and a red jumper, both covered in dog hair, and the hallway, while enormous, had such a homely feel that I relaxed.

'Should I take my shoes off?' I asked.

'Oh, dear me, no, I'm sure our floors are absolutely filthy, and they're freezing as well – that's the problem with all this marble. Let's go through to the snug, at least there's carpet in there and it's right next to the family kitchen, so it's actually warm.'

I followed her through heavy doors and dark corridors until we emerged into a bright and cosy room, cluttered with squashy sofas, colourful rugs and at least seven small side tables. I sat down and, as Lavinia went to get coffee, reflected how at home I was beginning to find myself in the most grandiose surroundings. My little boxy house felt a million light years away. Timothy, I thought, would be furiously jealous if he could see me now.

Lavinia soon returned, not only with coffee but several plates of biscuits and cakes.

'The children will be back soon,' she said, 'and they're absolute *locusts* when it comes to this sort of food, so do let's make sure we've had plenty before they return.'

We piled up our plates and fell into conversation. We clicked instantly and were soon howling with laughter over an

embarrassing situation she had got herself into at The Curious
Badger.

'Honestly Penny, poor Cecil didn't know what to do with
himself. I couldn't give a hoot about that sort of thing, especially
since giving birth, but he didn't know where to look. Now when
I go in, he sort of thrusts drinks at me frantically in the hope that
I'll sit quietly in a corner with no replay. Not a bad result, when
you think about it.'

We had been laughing so much that we hadn't heard the
clock, but soon the children burst through the door and, as
predicted, fell on the snacks as if they hadn't eaten for weeks.

Much as I could have stayed in that parlour all day, after an
hour or so it was time to leave.

'Come on, you two, I said we'd be home for lunch, and you
don't want to get me in trouble with Pilar, do you?'

They hugged Toby and continued chattering to him so
animatedly about his upcoming birthday party that Giles
relented and let him come along in the car to drop us off.
Lavinia and I hugged, and I felt sure that I had made a firm new
friend in her.

After a simple pasta lunch around the kitchen table, we all still
had plenty of energy. The twins couldn't stay in their chairs,
and I must say I felt their happy energy galvanising me as well.

'What are we going to do now, Penny? I want to look at the
Christmas tree all day, it's so beautiful.'

'I know, Phina darling, but I think we should go outside for
a while. It's such a sunny day. Let's go and collect some
greenery and we can make some more decorations. I'll teach
you a Christmas song all about the holly and the ivy if you like,
and we can sing it as we work.'

Bunny looked up.

'Actually, Pixie, that sounds marvellous, exactly what I

need. Well, maybe I'd better not join in the singing, I don't want to frighten all the little Christmas robins. But the crisp walk and the greenery: utterly gorgeous. I'll get ready, too, and join you all.'

Half an hour later, we were all ready, wrapped up in colourful scarves and gloves with big plastic trugs to stash our finds in. We strode out towards the woodland – well, it would be more accurate to say that Bunny and I meandered, and the twins scampered. The sun and cold air on my face washed away any vestiges of hangover, and I felt a great wash of well-being come over me. The children proved quick learners and soon they were singing joyfully:

> 'The holly and the ivy
> When they are both full grown
> Of all the trees that are in the wood
> The holly bears the crown.'

'You're wonderful for all of us,' said Bunny, reaching up to cut down a particularly long tendril of ivy and curl it into the trug. 'I haven't felt so cheerful for a long time and the twins are simply flourishing. I'm even feeling a bit less sick.'

'Any news from Ben?'

She shook her head.

'He says he's overwhelmed with work and can't make it down. But hopefully he is coming for the scan – it's booked for Thursday. Maybe once we see the baby on a screen, we'll feel better about the whole thing.'

'I'm sure that will help,' I replied, not entirely sure if I was right, but not knowing what else to say. I moved on quickly. 'Don't you have to go back to London for the scan with your doctor there?'

'Why would I do that?' asked Bunny, looking confused.

'Well, normally you're just registered with a doctor near your home, and you have to do everything there, unless it's an emergency. I'm just impressed that they let you do it here when you're on holiday, that's all.'

Bunny looked slightly abashed.

'Oh, I see! Well, we are *very* lucky, Pixie darling, and our doctor is terribly helpful. He has a practice down here as well, as there are heaps of us buzzing between London and Dorset, so he does a couple of days a week here and the rest in Harley Street.'

The mists cleared. Of course, Bunny would have a private doctor, no pesky NHS regulations for her. And with all the wealthy families who spent some of their time in this part of the world, her doctor was presumably laughing all the way to the (Sand)banks.

'Sounds perfect,' I said, wondering for the millionth time if I'd made all the wrong choices in life.

'It does help,' agreed Bunny. 'Anyway, let's not talk about that now. Did you have fun with William last night? He's a terrific father-in-law, I adore him.'

'Yes, we had a lovely time, but I'm going to be careful around him from now on. Doesn't he get hangovers?'

'I *know*, it's like some kind of superpower. Mind you, Lando had a very strong stomach at one point, although he drinks much less now.'

She paused.

'I want to tell you, dear Pixie, because I do so feel that you are part of the family now and it seems dishonest, somehow, not to. About a year ago, Lando had a breakdown. He had been burning the candle at both ends, working and partying more than one man could handle. Very good at both, but not really *him*, if you know what I mean, although everyone bought into it for a long time. Party boy Lando. He believed it, too, I think, and kept going – until he didn't.'

'Is that why he lives down here now?'

'That's right. He was in hospital for a while, then they tried to woo him back to the City. Breakdowns aren't all that uncommon, you see, and people often go back to exactly what they were doing before.'

'Until the next time?'

'Yes. Some of them are in a toxic cycle of work, play, breakdowns, heart attacks and scandals which they can't get away from. I worry about Xander, but maybe he can find a nice girl who will help him out of it.'

'And Lando got himself out?'

'He did. He was one of the lucky ones. He refused to go back – he'd already made pots of money and wasn't greedy for more – rented out his London pad and moved permanently down here for some peace and quiet and to pursue his interest in wood sculpture. William is here now, too, so until we descend at various points during the year, the two of them potter around quite happily with Pilar looking after them.'

'The house is absolutely beautiful.'

'Stunning, isn't it? He had a vastly ambitious girlfriend – Zara – who harboured ideas of shooting parties or something, I think, and rather liked the idea of being lady of the manor, so she pushed him into buying it and then masterminded the refurb. I can't deny she did a good job, but I was very glad when he kept the house and ditched her.'

Questions raced through my head, but I didn't want to be meddlesome. Well, I *did* want to be, but I didn't want to *look* that way, was closer to the truth. Happily for me, Bunny was clearly in the mood for telling all, and didn't need any prompting from me.

'He used to be huge fun, always buying drinks and whisking us off on yachts, but he's so serious now. I do hope he finds some sort of middle ground, I'm not sure he's happy – too busy proving that he's not a party animal anymore and – *I* think – rather scared of enjoying himself in case everything comes crashing down around him again.'

'He wasn't happy last night.'

'No, Xander was being *awful*, trying to make him drink and lead him astray. Xander just doesn't get it. He's my brother and I love him, but he's much more armour-plated somehow. Slick. He doesn't have an artistic bone in his body and can't understand why Lando doesn't want to plunge back into the City cesspit and carry on piling up the cash. Anyway, I still adore Lando, I only hope he finds his way. For all that he seems to want to behave like some sort of spartan monk, there's still a living, breathing man in there somewhere. I'd hate for him to turn to dust.'

We started to tackle a particularly beautiful but vicious piece of holly and the twins rushed over to advise.

'Mind that bit there, Penny, it's going to spike you. Cut some more, cut some more, I want to put it everywhere! Get the berries, those ones up there.'

I snipped away gingerly, and we stuffed our trugs to overflowing.

'Come on, everyone, it's getting cold. Let's get ourselves home, put these in some water and have a hot drink to warm ourselves up. On the way, you can tell me your favourite things about Christmas.'

Seraphina was first to pipe up.

'Oh Pixie, I adore all the presents. They look so pretty under the tree, and you never know what they are. I can *never* guess.'

'It sounds to me as if you like them better wrapped than unwrapped.'

She gazed at me, her huge brown eyes serious.

'Oh *no*, I *love* unwrapping them too.'

We all laughed.

'What about you, Caspy? What's your best thing about Christmas?'

'It's very hard to only choose one.'

He shook his head solemnly, and we walked in silence for a few minutes as he pondered his answer.

'I think – I *think* – it's probably the tree. I love decorating it and I like it there in the day and when we put the lights on. And I like the new and the old decorations. Yes, the tree.'

I gave him a squeeze.

'I like the tree, too, darling. But I think my favourite thing is the singing. All the carols I learnt at school and can remember – well, most of the words to. But also the pop songs.' I burst into a brief, slightly tuneless, rendition of Wham's big Christmas hit, then stopped when I saw the looks of bewilderment. 'Never mind, I'm sure you'll learn to love them. I like singing with the children at school too. I always cry when they do 'Little Donkey' and I've been teaching for years.'

'Oh, oh, we know 'Little Donkey'! Come on, Cas, let's sing it for Pixie.'

As they piped the dear, familiar song, I did indeed feel tears pricking at the backs of my eyes. Would I ever hear my own child sing this? I wondered sadly, before squaring my shoulders and conjuring up a mental image of an exciting, childfree life in India. It didn't look very Christmassy.

'What about you, Bunny?'

She started, as if her mind were a million miles away.

'What, darling? Oh, my favourite thing about Christmas? Gosh, erm, let me think. I suppose...' She paused, gazing at her children scampering across the frosty ground, now singing lustily about a snowman. Then she smiled. 'It has to be the children, doesn't it, watching them enjoy it? I never thought it would happen to me, but all my favourite things now seem to be connected to the children.' She placed her hand briefly on her stomach. 'Maybe another one will add to that.'

'I'm sure it will. And imagine, you could have a singing trio, work your way to being the new Von Trapp Family Singers.'

'Oh God, Pixie, that would mean me joining in, and no one wants to hear that, I can promise you.'

As we approached the house, I noticed a figure sitting on the bench outside, but I couldn't make out who it was as they were hunched over, their head in their hands.

'Who's that?' said Bunny.

'I can't see from here. They don't look very happy.'

Of course, the twins realised immediately and shouted out:

'Uncle Lando!'

He didn't look up and before we could stop them, they ran over to him, full of excitement about their walk. Bunny and I hastened our steps as they pulled at his arms and he lifted his leaden head. Even from several metres away, I could see how grey and drawn he looked. Bunny ran the last few steps and tried to shoo the children away, but they just got more excited, pulling at her sleeves and tugging at the basket she was holding. Stepping in when parents are there is one of the most difficult things to do elegantly, but sometimes it was necessary and Lando had dropped his head again. I went for the 'ripping the sticking plaster off' approach, and adopted my briskest tone:

'Go and find your Uncle Xander, you two, he would love to hear your new song. I bet you can remember all the words for him, and he'll be really impressed. Take your trugs and ask Pilar to put the greenery in some water. I'll come...' I trailed off and glanced at Bunny. She screwed her face up and made a little beckoning motion. '...Mummy and I will come soon and the quicker you go, the quicker we can come and find some biscuits.'

Galvanised, they skittered off towards the house, shrieking for Xander, and Bunny and I, in silent agreement, sat down on either side of Lando.

'Lando, darling, what's wrong?' she asked, putting her hand on his shoulder. 'You look absolutely desperate.'

He raised his head and stared in front of him.

'It's this *bloody* Nativity scene for the church. It's so nearly finished, but I can't get *bloody* Mary right.'

'Sounds like a Bloody Mary might be what you need.'

He didn't even try to smile at her quip.

'Seriously, Bunny, I'm running out of time – it's got to be delivered on Christmas Eve. I should never have embarked on such a huge project. I'm not ready, I'm not good enough.'

He raked his hands through his hair, the picture of despair. Bunny looked at me helplessly.

'What do you need?' I asked.

Lando turned his head and glared at me.

'Need? Oh, only about another six months and some actual *talent*.'

'Well, judging by the work of yours that I've seen so far, you certainly have the latter. Time clearly isn't on your side, but there must be something else that would help?'

'I suppose it might work if I had a live model. But that's not going to happen at such short notice.'

We all sat in silence for a moment, me with an impending sense of dread as I anticipated how a solution could be found. It didn't take Bunny long.

'Well, Pixie can do it. Can't you, Pixie?'

'Er, well, I'm meant to be here as a mother's help. What about the children?'

'You can do it after they're in bed maybe, or for the odd hour during the day. I'm the mother you're helping, and it would be a wonderful help to me to see Lando less stressed. That *would* help, wouldn't it, darling, if Pixie sat for you?'

Lando looked as dubious as I felt. He probably didn't see many Madonna-ish qualities about me, and I couldn't blame him. But, after a moment, his lips lifted in a slight smile.

'Yes, yes, that would help – if you were willing, of course? It wouldn't be many sittings.'

'Of course I'll do it. I'd be glad to,' I lied. I couldn't actually imagine anything worse than being shut in that tiny studio with the bad-tempered, humourless Lando for hours on end, but Bunny did have a point – I was there to help her, not to dictate what that help entailed.

'Marvellous! Then it's all sorted. Lando, you can stop looking so glum and let Pixie know exactly when you'll need her. Come on, let's get back up to the house before all this greenery we've collected starts to wilt.'

I followed her, wondering what exactly I might have let myself in for.

EIGHT

The sitting was not mentioned the next day at breakfast, which was a blessedly subdued affair with no surprise 'mother's help' jobs launched at me. Having avoided all alcohol the night before, I was feeling fresh and enthusiastic.

'Come on, you two, tear yourselves away from Paw Patrol. Let's go and get dressed and then I shall get out my special, mystery, super-exciting box. We've got work to do.'

As hoped, this fired the twins up and within twenty minutes we were sitting at the kitchen table, their eyes shining with excitement and me clutching the large plastic box, wrapped in colourful festive paper, that I had received from the courier. That had been an extravagance, but I couldn't possibly have brought it on the train, and I knew it had the potential to save Christmas.

'What else is in it, Pixie? Oh, do show us.'

'Well... I have one of these...'

I slowly extracted an item from the box, producing it with a final flourish, then watched their faces fall.

'A loo roll. That's not very exciting.'

'Ah ha! But it will be when you see what we can *do* with this humble loo roll.'

I went on to produce tub after packet of Christmas crafting bits that I had collected over the years. Sequins, cotton wool, shiny paper, scraps of fabric, ribbons, plastic jewels, stickers, buttons, metallic pipe cleaners, tiny bells... It was a box of delights, and I loved getting it out each year to show my classes. Phina and Caspy's expressions changed from disappointment to delight as I brought out each new treasure, and they laid them out reverently on the table, alongside an array of plain tubes and boxes, ready to be transformed. Soon we were making Father Christmases to add to the tree, and I had commanded the voice-activated speaker to play a selection of cheesy tunes. This is how Bunny found us when she popped in to make a cup of camomile tea.

'Oh, look at you all, how marvellous. I don't think I've ever seen anything so lovely and festive. How on earth do you do it, Pixie? I think you're terribly brave.'

I laughed.

'Well, it is what I do for a living. I think you're amazing producing those beautiful watercolours. How are they going?'

'Very well, thanks to you. I do feel such *relief* that I can get on with work and not worry about anything else.'

'Mummy, look!' said Seraphina, holding up her creation, which was dripping claggy bits of glue-soaked cotton wool on to the vinyl tablecloth I had thankfully remembered to put down.

'Phina, that is absolutely perfect,' said Bunny, and her daughter beamed. 'I hope that once it's dry it's going on the tree?'

As they talked, I watched them, thinking how much I already loved these dear, funny children with their brightness and instinctive love of life. The familiar ache started to seep through me, for my own children, my own kitchen table, my own eclectic, beautiful Christmas tree. But before the tears could start to fill my eyes, I pushed the feeling down firmly. No. This wasn't what I was doing anymore, hankering point-lessly after something that wasn't meant for me, suffering need-less pain when stoicism was what was required. After all, I should be happy and excited: my life was going to be all about adventure from now on. I forced myself to think about the images of India my parents had sent me – the colourful markets, hazy views of mountains, the sunsets, the primary school I might teach at, not so unlike an English one in many ways, except for the bare yard they had as a playground. My spirits lifted fractionally, and I nodded firmly. *That's better, Penny.*

Soon, Bunny returned to her work and the three of us continued with ours. By lunchtime, we had produced a small army of Santas, some rather wonky pipe cleaner reindeer and some bejewelled boxes, perfect for putting small presents in. We had started studding oranges with cloves, but it hadn't been as easy as the Instagram posts make it look, and we had been left with a mushy mess, no good for any Christmas tree but which scented the air beautifully, regardless of how they looked. Lunch was a quiet affair, just me, the children and, briefly, Bunny. The weather had turned grey and sleety while we were eating, and I had to turn the light on.

'Right, it doesn't look nice enough for us to go out this after-noon. You've worked hard this morning, but we can't hang the decorations yet as they're still drying. So...'

I widened my eyes at the twins, and they giggled in antici-pation of what might be coming next.

'So... how about we find a very Christmassy film to watch – and make some hot chocolate to have with it?'

They exploded into an excited clamour.

'Oh, hot chocolate, I *love* hot chocolate! Can I have mine with marshmallows – and unicorn sprinkles like Cecil does?'

I remembered the spectacular drinks the landlord of The

Curious Badger had produced and wondered what Pilar had in the cupboards that might compete.

'Can we watch Frozen? Or Frozen 2? Or both?'

'No, no, I don't want to watch that again. I want to watch the one where the dog gets dognapped.'

'Noooooo, that's too scary. Oh Pixie, *please* can we watch Frozen?'

I sat down on the sofa between them and drew them under my arms.

'Let's do one thing at a time, shall we? We'll get the hot chocolate sorted first – I'm not sure I can manage a Cecil Special, but it will still be delicious. As for the film, maybe you'll let me choose? I have something in mind that I think you'll *both* love.'

Fifteen minutes later, we were tucked up under soft fleecy blankets, sipping drinks that we had adorned with squirty cream and colourful hundreds and thousands, and starting a crowd-pleasing film about singing chipmunks. Even I liked this one and I sank into the arm of the sofa, feeling utterly content. That wasn't to last. After about twenty minutes, the door opened, letting in a gust of chilly air, and in stalked Lando. He sat down on the chair next to me. I fought the instinct to stand to attention – Timothy would doubtless have had something caustic to say about my sloppiness – but smiled at him and was, to my surprise, rewarded with a smile in return.

'You three look very snug there. What are you watching?'

'It's very cerebral, all-singing, all-dancing chipmunks. You'd love it.'

'Hmm. Maybe. But for now, I have to work. I only came in to arrange a time with you for our first sitting. Would tonight after supper do? I've checked already with Bunny that she can free you up.'

There goes that excuse.

'Yes, this evening is fine, although your father said he was having a friend over and invited me for drinks.'

'Don't worry, we'll be finished in time to get to that. I'm sure my father won't let a drinks party finish any later than about midnight.' He smiled wryly.

'Great, thank you. Do I need to bring anything or, I don't know, *do* anything?'

He looked puzzled, and I started gabbling.

'I mean, you want me to be Mary, but should I wear anything special? Not that I have a halo tucked away in my suitcase, but maybe a dress or something? As for the rest of it...'

'Yes?'

I had been about to make some inappropriate quip about being heavily pregnant and virginal and now I stared at Lando in horror as my brain caught up with my mouth.

'Nothing, nothing. I could... put my hair up...'

I trailed off miserably.

'Your hair's fine. Nice, actually. And no need to dress up. I have something for you to wear, if that's all right?'

I nodded mutely, silenced by the double whammy of my gobbledegook and his compliment – *was* that a compliment? It had passed by pretty quickly.

'Good. I'll see you later then. Enjoy the chipmunks.'

And he was gone. Thankfully, the film was so absorbing that Phina and Caspian had barely noticed or acknowledged their uncle's presence, so there were no awkward questions. I let myself sink into the tumult of thoughts and feelings that were chasing around my brain and body, pushing off the blanket which was suddenly too hot.

NINE

Lando wasn't at supper that evening, which made me even more nervous as I kept worrying that I was taking too long and he would be sitting in his studio tapping his watch and wondering where I was. Regardless of this, there was no question of turning down Pilar's death by chocolate, but as soon as I had finished scraping the glaze off my bowl, I set off. Far from impatient, Lando's face creased into a puzzled frown when I pushed open the door, once again breathing in that clean, woody smell. I wondered if I should remind him why I was there, but he put down his tools and smiled.

'Penny. Thanks for coming. Sorry, I was rather absorbed there. I can lose hours when I'm working.'

'Is it the Nativity you've been doing?'

'No, I'm making Christmas presents for the children, little models of this house to hang on the tree. I thought it would be a nice memory for them. I'd show you but they're not finished.'

'I'm sure they'll love them. It's such a beautiful house, I'm not surprised you want to recreate it.'

'I suppose it's an attractive house. I like it well enough, but it doesn't suit me. It's a family house and obviously I'm not a family man. I'll be putting it on the market after Christmas, hopefully for a quick sale.'

'Oh, I see. Where will you live?'

'I'm sure that my indiscreet sister-in-law has told you about my breakdown?'

I gave a tiny, awkward nod.

'Obviously I need a very quiet, secluded life, and although I have that here, it is criminally wasteful to keep this house for myself and my father. I am going to move to Greece, get a small place there, do my work, live simply and not cause anyone any worry.'

Another one running away, I thought, and wondered if he'd considered India. But instead, I asked him, 'Where will William go?'

'I'm sure Ben can find some space for him; they've got plenty of room and he'll like living in London.'

I nearly blurted out that everything could change, with another baby on the way and William freshly in love, but managed to bite my tongue.

'Your breakdown – wasn't that because of work? Now that you're here and doing something you enjoy, something less stressful, don't you think that family life might appeal?'

I'm asking for a friend...

Without replying, he stood up and went to a large box, from which he took a length of heavy fabric.

'I'd like you to wear this, if that's okay. I can pin it if you stand up.'

I did so, taking my cue to shut up on the subject of his personal life. I don't know why I was having to push away disappointment. After all, here was a kindred spirit in the 'moving away and eschewing the thought of a family' camp. I should be celebrating. I tried to smile.

'Are you all right, Penny? You don't look well.'

'Er, yes, fine, I'm fine. Let's get draped, shall we?'

I stood up.

'Can you drop your shoulders? They're up by your ears. And stand naturally – I won't stick pins in you, you don't need to worry.'

How could I tell him that it wasn't the pins making me tense but his sudden proximity? The brush of his hand against my cheek as he tucked the cloth around my shoulders, the warm scent of coffee and wood shavings that drifted from him, the curl of dark hair I had a sudden longing to tuck behind his ear.

'I think you'll need to take your jeans off.'

'Huh?'

'Your jeans. Sorry, but they're bulking out your silhouette too much under the fabric. Would you mind taking them off?'

He turned towards his workbench, and I started fumbling around for the fly button, trying not to dislodge the pins he had already arranged; partly not to spoil his work and annoy him, but mainly because I didn't want the whole lot to fall off and display my pale, dimply thighs and substantial, yet comfortable, black cotton pants. I managed to wriggle free and was draping the jeans over a chair when I realised that, as the cloth only fell to just above my ankles, my feet clad only in socks – comedy Christmas socks, of course, with cheery little elves eating candy canes – were on full display.

'Are you ready?'

'Um...'

He turned around and didn't even glance at the offending socks.

'Good. Much better without the jeans. Okay, come and stand over here, please.'

I shuffled over to the place he indicated and stood stiffly while he looked me up and down.

'I've got most of the body, it's the head and face I'm really interested in.'

That figured. Who would be interested in my neglected, biscuit-fed body?

'So, hold your arms however you're comfortable. Turn your head to the left a bit... and tip your chin up... look into the distance. That's it. I need you to hold that gaze.'

As I awkwardly tried to follow his instructions, I didn't think I could feel any more uncomfortable, but then he came close and started making tiny adjustments: a tendril of hair tucked in here, a microscopic lift of the chin there. I could feel his breath warm on my face and smell soap on his hands. I risked breaking my 'into the distance' gaze to look at his face as closely as he was looking at mine, noticing a dusting of freckles across the bridge of his nose and a small half-moon scar by his right temple.

'Can you look over there again, please?'

I jumped guiltily and resumed my gaze, hoping he couldn't hear my stupid heart, pounding away frantically, letting me down when I was so determined to believe that he was having Absolutely No Effect. I tried to conjure up another helpful and chaste vision of India and its primary schools, but now all I was getting was some sort of *Passage to India* fantasy: me on a large double bed, its muslin curtains drifting in the breeze, as Lando walked in through the door and closed the carved wooden shutters against the heat of the afternoon...

'Penny?'

'Yes, sorry, what?'

'You were miles away. I'm ready to start now, if you could hold it just like that.'

I had warmed up considerably and wanted to shrug off the heavy fabric but smiled weakly and tried to feel a bit more virginal as Lando started scraping away at a half-finished figure. It was about a foot tall, made of a glowing wood which rippled with different shades of brown, from lightest beige to a deep chocolatey hue. I kept letting my eyes dart over, fascinated by his concentration and delicacy as he worked. The peace soothed me, and I began to feel more comfortable.

'That's it, hold that.'

'Hold what?'

'You just smiled, just a little bit. It was perfect, beautiful. That's what I need, that's what I'm missing. Whatever you were thinking about, keep thinking. Please.'

Being described as both perfect and beautiful was enough for me, and I let the smile touch my lips again as I floated back to that Indian boudoir and let the story progress. Then another thought entered my mind. Seeing as Lando was patently unsuitable and very complicated, and had been upfront about not wanting a relationship, surely a small dalliance with him would not be remotely sensible – and therefore not breaking my own rules. Clever! Couldn't I maybe... enjoy him for a couple of weeks, as I got my ducks into a row regarding my adventure? Reality knocked gently at my brain, reminding me that he, too, would have to want this, but I brushed it away. At least I could *think* about him, under these new rules, and enjoy that. It was genius.

Sadly, I didn't have time to capitalise on this as Lando put down his tools and said, 'Okay, that's enough for one evening. You've been standing there for nearly an hour, you've been great, thank you.'

'An hour? It didn't feel anything like that long. Time flies, I suppose.'

'Isn't that meant to be when you're having fun? Can't imagine standing there in your Mary robe while I chip away is much fun, but *chacun à son goût.*'

I could feel my cheeks flush. Was he making fun of me? Maybe he saw my discomfort, maybe he was oblivious, but he carried on, 'Mind you, I suppose an hour's peace when you spend most of your time looking after small children probably *is* fun – so would you mind posing again? I'm nearly there, I think, and it *has* made a difference having a live model.'

I shifted from foot to foot. 'No, of course not, as long as it's all right with Bunny. I think I'll take this off now and put my jeans back on, if that's okay?'

'Oh, yes, of course. I'll unpin you.'

My decision to enjoy Lando's gorgeousness didn't really help with his closeness for a second time as he unfastened the fabric. I could feel my stomach leaping with desire and nothing would have felt more natural than to shrug the robe from my shoulder and let his warm hand replace it. But of course, Sensible Penny triumphed, and I stood stiffly, terrified of an accidental meeting of skin that might render me a hot mess of lust while Lando looked on, slightly embarrassed. His delicate movements intimated that he, too, was trying to avoid touching anything other than the pins, but I supposed that was more to do with avoiding hurting me than unleashing his own uncontrollable passion.

'All right, there you go. I'll go over there while you put your jeans back on.'

I managed this swiftly and pulled my shoes on over the shameful socks.

'Can I see Mary, or won't you let me until she's finished?'

'No, you can see her, come over.'

He handed me the sculpture, and I held it up to the light. Even to my eye, more used to finger painting than fine art, it was a thing of beauty. Her robe draped softly around her head and fluidly to the floor, her hands were slim and sensitive and her face radiant with peace and love. I didn't know what to say, without either gushing or being flippant, so I simply turned her over in my hands, running my fingers over the features.

'Do you like it?'

I looked up into Lando's face and saw that he really cared what I thought. I barely felt qualified to reply, but managed to stutter, 'Lando, it's... exquisite. I can't believe you've created this from a piece of wood. There's so much movement and emotion... I love it. The church is incredibly lucky.'

Gushing, then. Oh well.

'I'm so glad. Relieved. You're the first person who's seen any of it. I've been worried...'

I gazed into his eyes and smiled.

'You don't need to be. It's a work of art.'

He took it back and stared at it before hurriedly returning it to his workbench.

'Thank you. Obviously, it's not quite finished. But you've helped, Penny, you brought a kind of calm with you this evening, a reassurance.'

Having said this, he turned his back to me and started sorting through offcuts of wood, muttering something about their grain. I supposed that the calm he spoke of was more to do with my being so dull, and there was nothing much left to say. I felt I had been dismissed. Well, I was happy to go.

'I'll be off then. Are you coming up to the house for a drink with your father's friend?'

'No, I've got too much to do here. Night, Penny.'

'Night then.'

I opened the door to leave.

'Oh, and Penny?'

'Yes?'

'Nice socks.'

As I trudged back to the house, my mind was full and confused. On the one hand, there was the boiling attraction I was beginning to feel for Lando, and the exciting thought that I could throw sense to the wind and indulge that, in my mind if no other way. On the other was the stone-heavy lump of knowledge sitting in my stomach that I was, truly, rather a sensible person who brought calm and wore cheerful socks. Maybe I should accept that, I mused, and the consequences. Pixie might be propositioned by moonlight by dashing strangers with roses between their teeth, but Penny was hot chocolate and a sofa. Maybe I should return to my neat little house and my safe job, forget India, forget passion, forget adventure but without replacing those things with pointless yearning for family life. I should accept my lot and be some sort of community good egg: a nun without the trappings. These depressing thoughts took me inside the house, where I was instantly distracted. In the hallway were Bunny and Xander, helpless with giggles.

'Oh Pixie, there you are, darling. You've come back in the nick of time.'

'Why, what's going on?'

'It's William. The friend he's brought home is absolutely wonderful, but he is so starry-eyed…'

She went off into another peal of laughter, so Xander took up the story.

'It's fantastic really, but none of us has seen him like that. Daphne is running rings around him with her husky-voiced fabulousness. Do come and meet her.'

'Oh, I'm not sure. I'm quite tired from posing for Lando for all that time. I might go to bed early with a book.'

'Oh, please don't, Pixie. You're probably desperately low from spending all that time in silence while he chips away. This will be the most terrific mood-lifter, I promise. Even Pilar couldn't resist; she's in there pretending to tidy a bookcase. I keep trying to give her a drink and get her to sit down, but she won't have it – maybe you'd have better luck?'

It was hard to refuse Bunny when she laid her hand on my arm and smiled at me. It was good to see her happier; maybe the combination of this Daphne and William's besottedness was what I needed.

'All right, maybe for a bit then.'

We trooped back into the living room. William was sitting next to Daphne on the sofa, listening attentively as she spoke. They both looked up as we came in. Besotted he may have been, but William's immaculate manners didn't fail. He stood up.

'Penny, there you are, how wonderful to see you. Sit down, let me get you a drink and introduce you to my friend Daphne. Are you sure you won't have something, Pilar?'

She put down her duster as if she were relinquishing the crown jewels and smiled.

'*Bueno*, perhaps just a small sherry, *gracias* Señor Lord.'

I smiled my thanks to William and gave an awkward wave to the woman on the sofa, but Daphne rose and glided over to me, enveloping me in a warm, powdery-scented hug. For the second time that evening I was draped in fabric, but this time it was the slippery satin sleeves of her flowing, kimono-like robe.

'Penny, Penny, I'm *thrilled* to meet you.'

Her voice was deep and slightly raspy, full of warmth and humour.

'William said that you are already firm friends, so I hope that also means you are a friend of mine.'

'Oh, thank you, I hope so too.'

It was difficult to imagine this immensely glamorous woman dressed as an elf.

'Do you really work in the grotto with him?'

She drew me over to the sofa and plumped a few cushions behind my back as I sat down. William handed me a typically gigantic gin and tonic and sat down again on her other side. She took his hand, and he beamed as if he had won the lottery.

'I do. He is a peerless Father Christmas and I'm merely one of his lowly elf helpers, trying to support his good work.'

They gazed into each other's eyes adoringly, and I started to see why the others had needed to escape to the hallway to release their giggles. I settled for a slug of my drink, with which I successfully quelled the rising hysteria.

'So, Daphne, have you done any performing before?'

She and William looked at each other and laughed gently, in that special 'sharing a secret' way that lovers have. My bubbling giggles went flat. I was happy for them, but so sad for myself. An image of India obediently came into my mind, but I swiped left. I wasn't in the mood.

'Penny, Daphne is a *doyenne* of the stage. The elf gig is her gift to the children each Christmas. A very gracious one.'

'I'm sorry, I didn't realise you were an actress. What are your favourite parts?'

Daphne clutched at my arm, her myriad rings glinting and winking in the firelight.

'Oh Penny, what a *wonderful* question. Thank you for asking.'

I could see Xander beginning to double up again, but I was genuinely interested in Daphne's answer.

'Do you know *Abigail's Party*?'

I nodded. 'Yes – well, I've seen the TV version, anyway.'

'Then you will guess that I loved my time touring as Beverley. Such a *nuanced* role.'

I nodded vaguely, hoping she wouldn't expect me to remember too much.

'Or maybe Coward is more your thing? *Private Lives*, Amanda, terrific fun.'

'Oh yes, I've seen that a few times, I love that play.'

'Maybe we should perform a short scene?'

'Oh gosh, no, I don't think I'd be very good at that.'

'You'd be fabulous. But perhaps something less scripted would be fun. Charades! Oh, do come on everyone, Charades!'

She stood up and started organising us into teams before most of us had a chance to object. Pilar, however, was too quick for her, draining her drink and rising off the sofa with terrific aplomb and casting a '*buenas noches*' over her shoulder as she shot out of the room.

'What a shame she's gone,' said William, looking disappointed. 'She could have chosen Spanish films and books none of us philistines have ever heard of and won easily.'

'I think Pilar might think she's on the winning side, anyway,' said Xander, grinning. 'Maybe she needs some help in the kitchen—'

'Don't you dare,' said Bunny. 'Anyway, you know you can't resist showing off in Charades.'

He shrugged good-naturedly and Daphne allocated the teams: me with her and Xander, the other team comprising William and Bunny. I made a mental note to message my parents about this later. They would find the idea of us all gathered round playing a traditional parlour game hilarious but endearing and would probably be inviting their neighbours in for some of the same within the hour.

'All right, we have five minutes to scribble down some titles and then we will begin. William, I think that Charades really demands champagne, wouldn't you agree?'

He seized her hand and squeezed it.

'Daphne, you are a marvel. Back in a mo.'

Half an hour later, we were all screaming with laughter at the frantic gesticulations of our team members, quaffing champagne (all except Bunny, of course) and accusing each other of cheating.

'Sorry, but who put in *Bohemian Rhapsody*? How the *hell* am I supposed to mime that?'

'Well, it's not as difficult as *The Iliad*. Who put that in?'

Nobody owned up. I was glad, hoping to maintain the illusion that it might have been me. Of course, I only ever manage to come up with children's book titles for these things, and *What the Ladybird Heard* had been guessed quite quickly.

Even under Daphne's skilful direction, the game eventually

collapsed, and nobody had any idea how many points each team had, let alone who had won, but we were all exhausted and happy and more than a little drunk. I made the mistake of glancing at my watch.

'Oh no, look at the time! I'm going to go up. Thank you all for such a fun evening – and it was such a pleasure to meet you, Daphne.'

I was treated to another scented embrace before I tottered into the hall and began navigating the stairs, making full use of the banister to keep me on track.

As I got ready for bed, the excitement provided by the evening's fun and the lift of the champagne began to subside. I pulled on my pyjamas and sat on the side of the bed, feeling a distinct sense of coming down. An image flashed into my head of Lando's cosy, messy, wood-infused studio and I felt a powerful yearning to be there. It was not only I who had brought calm to him; I had also found it there myself, in the peace and the purpose. Did life have to be one thing or the other, I wondered, adventure *or* 'sensible'? Maybe it was possible to have both, to give up neither. I snuggled under the covers and started to read my book, but a thought kept creeping into my head, waving its brightly coloured 'good idea' flag. After several glasses of champagne, I should have known better than to listen to its siren call, but my defences were down, and it was very compelling.

Why don't you text Timothy? it whispered. *He's certainly sensible, and now that you've got more of an eye on adventure, maybe you'd be the perfect pair again? It would be better than trying to start again with somebody else...*

My feeble protestations were met with firm resistance, and the conviction that texting Timothy was a Good Idea became so strong that even my final vanguard suggesting that I at least waited until the morning was effortlessly dismissed. I reached for my phone.

TEN

I woke up earlier the next day than I would have liked but felt better than I would have expected. Maybe champagne was the answer? It would be very non-sensible to decide that, from now on, it was my only tipple. I allowed a few pleasant pictures of myself quaffing bubbly in various locations – admittedly, Lando's messy studio was one of them – to drift across my mind, when another picture rudely interrupted. My hand flew to my mouth and then to my phone. Oh no, I hadn't texted Timothy – had I? Even as I tapped in my PIN and opened WhatsApp, I knew that I had done it, not dreamt it. There it was:

> Hello. Just wondering how you're doing? I'm fine. Wonderful in fact! Having an adventure this Christmas. Be good to see you xx

I threw the phone across the bed, unfairly blaming it for the message, rather than my own, stupid, champagne-addled self. Almost immediately, I seized it back. *Maybe,* a tiny glimmer of hope whispered, *maybe he hasn't seen it yet. You can delete it, job done, then delete his bloody number and you're home free.* But no. There were the treacherous two blue ticks. He had read it. An hour ago, at least, according to the time stamp. I knew how this worked now. I would suffer an uncomfortable, churning mix of feelings in my stomach all day. On the one hand, hoping he would reply, which would end the suspense if nothing else, and on the other, hoping he wouldn't, because I really, really didn't want to get back in touch with Timothy. But what could I do? Other than send another message, withdrawing the first message, which felt a bit desperate, I was powerless to influence the situation. I would have to wait until he replied – if he replied – and style it out from there. All I could do now was to get a grip on myself and try not to think about it. To this end I switched the phone off, shoved it under a pillow and quickly grabbed my dressing gown to go down to breakfast. I was sure that the Lords would distract me soon enough.

I was first downstairs again, but it wasn't long before the family followed, William starry-eyed with love for Daphne, and even Bunny looking brighter. She drew me to one side and spoke to me quietly.

'Pixie, wonderful news! I have my three-month scan today and Ben is definitely coming. He's taken time off work and will be here in an hour or so. I'm so *happy*.'

I hugged her.

'That's brilliant, I'm happy *for* you. And how exciting to see the baby for the first time.'

I was also intrigued to meet Ben: Lando's brother, Bunny's husband, the father of those adorable children. They were beside themselves with excitement when they learnt that their father was coming, and deaf to Bunny's and my caution that their parents would be going out again almost as soon as he arrived. They zoomed through breakfast, then danced upstairs with me to get dressed, singing:

'Daddy, Daddy, Daddy, Dad-ahd-deee! He is coming to see-ee me!'

We were on the landing when he got in and I had to grab the twins' hands to stop them tumbling down the stairs in their haste to see him. They still managed to reach him before Bunny, and he scooped them both up, one in each arm, giving them a huge squeeze and kissing them until they shrieked. He threatened to drop them, provoking more screams, and eventually put them down, which was when I got my first proper look at him. There was no mistaking his resemblance to both Lando and William, with his attractive face and tall, slim body. But he had much lighter brown hair than Lando, slightly thinning, and there was something softer about his appearance, without being baby-faced. As the children grabbed at his trousers, clamouring to be picked up again, he waddled over to Bunny, who was waiting slightly awkwardly. He put his arms around her, and they shared a clumsy embrace before both turning to the children with, it seemed to me, some relief and fussing over them for a few minutes. I busied myself by studying the Christmas tree, knowing I would soon be needed to remove Phina and Caspy so their parents could go to the clinic. The sudden change of the laughter to wails gave me my cue.

'But why do you have to go already? You just got here.'

'I wanted to show you my loo roll Santa.'

I hurried over.

'Come on darlings, Mummy and Daddy have to go out and they can't be late.'

'But we don't *want* to stay with you, we want to go with them.'

I saw Bunny's stricken face and knelt down.

'I know, and I'm really sorry, but it's important that they go. I have something very fun in mind for us to do and you'll see Daddy soon – it's almost Christmas, remember?'

I received two identical, small smiles and I took their hands.

'Well done. Come on, say bye bye and we'll go and find Grandpa, who is going to help us with our next adventure.'

I hope so, anyway, seeing as I've only just thought of it.

Goodbyes were said and I moved the twins back through the house as quickly as I could, getting them to call elaborately for William.

'Now let's shout like parrots... like hyenas... like sparkly Christmas fairies...'

By the time we located him, they had rallied, and they perked up even further when they found him in an even better mood than usual. Grinning ear to ear, he produced a mini sack of gold coins from each pocket, which were quickly spirited away to a corner of the living room, where silence fell as the children started picking away industriously at the stiff gold foil.

'Benvolio been and gone, has he?'

'Yes. I'm sorry he didn't see you, they were in a rush.'

'Understood, understood. I can read an atmosphere well, Penny darling, and I am aware when couples need space.'

I didn't reply. I was too worried about giving away Bunny's secret.

'You look very serious indeed, my dear, so maybe what I have to tell you will lighten your heart as it has lightened mine.'

I was grateful for the change of subject.

'I do hope so. What is it?'

'The luminous Daphne – she allowed me a kiss last night. I now understand fully the expression 'walking on air', as I am ten feet up.'

'William, that's wonderful! Congratulations! I thought she was lovely, and very lucky to be the subject of your affections. I'm so glad it's working out for you.'

'As am I. But I feel it should be *you* telling me about some Christmas romance; I wonder if I could introduce you—'

'No, thank you.' I was firm. 'And right now, I want to ask you a different favour.'

'You have chosen the perfect moment. All my worldly goods? They're yours.'

I laughed.

'Not *quite* that big a favour. Actually, I was wondering if we could take the children to your grotto? I know the daytime cast isn't a patch on yours and Daphne's evening shift, but I think it would cheer them up.'

'What a splendid plan. And lunch afterwards – my treat.'

The twins were overcome with excitement at the prospect of visiting Santa's Grotto, and the last vestiges of disappointment at seeing their father so briefly fell away. How I wished my own worries could be soothed so easily.

William borrowed Lando's car, a modest and unwashed black Ford Fiesta, and we piled in for the short journey. The Santa on duty that day was a tiny, wizened man more suited to playing an elf, but with an infectious 'ho ho ho' and a heart-warming delight in seeing each child. As Phina and Caspy – who insisted on going up together – chattered away to him about their Christmas wishes, William filled me in:

'He used to be a funeral director, and very good at it he was too: exceedingly solemn and sympathetic, meticulously organised. Then he retired and handed the business over to his daughter and my goodness didn't we see a change in him. The life and soul now, presiding over the tombola at the village fete and never missing a chance to get dressed up, as if he'd been saving up his jollity all these years.'

He was certainly a successful Santa; the twins came away beaming and clutching brightly wrapped presents, the corners already slightly torn at the impossibility of waiting to see what was inside. We had lunch at a cosy Greek bistro, where the owner knew and loved William (although I suspected this was the case for every hangout in town) and lavished attention and food on us until we were dizzy and replete.

'What are we going to do when we get home, Penny?'

'Well, I don't know about you, but I am in the mood for a few rounds of Snakes and Ladders... and maybe a small den?'

Joyously discussing the layout of the den, which sofa cushions made the best walls and how many blankets would be needed, we headed home.

I had dragged everything into position and the three of us were sitting in the atrium of the den – I am a *very* experienced den builder – playing board games, when Bunny came in.

'Mummy, you're back! Is Daddy with you? Is he coming to the panto this evening?'

'I'm afraid not, darlings, but soon he'll be here for a whole week. He can't wait.'

'Come in our den, come in, come in, it's amazing. There's a skylight and everything.'

'I will, just let me go and make a cup of tea first. I won't be long.'

I heard Bunny's voice crack and saw the tears welling in her eyes.

'I'll come and give you a hand.' I stood up and turned back to the twins. 'Maybe we should have a snack in the banqueting hall part of the den, what do you think? Can you set up a special picnic?'

Delighted with this idea, the children raced off to get their bits and pieces of tea sets, all in mismatched patterns and sizes, but nonetheless ideal for the job. Bunny and I walked through to the kitchen, glad for once not to find Pilar there, although I was sure her advice would be sounder than mine ever could be. I flicked on the kettle and asked gently:

'Do you want to talk about it?'

A tear rolled down Bunny's smooth, pale cheek, followed by another, and another until she was sitting there, silent, and motionless other than the torrent of tears. I grabbed the kitchen roll, incongruently cheery with its Christmas pattern of snowflakes and robins, and pushed a couple of pieces into her hands, then busied myself with tea and snacks until she was ready to talk.

'Oh, Pixie,' she whispered eventually. 'Pixie, it's more terrifying than I could have imagined.'

'What happened? Ben is... coming back, isn't he?'

'Yes, yes – at least he says he is. But Pixie...'

She had stopped crying now and her pale cheeks had a tinge of grey.

'...it's another set of twins.'

Right on cue, Phina and Caspy rushed in, wondering where we were. I quickly filled their arms with packets of snacks which purported to be healthy and sent them back to the living room to continue setting up, then turned to Bunny.

'That must have been a shock,' I said carefully. This clearly wasn't news she was celebrating, and while I could understand why, I couldn't quite bring myself to commiserate either. I would have swapped places with her in a heartbeat. She looked up at me, her eyes wide and devastated.

'Don't think me a monster, Pixie. I know we're meant to think that every child is a blessing, and to be extra happy at news like this – double the fun and all that, but...'

She trailed off, her wan face a picture of misery. I sat down and took the limp hand that lay on the table.

'Tell me, Bunny, it's OK.'

She stared into her lap and spoke.

'All I can think about, all I can envisage, is *problems*. Ben obviously doesn't know what to say and God only knows what he's up to, anyway; my body took a beating from my first pregnancy, and I dread to think what this will do to it. Money is all right, I think, but another *two*... And Pixie, I'm so bloody *tired*. I already feel pulled in too many directions – how will I survive? The sleepless nights almost killed me last time, then the agonies of feeding, the treadmill of nappies and washing and worry. I don't know if I can *do* it again.'

Through my confused and conflicted feelings emerged one, stronger than the others, a deep sense of compassion. Feeling tears in my own eyes, I squeezed her hand.

'Bunny, of *course* you are scared and worried. There's more to having babies than lullabies and bunny rabbit onesies. If you're feeling dread – well, that's all right, and I think it's better that you're talking about it rather than trying to hide it.'

She went very still. Had I said the wrong thing? Offended her? The thick silence pulsed between us, before she looked up at me.

'Thank you. Oh, thank you, Pixie. I don't know what I'll – what we'll – do, I don't know what I can *bear*, but thank you for understanding, for not telling me I'm a wicked person.'

'Of course you're not wicked. Far from it. You're a loving mother and a human being. This stuff isn't straightforward. Come on, do you think you could *not* think about it for a bit? You don't have to right now. A spot of den making with those two might take your mind off it, and once the news has sunk in, then you'll have a clearer idea of how you feel.'

We took our drinks and headed back towards the living room and the playing children, doubtless both of us picturing what life would be like with another pair in the mix.

ELEVEN

The afternoon passed quickly, and Bunny put aside her distress and threw herself into the game, even creating a sort of bell-tower for the den out of some small, firm window seat cushions, that you could pop your head up through, like a meerkat. Of course, I was doing just this, two stick-shaped potato snacks wedged into my mouth like teeth, when Lando walked in. Again, I saw that glimmer of a smile cross his face, that led me to believe there was great humour behind that almost dour exterior.

'This looks like fun.'

'Come in, Uncle Lando. You can be the dragon.'

'I would like nothing more, but I've been sent to get you by Pilar. Early supper, before the panto?'

I glanced at my watch, horrified. The time had slipped by so quickly. I surreptitiously eased the snacks out of my mouth and crawled out of the den, telling myself that dignity was more a state of mind than body.

'Your uncle's right, it's later than I realised. Come on, let's get cracking.' I turned to Lando. 'I'll get them settled and I'll come and put all this away.'

'Don't worry, stay with them. I'll sort it. Excellent den, by the way.'

I grinned at the unexpected kindness.

'Thanks. One of my many talents.'

'I can imagine.'

Was he *flirting* with me? I didn't have time to think about it as the children dragged me off to the kitchen, the den forgotten and their minds now on tonight's panto, the breathless questions coming thick and fast.

'Do you think there will be *real* ponies? Can I have one of those sparkly spinny wand things? There will be ice cream at the interval, won't there? What can we wear, Penny?'

An hour later, we assembled in the hall. Everyone was going, including Pilar, who told me she loved panto, even if she found it completely *desconcertante*, which together we worked out translated as 'bemusing' or 'bewildering'.

'There are men as women, women as men and the audience are told to shout out things all the time,' she said, shaking her head. '*Muy extraño.*'

Daphne had taken Ben's ticket at the last minute and would meet us there. We piled into two cars for the short journey, and by the time we arrived, we were all as buoyant as the children. The red brick Victorian theatre on the edge of the village green was buzzing with activity. Families were milling around, their breath rising like smoke in the cold air, as they waited for latecomers and dug through bags or scrolled through phones looking for their tickets. I remembered the many times I had been taken to the panto as a child and felt a sudden longing for my parents. I switched my phone back on for the first time that day and sent them a quick message, with a photo of the colourful theatregoers. I resolutely ignored my mixed feelings about the fact that Timothy had still not acknowledged my text.

Many of the children had dressed up for the occasion, including our two. Phina was resplendent in a ladybird costume complete with a sticky out red tulle skirt, heart antennae and spotty net wings and Caspian had opted for a grey wig, blue boilersuit and fake glasses, which made him look like Einstein come round to plumb in your washing machine.

'Neither of you looks resoundingly Christmassy,' said Lando, 'but I admire your creativity.'

'You really should have dressed up too,' said Seraphina, twirling around. 'You could have come as Elvis.'

He roared with laughter. It was a treat to see him in such a good mood, but it wasn't doing much for my 'keep it casual' fantasies.

'What do you know about Elvis?'

'Lots. He sang about teddies and wore a sparkly white suit and ate hamburgers. I'd *love* one of those suits for Christmas.'

I think Lando might have whipped out his phone and ordered one on the spot, had Daphne not chosen that moment to turn up in an ankle-length leopard print fur coat and a cloud of perfume. She kissed everyone warmly before slipping her hand into William's and smiling girlishly at him.

'All right, we're all here,' said Bunny. 'Let's go and find our seats.'

We navigated our way past all the stalls selling garishly coloured merchandise. I ushered the children along gently with reminders that the tickets themselves were the treat, only to realise once we reached our third-row seats that various members of the family had stopped to buy different items. The twins were, to their utter delight, promptly issued with sweets (William), spinning LED wands (Bunny), more sweets (Xander) and glow wand necklaces (Daphne). I couldn't help laughing; their pleasure was so infectious.

'Just please no one send them home with one of the ponies,' I implored. I wouldn't put it past any one of the Lords to be found by the stage door later in the evening arranging for that to happen.

There had been a certain amount of negotiation as to who was sitting next to who. William and Daphne deemed themselves inseparable, and both twins wanted to be next to their mother. Xander insisted on an aisle seat in case he needed to rush out on urgent business, and Pilar sat next to him. Seraphina voted to have Daphne on her other side, guessing – perfectly correctly, as it turned out – that she would continue issuing sweets from various pockets and her sequinned handbag as Phina's own supply dwindled. Caspian, touchingly, wanted me next to him, so that meant Lando was on the end, and I had to have him on my other side. As we had been chattering and folding coats to tuck under seats, I could feel him watching me and eventually I turned to him.

'You're not still carving Mary, are you?'

'Sorry, I was staring.' He didn't sound remotely contrite. 'I like watching you with the children. You really love them, don't you?'

I softened.

'I do. I know it's only been a handful of days, but they're an eminently loveable pair, so funny and quirky and – well, perfectly adorable. Mind you, I like children very much in general – I couldn't do my job if I didn't.'

He opened his mouth as if he was going to say something else, but at that moment the lights dimmed and the safety curtain began to rise, revealing plush red curtains and a large sign hanging in front of them with 'Cinderella' in loopy, sparkling letters. All around me were giggles and whispers of 'It's beginning!' and I settled myself down to enjoy the show.

It certainly didn't disappoint. It was a panto in the best tradition, with all the old jokes and plenty of opportunities for the audience to join in. I was quite surprised to witness Lando's gusto as he shouted, 'It's behind you!' and booed the Ugly Sisters in their tall wigs and enormous, gaudy costumes. He roared with laughter at the cheesy jokes and gave every appearance of thoroughly enjoying himself. It was a marked contrast to the serious, almost grumpy, man I was used to seeing at the house. When the lights came up for the interval, I turned to him.

'I wasn't expecting you to be such a panto fan.'

He smirked.

'Love it. I've always loved it. Shame it's only once a year. Now, who wants ice cream?'

This was, predictably, met with a volley of excited shrieks from the twins, who swept everyone else up, so Lando soon had an order for eight ice creams, plus his own of course, although it was hard to imagine those toughened work hands pinching a tiny little spoon to eat up the mint choc chip.

'I'm not going to remember all of these; I'm going to need some help.'

I can never stop myself.

'I'll give you a hand.'

He didn't reply, just smiled and turned to edge his way along the row, leaving me to follow. I immediately regretted my willingness to volunteer as I shuffled after him. It had probably made me look all keen and puppy-eyed, but the truth was that I'm a natural helper and can't stop my eager little hand popping up when the call goes out. No wonder I got walked over the whole time – I practically had 'Welcome' printed across my back.

'Can you remember what everyone wanted?'

I had been so busy wallowing in my thoughts that I hadn't realised we had reached the usher with his tray.

'Oh, yes, I think so. Three vanillas, two chocolates, two

strawberries and a salted caramel if they've got one, otherwise another vanilla. And whatever you're having.'

'Impressive.'

My stomach flipped pleasantly, and although I told myself he was merely impressed by my mother's help skills, I couldn't help but feel that little flutter of hope, of promise, that was fanning a long untended fire inside me.

We were finishing our ice creams as the curtains opened again, on the wonderful, glittering scene of the palace ball. Boosted by the sugar and the sparkle, I settled down to enjoy the second half, whilst unsuccessfully attempting to ignore Lando's warm presence at my side. The arrival of the real Shetland ponies pulling the pumpkin carriage was so utterly adorable that I nearly managed it, but all too soon we had reached the singalong, and were nearly at the end of what had been a wonderful show.

'Now, you gorgeous lot,' said one of the Ugly Sisters, who was about six foot four, built like a wrestler and clad in a lime green ballgown decorated in flashing, multicoloured fairy lights. 'It's time for you all to join in. *I* know *you* all know about my lovely coconuts, so don't think you can get away with staying quiet. Everybody up!'

As we stood, a song sheet descended from the lighting rig with the familiar words. We sang obediently:

> *I've got a luverly bunch of coconuts*
> *There they are a-standing in a row*

Of course, our attempts were barracked and ridiculed in the finest panto tradition, but eventually it was time for the finale.

'Hold hands, everyone,' roared the Ugly Sister. 'Grasp your

neighbour, take your opportunity, it is Christmas, after all. Now sway!'

Caspian seized my hand immediately, but the awareness of Lando on my other side felt electric. I glanced up at him, and he lifted his hand towards me in invitation. Shyly, I slipped mine into his, and he gave it a little squeeze as the music started up again and the audience sang with gusto, swaying along in time. I felt as if someone had thrown a noose around my neck and was slowly strangling me. All I could think about, all I could feel, was Lando's hand holding mine. All my other senses seemed dulled – the music distant, the shouts from the stage echoing far away, Caspy's hand like a feather in mine. My entire being felt as if it was pulsing down my left arm and I feared my hand would be red hot and that Lando could feel my heart beating madly through my palm. I croaked my way to the end of the song, and as I was stumbling through the final chorus, Lando shifted his grip, lacing his fingers through mine. Now I went cold, the sudden intimacy shocking me, and I stopped singing altogether, feeling dizzy as the heat now returned to my body, flushing my face. I prayed my hand wasn't sweaty; I didn't think I could bear to see Lando wipe his on his jeans when we were finally allowed to release the hold. After what felt like several months, the song finished on the seventh repetition of the final line:

Roll a bowl a ball a penny a pitch!

Our hands were freed to clap and wave as the actors took their bows, and then I busied myself organising coats and hats and gloves and scarves, making more fuss than I usually do to ensure the children were warmly wrapped up, buying time to let myself settle. When we stepped outside, the cold air helped refresh me, and by the time we reached the cars, I had enough presence of mind to make sure that I was in a different vehicle from Lando. I piled in with William, Daphne, Pilar and the children. We drove home listening to Daphne's tales of her years on the stage, some of them far too scurrilous for Phina and Caspy's ears, but so funny that I couldn't stop laughing long enough to ask her to tone them down.

Although it was late when we arrived home, the twins had far too much adrenaline – and sugar – coursing through them to sleep. They skipped in singing the coconut song joyfully at the tops of their voices.

'Oh dear, I don't think I can keep my eyes open a second longer,' said Bunny, who was looking exhausted, but happier than she had been earlier.

'Go to bed,' I said. 'I'll gladly stay up with them for a while. They need to wind down and maybe a late night will mean a late morning.'

'You are a genius, and too kind. Thank you, dear Pixie.'

She kissed them goodnight and disappeared upstairs. Xander had vanished with some champagne and his phone almost as soon as we arrived, and William was still wearing his coat.

'I'm going to run Daphne and Pilar home,' he said, clinking his car keys.

'Goodnight then,' I said. 'I want to hear some more stories from the theatre next time, please.'

I followed the children into the kitchen, where they were sitting on the spotless floor by the warm Aga, the closest place they could find to help them recreate Cinderella. Lando was filling the kettle at the sink.

'All right, you two, how about some milk and gingerbread men and a quick game, to help you get ready for bed?'

'Oh, yes please, Pixie. I want the gingerbread girl.'

'You got it!'

'You will stay and play, won't you, Uncle Lando? I'm going to get Hungry Hippos and it's much, much funner with four. But I want to be the green hippo.'

Lando looked at me.

'Oh, I'm sure Penny doesn't want me hanging around, she's already got you two to look after.'

'Oh please, Uncle Lando, please!'

'No, do stay,' I said. 'Hungry Hippos is definitely more fun with four. But you have to be the yellow hippo.'

The children shouted, 'That's the *worst* one. You'll never win.'

Lando regarded us solemnly.

'Well, with a challenge like that, how could I refuse?'

Soon we were sitting around the kitchen table, all bashing away furiously at our hippos, raising squawks and whoops of dismay or victory as they gobbled the little plastic balls. As Seraphina reset the game for the third time and Lando chased after an escaped ball that was dangerously close to being lost forever behind the fridge, I allowed myself a moment's reflection. Having decided that I could have a torrid fling with the attractive but bad-tempered man, even if that fling were only imaginary, I now had to recalibrate. Tonight, I had seen a different, unexpected side to Lando; he had been relaxed, fun, good-natured, warm. Although you would think that this was a good thing, I disagree. When he was in the 'grumpy but gorgeous' box, I felt safe – I could fantasise about him in a sort of 'film star' way but had no desire actually to get to know him, or to have to worry about any deeper feelings. Seeing him in this new light, particularly interacting with the children who he obviously adored, had confused and upset me. The superficial images in my head were being nudged aside by something more meaning-ful, flashes of a shared future, and this was precisely what I had promised myself I would avoid. I felt almost cross with him for being so lovely; he had gone off-script and that made it difficult for me to stick to my resolutions. But as I looked up to see three expectant pairs of eyes waiting for me to position my trigger finger for the next round of Hungry Hippos, I comforted myself with the thought that all I had to do was keep all of this firmly in my head, which shouldn't be difficult. It simply mustn't spill over into real life. What would Lando see in me, anyway? And surely, I could ignore the nagging inner voice insisting that my desire for husband, children and home was as strong as it had ever been, and would offer me far more adventure than a new start in India could ever hope to? *Keep going, Penny*, I told myself. *Keep yourself safe.*

Two riotous rounds later and I noticed that the children's reactions were slowing, their shouts quieting. I knew I'd be unpopular, but my years of experience with children had taught me that it was always better to make them leave the party before they thought they were ready to.

'Come on, you two, time for bed. I'm sure there'll be plenty of time over the holiday for a rematch.'

Their complaints were token, and they bid Lando goodnight with little fuss. I shepherded them upstairs, through a very quick shower and toothbrushing, then one quick story. Eyelids were closing even before I had finished reading. I kissed them goodnight, then went back downstairs to tidy up. Was a part of me hoping that Lando would still be there? Of course, it was. I was even wondering how – or whether – to suggest a cup of tea. I was as bad as the children at knowing when to stop, and the thought of continuing the evening in the company of the 'new' Lando was enticing. But my hopes were dashed. The kitchen was empty. I was saved the job of tidying up, as he had put the game back in its box and removed our cups and glasses to the dishwasher. Damn him for being helpful and considerate on top of everything else that evening. I opened the back door for a last breath of freezing air and could see a light burning in Lando's studio. A vision of that cosy, busy space came into my mind, and I pictured him hunched over his carvings, as I had first met him, pouring whatever complicated emotions he was experiencing into the wood. I longed to go to him, to understand him, to get to know him. But, instead, I closed the door and took my exhausted mind and body to bed.

TWELVE

Breakfast the next morning was unprecedentedly quiet – just me and my thoughts and a text from Dad in response to the photo I had sent last night:

> Looks very festive and cold. It's 30° here! You might be surprised to hear that we are also going to see a panto, a local group puts them on every year, but they're a bit different from the ones at home. I'll send you the link xxx

I clicked through to read the article he had sent while the kettle boiled. There was still no reply from Timothy, who was clearly ignoring me. After ten years together, it seemed harsh, but I couldn't pretend I wasn't glad at the same time: I wished I had never sent that message. I decided that if there was no word from him today, then I would put it out of my mind completely. I had looked in on the children before coming down, but they were fast asleep, and it seemed a good idea to leave them that way, after their late night. I had been expecting to see Bunny, who was usually an early riser, so before I settled down to eat, I went up and knocked gently on her door. The 'come in' was barely audible and I went in to find her still in bed, the room dark.

'Good morning. Are you all right? I wondered if you'd like any breakfast?'

'Pixie, you are kind to think of me.'

Her words ended in a sob, and I went to sit on the bed, taking her hand.

'Bunny, what's wrong?'

'Oh Pixie, I feel so dreadfully sick. I've been throwing up for an hour, although there's nothing left to come out. And I'm so... hopeless.'

She started crying in earnest now, and I leant over to hold her shaking body, soothing her as I might have done one of the children, stroking her hair and muttering words of comfort. As she calmed down, I decided to start in a practical way. As ever.

'What normally helps with the sickness? Do you need to eat something?'

She nodded.

'It does help, but I couldn't face getting out of bed and going down.'

'I'll ask Pilar to prepare something, and I'll bring it up. I won't be long.'

Ten minutes later, I returned to the room with a plain breakfast to find her sitting up in bed looking, frankly, appalling. Her hair was lank, her face grey and her eyes so painfully sad that it was all I could do not to burst into tears myself. Instead, I encouraged her to eat and was soon rewarded with a tiny bit of colour in her cheeks.

'Thank you, Pixie, I do feel better. Sorry for being so silly.'

'Not silly in the least. You've got a lot to contend with at the moment – the pregnancy, your work, the twins...'

I trailed off, not wanting to mention her husband's apparent ambiguity, but she didn't shy away.

'And Ben running away. Yes, it's a lot. And Pixie, I feel so dreadfully guilty about the twins. I must, must get these commissions finished, that's one thing, but now with the sickness, and the prospect of two more babies... I feel like I can never give them the time and attention they deserve, and I'm missing out on their childhood too.'

Fat tears started rolling down her cheeks again. I wasn't sure how to comfort her, because I knew I would feel exactly the same in her situation, and I liked her too much to offer empty, meaningless words. I went for robust but sympathetic.

'Bunny, I am so, so sorry. It's a very difficult time for you. All I can say is that the twins really are fine, so don't disappear off down a rabbit hole of imagining their wan and weeping little faces as it truly isn't how it is. They're fast asleep right now, anyway, after their amazing outing last night. I'm also sure you will feel better once the nausea settles. What happened last time you were pregnant?'

'It did stop – around this sort of time actually.' She brightened. 'Maybe I haven't got much longer of feeling this bloody awful and then you're right – everything will be easier. I wish Ben were here.'

'I know, but right now he's doing whatever he needs to. You can't do anything about that right now, so concentrate on what you *can* control. How much longer until you've finished the commissions?'

'Oh Pixie, you're so wise. I could get them finished today if I can work uninterrupted. That would be marvellous. I feel better already.'

'Good. Then finish up your breakfast, have a long shower or bath and get busy. Phina and Caspy are absolutely great and will love to see you later, when you're ready for them.'

I left her in peace and went to tidy up the twins' room and

gently wake them. As I folded little clothes and stacked teddies, I allowed my mind to wander to forbidden territory. How much I loved this domesticity, these routine, caring jobs which held no real excitement or status but which I longed to fill my days with. Doing this job was giving me a small flavour of what it was like to be a mother, and all that did was to tear at the void inside, emphasise the hollowness. Would moving to India, seeking adventure, really manage to fill it, to satisfy me? I suspected not; one's true personality does have a way of pushing through. But what else to do? I couldn't, simply couldn't, put myself through more hope and heartbreak. That, the loss of hope, had proved more painful than anything. At least if I set my sights on a different kind of life, one that didn't include family and home, I wasn't setting myself up for a fall. And maybe acceptance would come. Neither child had stirred as I had bustled around the room, but now I twitched the curtains open, determined to channel my best affectionate-but-detached Mary Poppins. My resolve wavered instantly, as they blinked sleepily against the milky morning light and rubbed their eyes, snuggling back down again into their cosy beds.

'Come on, you two,' I said softly. 'Time for some breakfast and then we can think about what to do today.'

Fifteen minutes later, we were downstairs, having breakfast and reliving the best parts of last night's panto. Pilar had joined in to discuss how on earth the second Ugly Sister managed to pile her hair up so high and keep it there, when Lando came in.

'Morning all.' He plonked a strong-looking coffee on the table and sat next to me. 'Look, Penny, I'm sorry I vanished last night. I had a phone call I had to deal with.'

'Who was it, Uncle Lando?' piped up Seraphina, waving her spoon excitedly. 'I *never* get phone calls. Will they phone me, please!'

He smiled.

'Just an old... friend. I didn't really want to talk to her actually, so I'm sure you wouldn't. I'm sure we can find someone much nicer to give you a ring, if you'd like that?'

'Yes, please.'

They started chattering about who they would like to find on the other end of the phone, and I took my opportunity to study Lando. He seemed still to be in good spirits, but tired if that mud-like coffee was anything to go by. He might not have welcomed 'her' phone call, but it looked like it had kept him up, one way or another. I pushed aside the encroaching questions and broke into their chatter.

'I'd particularly like a chat with Father Christmas, I think. I'd ask him for a ride on his sleigh. Talking of which...'

Four little eyes popped with the excitement that a mention of FC always brings.

'I heard that there is a Winter Wonderland not far from here? Somewhere you can go and see his workshop, and the elves, and even a reindeer or two. Is that right?'

To my surprise, their faces fell.

'We really wanted to go, Penny, but Mummy said it's impossible to get tickets if you didn't buy them at Easter. You didn't, did you?'

'No, I'm afraid not. I'm so sorry, I didn't know. I saw an advert in a magazine yesterday and thought it looked like fun.'

The mood had dipped considerably, and I felt terrible. Then Lando spoke.

'That's not the one being held at Marshingham Grange, is it?'

'Yes, that's right. About twenty minutes from here.'

'Right, don't any of you go anywhere.'

With these enigmatic words, Lando darted from the room, only to return a few minutes later clutching his phone and wearing a big smile.

'Erm, anyone here still interested in a Winter Wonderland today...?'

The twins and I answered resoundingly: yes, yes, yes!

'Good, because it just so happens that the owner of Marshingham Grange is a friend of mine, who would love to invite us for morning coffee – as long as we go through an enchanted forest, sweet factory and Santa's workshop first, that is.'

The ensuing squealing was ear-splitting, but it was a joy to see the twins' happy faces. They rushed off to find their coats and shoes, and as we proceeded towards the hallway at a more stately pace, I said to Lando, 'Thank you, they're so thrilled. And they'll love that you're coming too.'

As will I.

'Well, George is a very old friend and I've got a few favours to call in. Not that he minds, he adores children – he's got five of his own – and arranges for this wonderland thing to be held in his grounds every year. As for me coming, it does make things very tight for time. I was wondering...'

'Yes?'

'It would help me relax a bit if you'd agree to pose again tonight.'

I remembered the last evening I had spent in his cosy, calm studio and didn't need to think about my answer.

'Of course I will. I just need to fit the timings in with Bunny and the children.'

He nodded and we turned our attention back to the twins, doing up zips and searching for a lost mitten.

The drive to Marshingham Grange wasn't long, but was well signposted, and Phina and Caspy grew louder with every notice they saw. When we swept past the main entrance, they shouted with that panicky disappointment that afflicts children so readily. Lando spoke up.

'Don't worry, calm down. My friend George told me to go around to a different entrance because we don't have tickets. We'll park up near the house, then walk down.'

I could feel the twins' anxious tension as we drove around the long walls before turning right up a short drive that led to tall gates adorned with wrought iron oak leaves and rearing stags. Lando hopped out and tapped a few buttons on a keypad next to the gates, which started to swing open slowly. We drove along a winding road, through paddocks then woodland, before emerging at a huge, honey-coloured stone house. A short, portly man appeared through a door at the top of some central steps, then came trotting down towards us. As we got out, he greeted us with great enthusiasm, hugging Lando and slapping him on the back, pumping my hand up and down and jostling the children's shoulders warmly.

'Hello, hello! Welcome to Marshingham. And Merry Christmas, of course! Sorry to make you use the service entrance. Lando, you look very well, good to see. Yes, well done. And absolutely *super* to meet *you*, Penny.'

He beamed at me, and I beamed back. It's so infectious when someone is so obviously glad to meet you, although I wasn't entirely sure why.

'Now then, I know you two' – he gestured to the children – 'won't want to wait a second longer to get to that magical forest, but promise me you'll come back up to the house later? I believe there is some fresh gingerbread for the taking...'

Phina and Caspy nodded vigorously.

'And I very much look forward to getting to know *you* better, Penny. Right. Off we go!'

He set off at a brisk pace, and we hurried to follow him.

'George seems nice,' I said to Lando, as we skirted some rose beds, barren at this time of year but nonetheless immaculately kept. 'Very friendly.'

'Mmm, yes, he's being a bit over the top, I'm afraid. I think he assumes you're my new girlfriend, come along to rescue me from my miserable bachelor's existence. George thinks that no one could possibly be happy without a rosy-cheeked wife and hordes of children. Don't worry, I'll put him straight, save you an interrogation.'

I bit my lip in embarrassment. It wasn't my mistake, but all the same Lando's crushing summary made me feel slightly ashamed, as if I had somehow presented myself as suitable marriage material and been found wanting. To add to my shame, I was secretly relieved when Phina tripped over and banged her knee. I rushed over to her and fussed far more than I would do normally, then took her hand and stayed well away from Lando.

The winter wonderland was as wonderful as its sold out status suggested. From the moment we stepped through the icicle-hung archway, magic surrounded us. Cheerful elves and pretty snow fairies guided us along snowy paths which led to dimly lit jewel caves, full-size gingerbread houses and crystal pergolas, all holding new wonders. We helped mine diamonds, print snowflake wrapping paper with little carved blocks, assemble wooden toys and make – and eat – sweet, spicy gingerbread. An hour or so later, starry-eyed with festive dreams and our tummies full of lunch and sweet treats, we were led to a log cabin, smoke pouring from the chimney. The door opened and there stood a smiling woman, dressed in red edged with white fur.

'Hello, my dears, have you come to see Santa Claus?'

'Yes, yes, we have. Is he there?'

'Oh yes, of course he is here, and he is looking forward to meeting you, Seraphina and Caspian.'

'*How does she know our names?*' whispered Caspy, eyes wide.

'*Magic, of course,*' I replied in a whisper. '*Or maybe the elves told her. I think this is Mrs Claus.*'

She continued: 'Before you come in, there is a job he would be so grateful if you would do. He has been so busy sorting out all the presents and polishing up his sleigh that he hasn't had time to give the reindeer anything to eat. Could you do that?'

I didn't know if the twins would be able to get the words out, so great was their excitement, but they finally managed to gasp, 'Yes, of course we'll help.'

'I *love* reindeer,' added Phina earnestly.

I caught Lando's eye over her head and smiled, receiving in return a matching smile of pure joy at seeing the children's wonder. For a moment our eyes locked, then I looked away sharply. Maybe we were sharing this beautiful time together, but I didn't want to be mistaken again for an eager wifeling.

We followed Mrs Claus around to an enclosure where three real reindeer stood, their coats thick and shaggy, magnificent antlers rising from their huge heads. They turned round as we approached, their warm breath puffing clouds into the chilly air. The twins were agog, and I was impressed, too, by these lovely creatures. Mrs Claus collected a small sack and beckoned us over to the fence.

'Come on, my dears, don't be afraid. This is Cupid, Blitzen and Dancer. They're very friendly.'

We approached slowly, more in awe than fear, and took the handfuls of hay we were offered, holding it out on flat hands as instructed. The animals meandered over and gently snatched it from us, causing little cries and giggles of pleasure. I gingerly stroked Blitzen's velvety nose and was rewarded with a nudge and whicker. Soon we were all more confident and we stood for several minutes feeding and stroking the docile creatures.

'Let me take a photo,' said Mrs Claus, holding her hand out. I gave her my phone, and she took several pictures of the four of us.

'Let me see, let me see!' said Phina, pulling at my arm as I took the phone back. I crouched down to swipe through the pictures, which were lovely, showing us purely happy at this simple pleasure of communing with the reindeer. Try as I might, no colourful vision of India would come to chase away my longing as I looked at our shining faces and the family-like scene. I stood up and was about to stuff the phone into my pocket when Lando's hand covered mine to stop me.

'Can I see?'

'Oh, of course.'

I lit the screen up again and tried to hand him the phone, but he leant in instead, studying the photos as I moved through them.

'That's a good one,' he said. 'Will you send it to me?'

'Er, yes, if you like.'

'I do like. Thanks, Penny.'

He went back to join the children for a final pat of the rein-deer, leaving me flustered. Why did he want the picture? I suppose it was for the children; he could always crop me out. But I looked again at the image he had asked for, and both chil-dren had their backs to the camera; tired of being photographed they had returned to the animals. He and I, however, were smiling straight into the lens. I shrugged and pocketed the phone as Mrs Claus said:

'OK, time to say goodbye to your new friends, I think Santa is ready for us.'

Waving to the reindeer and promising to leave them specially juicy carrots on Christmas Eve, we returned to the front of the house, where a smiling elf was waiting for us. She ushered us inside through a hall decked with tinsel and candy canes and into the grotto where the biggest, jolliest Father Christmas I had ever seen sat waiting, chuckling and grinning.

'*He doesn't look like he did yesterday,*' whispered Caspian. '*He's completely different.*'

I bit my lip, not sure how to answer this perfectly accurate observation. I was most relieved when Lando squeezed Caspy's shoulders and said, 'You're right. You never know who the real one is, that's part of the fun. He's so busy that he has to have lots of helpers at this time of year to find out what all the children would like in their stockings. But I think he *must* be the real one, remember the reindeer?'

I smiled gratefully at him as Caspy nodded vigorously and stepped forward.

'Thank you,' I said. 'What a wonderful answer.'

'I love seeing them so happy,' he replied. 'God knows life gets hard enough as you get older, so you've got to keep the magic going as long as you can.'

'Don't you think there's room in all our lives for a little magic?'

He didn't answer at first, but caught and held my gaze with an unreadable expression. I began to feel flustered, dizzy, but couldn't drag my eyes away from his. Eventually he spoke.

'I didn't used to think that, no.'

I was saved from answering by the children bouncing back over, each clutching a brightly wrapped present.

'He *is* the real one, Uncle Lando, you were right.'

'He said the reindeer would remember us and take him extra quickly to our house.'

Chattering and waving, we left the log cabin and the enchanted forest, to cross a vast lawn back towards the house, where George was waiting for us.

'You all look like you've had a wonderful time,' he said, ushering us into an immaculate blue and cream room where on a low table between squashy sofas stood a four-tier cake stand laden with macarons, tiny, iced cakes and biscuits thick with chocolate. We sat down and he started to pour tea and hand out delicate little plates for us to load up with goodies. 'Even you look cheerful, Lando – a bit of our woodland magic must have rubbed off.'

'Something like that,' he answered drily, taking a biscuit.

'Uncle Lando *has* been more cheerful,' piped up Seraphina, who had somehow already managed to get more icing around her mouth than had surely ever been on her cake. 'He's smiling much more than he used to.'

George looked pointedly at me and gave me a huge, theatrical wink.

'I'm not remotely surprised,' he answered.

I didn't dare look at Lando, but busied myself wiping the children's faces and fussing over non-existent crumbs. Surely, Lando would put George straight, explain that I was just the mother's help, not the future Mrs Lord, but instead he asked about George's children while I was left confused, my mind whizzing through a million different thoughts, of which my imminent Indian adventure was the very least.

When we arrived back at the house, we found Bunny looking vastly better, having managed to both finish her difficult commission and get some rest. She and the twins fell into each other's arms, and I was so glad to see their delight in one other.

'Pixie, thank you for today. I was simply in *despair* this morning, but everything seems lighter now. I'll take my darlings from here, it's been too long since I've sat with them at teatime and put them to bed and I can't wait. I've got Pilar to shore me up if I fail too terribly.'

I turned to Lando.

'I can come and pose now then, if you'd like? I don't think I could eat a morsel of supper after that wonderful tea George gave us.'

He agreed, and we walked together towards the studio

without speaking. For once my tendency to gabble and fill silences had dried up, and as he held open the door to that fragrant haven, I wondered what further magic the day might hold.

THIRTEEN

The heavy atmosphere between Lando and me didn't lift as he draped the robe around me again. If anything, the brush of his hand on my skin as he fixed the pins was even more electrifying than previously, and I was at once terrified that he would notice my rising desire and desperate to spill it all out. As he went over to his workbench, I relaxed a fraction and let my mind wander back to the day we had spent together, a day of simple pleasures and easy company, punctuated by that lingering gaze and the confusion over why he hadn't corrected George as to the reason for my presence.

He worked for nearly an hour, then placed his chisel down, picked up the figure and rubbed it all over with a soft cloth.

'Penny? I think she's finished.'

'May I see?'

'Of course.'

I took the carving from him and turned the warm, smooth wood in my hand. I'm no art critic, but even I could tell that this was spectacularly good. Beautifully and sensitively carved, the fabric had fluidity and Mary's face radiated peace and love. Her lips curved in a soft smile and her eyes, whilst gentle, held the faintest whisper of humour.

'How is it possible?' I said, looking at Lando in wonder, seeing this man who could be so grumpy that it verged on being curt, in a different light. 'How can you create something so – *alive* – just from wood? It's absolutely beautiful.'

'I'm glad you like it. I hope the vicar feels the same.'

'I don't see how he could fail to. But Lando...'

'Yes.'

'She does look very like me. I didn't think you were doing a portrait.'

It was true. Although I could never hope to achieve such glowing serenity, Mary's face was unmistakeably mine.

'Neither did I, and I hope you don't mind. But...'

He paused and turned to his workbench, shuffling around some papers and tools in what seemed to me to be a completely unnecessary way. I waited.

'... well...' He turned back to me. 'Your calmness and peace... you sort of radiate it, you know, Penny. I thought it was only with the children... You're fun with them, but you soothe and settle them by – just by being the way you are. I thought maybe it was a professional thing, being a teacher. But you brought that here with you too. It infused my work. How could it not?'

He shrugged and looked so perplexed that I almost wanted to laugh, while at the same time being incredibly moved by his words. What beautiful words, when I thought of myself as dull and sensible. I cleared my throat.

'Gosh, thank you. I don't know what to say. I'm glad I could help.'

'Yes, well, you have.'

'OK... I'll change out of my robe then and get off. Get on my way, I mean.'

Stop wittering, Penny. He knows what you mean. That sexual tension you think is in the air? All in your own head.

'Right. Yes, you'd better do that. Actually, I wondered if you'd like a drink. To celebrate. I'd like to celebrate finishing Mary. If you'd like to stay. You don't have to.'

I resisted the temptation to make a snarky comment about not being able to refuse such a gracious invitation, which I didn't think would fit with my new, serene persona.

'Thank you, I'd like that.'

He disappeared through the door at the back of the studio whilst I hurriedly shed the heavy cloth and tugged my jeans back on. He reappeared carrying a bottle of champagne, no less, and two glasses.

'Champagne? How delicious.'

'I hope that's all right? You haven't developed a taste for all the fragrant liqueurs my father has been pouring down your throat?'

'No! Well, they are delicious, but absolutely lethal. I don't know how he stays so chipper. No, champagne is lovely, thank you.'

'I hope it's all right,' he said, easing out the cork with well-practised skill. 'Time was I would have drunk it before it had had time to chill, but this has been in the fridge for weeks since I was given it.'

He poured out the sparkling liquid and handed me a glass.

'To Mary.'

'To Mary.'

'Oh, sorry, do sit down. Er, there aren't many places. Look, sit here, Garbo won't mind.'

He scooped the little dog off a tatty but comfortable-looking bucket chair and waved me into it, then perched on his work chair. I tucked my feet up and had another sip. I decided I was feeling daring – adventurous, even.

'So, when was it you would have drunk warm champagne? Sounds like desperate measures?'

'Yes.'

I wondered if he was going to divulge any more, or if I had overstepped the mark in asking. I stayed quiet and waited. He continued.

'Well, I used to work in the City, as a broker. It's a stupidly fast-paced life and fuelled by adrenaline, booze and various prescription and non-prescription drugs. They weren't really my scene, but the adrenaline and alcohol were a toxic enough mix as it turns out. For a few years I loved it. I was making money hand over fist and having a ball – in that world, work and play mix almost constantly, until you can't tell which is which or where to draw the line. Hitting nightclubs with clients until four in the morning becomes as crucial as getting into the office at five to beat the competition and spot the best deals. You have no idea who your friends are, or why people want to be with you, and when you're partying hard on a superyacht in the Med, you don't really care. For a while, anyway.'

I nodded in what I hoped was a wise and understanding way, but it was so far removed from my sensible, pedestrian life as a primary school teacher that I found the permutations of it hard to grasp. As you know, I like cheese on toast in front of cosy crime dramas, so what could I possibly say about yachts and stock markets? He continued.

'Anyway, long story short, I burnt out. It's not uncommon, or unexpected. For me it was pretty severe – a full breakdown that required a hospital stay then recuperation down here. At first, I anticipated returning to London as soon as I was strong enough, as did everyone else, but I found I didn't want to. The peace here, and the chance to explore my art – and discover I'm reasonably good at it – were more of a pull than the city ever had been. So I stayed. That's it really.'

'Xander wants you to go back.'

'He does. He's lost his partner in crime, and I made him a lot of money. I like Xander, but I don't want to work with him again. I hope that he sorts himself out, otherwise he'll be the next one detoxing and reassessing – although I suspect he'd just reassess himself straight back into a wine bar.'

'But you're not going to stay here, in Dorset?'

He held my gaze for a moment, then looked down at the dog in his lap.

'No. The plan is Greece. Even more solitude.'

I felt ridiculously disappointed. After an atmosphere verging on intimacy had developed between us, I somehow felt he might revise his plans... Would I ever learn? He continued.

'Although I wouldn't recommend a breakdown, looking back it came as something of a relief. I didn't want to carry on the way I was, but I'd lost sight of how to extricate myself. Now I want to get away from all the memories.'

'Are you still worried you might be tempted back into it?'

He thought for a moment before replying.

'Sitting here, working, healthy, talking to you, being with my dogs – no. It's infinitely more valuable and precious and I don't want to jeopardise my recovery, not for a second...'

'But?'

'But I know how easy it would be to be tempted. To be persuaded back for one more deal, or one more party, and how quickly I could slide back into my old life. I know I seem quite... dour, but I know what can happen if I enjoy myself too much.'

I drank some champagne and considered what he had said.

'I think I understand that. But aren't you in danger of throwing the baby out with the bathwater? Life *is* to be enjoyed: would you be cutting yourself off too much in your Greek wilderness?'

'Maybe.'

It obviously wasn't up for discussion, and I didn't say any

more. I didn't want to look as though I was presuming to try to make him stay. He suddenly smiled.

'Are you artistic, Penny?'

I laughed.

'Me? I'd love to be, but I'm hopeless. I'm all right at crafts, for the children, but not real art. My Reception class mocks me when I try to draw anything.'

'Would you like to have a go at wood carving?'

'Oh gosh, I wouldn't know where to start.'

'Well, I'll show you. What would you like to make? Maybe something festive?'

'All right, I'll give it a go. I'll make... What about a bell?'

I tried to think of the simplest shape I could.

'Hmm, a bell would be difficult to hollow out, and with the clapper... You could try a star?'

'Oh yes, I'd like that, but it sounds difficult...'

'Not at all, come over here.'

I stood up and walked shyly over to his workbench, sitting down at his chair. Lando started rummaging in a drawer, muttering to himself, before producing a block of wood about ten centimetres big.

'Okay, so, this is lime wood – it's really easy for beginners as it's soft but strong. I want you to take it and use your senses to experience it.'

I looked at him slightly askew, and he gave me a nod, his face serious.

'I mean it. Touch it, smell it, look at the way it has grown.'

It felt strangely intimate to be examining the wood in this way as he watched me closely, but I persevered.

'It's warm, isn't it? And smoother than it looks,' I said. 'There's more colour variation than I noticed at first.'

He nodded again.

'Good. Now I want you to close your eyes and picture the

star you want from the wood. Not the star you're going to make, but the star the wood is going to give you.'

I raised my eyebrows but managed to stop short of rolling my eyes. This sounded like one of those things people say – and maybe believe – that is utterly inaccessible to me. I'm more pragmatic, I like to get on with things, rather than getting all woo-woo about them.

'I mean it,' Lando said. 'Give it a try. Close your eyes and imagine that there is a beautiful star inside the wood that you are going to release.'

Not wanting to shatter the atmosphere, I shut my eyes and obediently visualised a star encased in the block of wood. The star was very like one I had seen in Present Box, rather than some beautiful creation of my imagination, but I didn't suppose that mattered, especially for a beginner. I turned the wood in my hand and was surprised to find that my mental picture and the physical object somehow started to merge. Lando's quiet voice broke in.

'Are you ready?'

I opened my eyes and blinked a little.

'Yes, I think so.'

'Good. Now, for more complex sculptures I make a clay model first, but I think we can skip that stage.' He handed me a pencil. 'Draw your basic star shape onto the wood.'

I took the pencil gingerly, then put it down on the workbench.

'I honestly don't know if I can. I'm hopeless at drawing.'

I felt slightly panicky now, and sorry that I was ruining the moment, which had all the hallmarks of a romantic scene like the pottery one in *Ghost*, but was instead making me anxious at my own inadequacies.

'Penny, it doesn't matter if you get it wrong, if it's not perfect.'

He picked the pencil up and pushed it into my hand, wrapping my fingers around it. Did he know the shockwaves his touch was sending through my body? I looked into his face, so earnest, and wanted to reach up and stroke his cheek, draw him to me and kiss him, this gorgeous, complicated man. For a moment, a heart-stopping, slightly sickening moment, I thought I was going to do it. Much in the way I had visualised the star in the wood, I could see myself touching him, kissing him. I could feel it, almost as if I had actually done it. Maybe he moved an inch towards me; did he? I knew I was flushing, could feel my hand sweaty around the pencil, my lips parting. Could I step into adventure? Not this time. A flurry of thoughts thudded down on me, deadening my ardour and snapping me out of my vision.

You're making a fool of yourself, Penny – and there's no fool like an old fool.

Don't get involved with another man, it'll end in tears.

Lando doesn't want you, *why would he? Look at you.*

You have to protect yourself, Penny, be careful, be careful, be careful.

I tore my eyes from his and addressed the block of wood with determined cheeriness.

'Okay. Come on then, Star, time to let you out. Here goes!'

I started dabbing the pencil at the wood, until a convincing-looking star shape emerged. I held the finished product out proudly towards Lando, who took it and scrutinised it.

'That's very good.'

I nearly burst with pleasure.

'Your proportions are a little wonky here... and here...'

I deflated slightly as, with a few deft strokes, he straightened up my star and made it look a hundred times better.

'Now, I'm going to show you how to use the chisel.'

I watched closely as he smoothed the wood away under the sharp blade, his skilled hands and confidence sending shivers down my spine.

'Would you like a go?'

'I beg your pardon?'

I was shaken out of my reverie abruptly, then realised he was handing me the tool.

'Oh, yes, thank you, great.'

I tried to emulate his movements, whilst picturing the as yet unrevealed star and, to my delight, a shape began to emerge. Lando offered gentle guidance: muttered comments and occasionally a hand on mine to guide the chisel correctly and coax the shape from the wood until, eventually, I was holding a star in my hand – crude maybe, but a bona fide star. I looked up at Lando and beamed.

'Look at that! I did it!'

'Of course you did, well done.'

He looked as pleased as I felt, and we grinned at each other as proudly and dizzily as if it had been a new-born baby rather than a little wooden star that we had created together. He showed me how to sand it, then took it from me in exchange for a fresh glass of champagne as he brushed it all over with oil.

'There you go, that needs a little while to dry and then you can take it. I'll bring it up to the house tomorrow. Would you like me to make a hole in it so you can hang it?'

I nodded, suddenly feeling shy now that I had nothing to occupy me other than my drink.

'Yes, thank you. Although I'm not sure it deserves its place on that tree with those beautiful decorations.'

'You do yourself down a lot, Penny. You shouldn't. Your star is a work of art. A simple one, maybe, but a work of art nonetheless, and it deserves its place to shine.'

'Don't you think it's a bit – boring?'

'No, Penny, I don't. It was created with care and vision; it brings pleasure to look at and to touch and it represents light and brilliance. Its wood came from a living tree, and it was hewn into shape by us working together. It has a story, a presence, as much if not more than any of its flashier relations. It is rich in its humility. Do *you* think it's boring?'

I shook my head, stared fiercely at my knees, trying to force down the tears that were springing to my eyes, so moved was I by his words.

'No,' I whispered. 'I don't. I think it's wonderful.'

He put a finger under my chin and tilted my face up so that I was looking into his sincere brown eyes.

'So do I,' he said.

This time only one thought filled my head: *He's going to kiss me. Oh, bloody hell, he's going to kiss me.*

The rest of my brain was a sort of background buzz of panic and excitement and terror. It reminded me of being at university, just starting out in life and romance, that heady mix of feelings when you knew exactly what was about to happen but hadn't had time to *think* about it, and your friend is saying, 'Don't *think* about it, Penny, *enjoy* it' and you're going: but what if, what if, what if? And all those thoughts and feelings race through you in a millisecond, and then he's kissing you and everything fizzes and you're not sure if that's in a good way or not.

Except he didn't. One minute he was absolutely going to and the next the brown eyes gazing soulfully into mine were somewhat different. I let out a scream of laughter as the tension shattered.

'Garbo! What do *you* want?'

She definitely grinned at me as she clambered up onto Lando's shoulders and settled with a sigh. He reached up and stroked her silken back, smiling ruefully.

'I'm afraid my chaperone here is a creature of habit and it's time for her to go out before bed. You could set your clock by her.'

I felt a curious mixture of disappointment and relief as I stood up.

'It's time for me to get back, anyway, it's going to be another busy day with the twins tomorrow. They have a birthday party to go to.'

Lando looked as if he was going to say something else, then changed his mind.

'Got it. Come on, we'll walk you up to the house.'

I gathered my things together and followed Lando and the dogs out of the cosy, messy studio and into the freezing night air.

FOURTEEN

The dogs kept haring off through the night after imagined foes, so I bade Lando a chaste and chilly goodnight at the back door and scuttled thankfully into the warm house and up to my welcoming room. I went to move my laptop, which was sitting open on the bed, and of course the bloody thing leapt keenly into life, shining a website at me all about how to rent property in India. Crossly, confused, I clicked it shut, only for my email inbox to be revealed, with a new message from my mother marked 'High Priority'. I wasn't particularly moved by this as she does it with all her emails, flagging them up to be sure you don't dare miss them. If she could, I'm sure she'd have a little red flag to wave in real life, too, just so that you were in no doubt that unmissable pearls of wisdom were about to drop from her lips every time she spoke. It was the subject line of the email – 'WE NEED TO TALK ABOUT YOUR MOVE' – that put me off, and with a muttered 'sorry' I slammed the laptop shut and stuffed it under some clothes on a chair.

As I got ready for bed, I tried to think about other things, but my mind kept relentlessly returning to the evening I had spent in Lando's studio. Had I imagined those two near kisses?

Or was I nothing but a hormonal, desperate, nearly middle-aged embarrassment? As I undressed, showered, brushed my teeth, got into bed, my mind swung from one thing to the other. One moment I was so sure that the zing between us had been real, the next I was cringing at my hubris in thinking that Lando could possibly fancy me. I would let my imagination run away with me for a while, picturing – *feeling* – the kisses, then would bring myself back down to earth with a crash, remembering why I had sworn off men and how unpleasant I had initially found this object of my fantasies. As I picked up my book and forced myself to concentrate, I decided that first impressions count. *Trust your gut*, isn't that what everyone says now? Well, my gut was churning unpleasantly, so I concluded that I was better off as I was: tucked up in bed, alone, with a good book. I should have tried telling that to my dreams, which raged all night with torrid and romantic scenes and left me quite worn out by the morning.

Breakfast was busy that day as, unusually, everyone was there together including, to everyone's delight, Daphne, who was radiant in the most glamorous item of clothing I have ever seen in real life, a peach silk floor-length robe trimmed at the sleeves and neck with billowing ostrich feathers. As she wafted across the room, coffee in hand, William stood next to me, where I had stopped, stunned, clutching my bowl of porridge.

'Isn't she ravishing, Penny? Am I not the luckiest man on earth?'

'She's wonderful, William, I'm so happy for you. But I think I'm a little bit in love with her myself.'

He laughed and crossed over to sit with her, and they both managed to eat breakfast one-handed, as they didn't stop holding hands the whole way through.

I was nervous but excited about seeing Lando, and I

huddled in a chair with a magazine, half wishing he would turn up and half dreading it. But turn up he did, last of everyone. He greeted the room with an uncharacteristic smile, then passed by me and put a hand very briefly on my shoulder.

'Morning, Penny.'

I felt the redness rush to my face as I managed to choke out a 'good morning' in return, then saw Bunny looking sharply between us. Fluffy and ditsy she may appear, but she was nobody's fool.

'How did the carving go last night?' she asked.

'Wonderfully,' said Lando, shaking out the newspaper. 'I think we're there with Mary, thanks to Penny.'

I was saved from saying anything by my phone ringing in my dressing gown pocket.

'It's Lavinia. I wonder why she's calling so early; we're seeing her later at the party. Hello?'

'Penny, thank goodness. I'm in an awful fix and I wondered if you could help?'

'Of course – if I can.'

'Thank you. You see, the place is half under water, God only knows what's happened. Giles is looking into it, but we can't possibly have Toby's party here now. Could you possibly ask Lando if we can have it there? I absolutely *promise* that we will leave the place exactly as we found it. Better, if anything.'

'Oh Lavinia, poor you. Yes, of course I'll ask. He's right here, hang on a moment.'

I looked up to see the entire family looking at me, wondering what drama was unfolding on the other end of my phone. My eyes met Lando's. I quickly explained what had happened. He rolled his eyes but smiled.

'Yes, of course she can have Toby's party here, but tell her if all the parents are coming as well, I'm locking the drinks cabinet. Does she need any help getting things over?'

I ignored the flabbergasted faces of the others as Lando

calmly returned to his breakfast, and I spoke again to Lavinia, then slipped the phone back into my pocket.

'She's so grateful, thank you, and says she can bring over everything herself. She'll just need to borrow the kitchen to finish off the cake and make the sandwiches – would that be all right with you, Pilar?'

She nodded vigorously.

'*Claro qué sí.* I can help make them, too, please tell her.'

'Thank you so much, I will. As for the rest of it, apparently there's an entertainer who does almost everything, so it should be a doddle.'

'Oh God, Pixie.' This from Bunny. 'I know you're a wonderful teacher, but have you ever *done* a child's birthday party? They are *hell*, no matter how many entertainers you have. Food everywhere, tears, sick, everything ends up sticky. Sorry, Lando, but that's how it goes.'

He shrugged.

'I'm sure it will be fine, as long as the children enjoy them-selves. You know I don't care about the cushions, or whatever.'

'You just wait,' said Bunny darkly. I stifled a giggle. Bunny was lovely, but I couldn't imagine her corralling hordes of excited children at a sugar-fuelled birthday party.

'You seem very relaxed about this,' drawled Xander. 'I didn't realise you were so fond of Lavinia. Or maybe it's someone else making you feel the party vibes?'

He looked at me meaningfully and the hateful flush filled my face yet again.

'Oh, do shut up, Xander,' said Bunny to her brother. 'Seeing as you're a self-styled party animal, you can be in charge of looking after the parents.'

'Suits me,' he replied. 'Are you going to be leading the conga, Lando? I assume you *are* going to help out?'

'I'll help where it's needed,' replied Lando evenly. 'Just

make sure everyone gets their children home safely, Xander. I'm confiscating car keys after half a glass of wine.'

Xander opened his mouth to make some doubtlessly cutting remark, but Bunny stepped in.

'Quite right, Lando. I'll keep an eye on that too – and on this one.'

To give him his credit, Xander grinned good-naturedly.

'All right, all right, responsible fun it is. But it's not like the old days.'

'Thank God,' said Lando and Bunny in unison, and the ensuing laughter set the scene for the day ahead.

Lavinia arrived an hour or so later, her huge car laden down with party paraphernalia, which we all helped to carry in. Pilar looked askance at the piles of food as they were carried into her kitchen, but somehow managed to stash it all away in the fridge and cupboards.

'I can't thank you all enough for your help,' panted Lavinia, hefting two huge bags filled with wrapped presents out of the car. 'It's bad enough that poor Toby was born so near Christmas – not his fault, obvs – but with the flood I could have *wept*.'

I helped her with the bags.

'Has Giles found out where it's coming from yet?'

'I don't know what it is, but he managed to turn it off. The water was going down when I left, but it's a big clean-up job. Oh well, new carpets for Christmas, I suppose.'

I was impressed by how sanguine she was but thought that having a huge wodge of family money behind you couldn't hurt in these situations.

'Well, as far as Lando is concerned, his casa seems to be your casa.' That strangulated bit of Spanglish earned me a glare of mock disapproval from Pilar. 'What on earth are all these presents, by the way?' I asked, putting my bag down with some relief.

'They're the going home presents. I always go overboard, can't help myself. They're little devils, most of them, but so sweet to see them enjoying themselves.'

I grinned, thinking of Bunny's words earlier, and wondered whose children's party philosophy would still be intact by the evening.

Lavinia, Pilar, the children and I spent the day buttering bread for sandwiches and decorating a large cake. The rest of the Lord clan had vanished for this part of the proceedings, except for Xander, who had spent a jolly half hour setting up a parents' bar in Lando's little-used study. The room was styled to such perfect National Trust specifics with its polished wooden furniture, book-crammed shelves and masculine *objets* that I wondered if we should be charging entry.

'Gorgeous, isn't it?' sighed Xander, plonking down bottles on the leather-topped desk. 'I'd love a man cave like this, but Lando never comes in, far happier knee-deep in wood shavings. All decorated by his ex, Zara, who held lady of the manor aspirations for a while.'

I couldn't resist taking the bait, and summoned up my most casual tone of voice.

'What was she like?'

'Zara? Absolutely stunning, but a total bitch. Ditched Lando precisely when he could have done with a soothing hand on his brow and belted off to find someone else to keep her in Jimmy Choos. She even tried her luck with me, but although I look stupid, I know a good woman when I see – or don't see – one.'

'And you see one in whoever's at the end of your phone all the time?'

He reddened.

'Hmm, well, I don't know about that. Probably too good for me, but maybe one day I might even reform a bit.'

I grinned at him.

'Aw, no, don't ever change. Well, not *too* much...'

His merry laughter echoed behind me as I left the room in search of a balloon pump, mulling over what he had said about Zara. It sounded as if she had gone for good, which was all I needed to know. Not that I was that interested, you understand.

At two pm we were ready. The tea table was laid out, balloons blown up, ball pool filled (yes, Lavinia had brought a ball pool) and anything small and breakable removed to safety. The entertainer, Miss Magick, had set up her stall in a corner of the big living room.

'Is she really meant for children's parties?' I whispered to Lavinia. We watched the slender woman in the long, clinging black dress swishing her waist-length platinum blonde hair as she laid out crystals on the purple satin cloth she had placed over a table. 'I was rather expecting a green wig and trick washing machine.'

Lavinia stifled a giggle.

'I know what you mean, but she came highly recommended. Apparently, she's sort of two for the price of one: once she's finished with the children's act, she'll read tarot cards for the adults.'

I was saved from having to think about this by the doorbell: our first guest.

The little partygoers arrived thick and fast and soon Lando's beautiful house was a melee of overexcited children and parents who seemed determined to renege all control over their offspring and make straight for the bar and a good gossip about who might be getting a divorce in January. I appointed myself cloakroom monitor and tried to make orderly piles of adult and children's coats, tugging all the sleeves of the latter the right way out. I didn't spend four years getting a teaching degree for nothing. Lavinia was supervising the ball pool, although this seemed to involve more getting in and chucking balls at the children with evident enjoyment than actual supervision. Pilar was cloistered in the kitchen, claiming she was putting the final touches to a tea I thought was all organised, but I couldn't blame her; this was definitely not her circus. Xander was being the perfect host to the parents, and had already swiped a few car keys, replacing them with the card of the local taxi company, which was going to have an early Christmas with all this business. William and Daphne had excused themselves for an afternoon at a five-star hotel in town, and who could blame them? Bunny, to my great surprise, had set up a little art station in a corner and was doing rapid sketches on demand for the children to colour. No request seemed to faze her, and she had some colour in her cheeks for the first time in days. I hoped she was feeling better both physically and mentally. Lando had yet to put in an appearance. Most of the guests must have arrived, I decided, and was about to go and ask Miss Magick to get started, when the doorbell rang again. I opened up and there was a very tall woman dressed in a voluminous patchwork coat and carrying a rather incongruous and extremely expensive Hermès handbag. At her side was a small and miserable-looking little girl.

'Hello, are you here for the party? Come in.'

I stood aside and the woman swept past me, dragging the child behind her. She removed both their coats and handed them to me. It was all I could do not to bob a curtsey.

'Are you in charge?'

'Er, sort of. Hello, I'm Penny, welcome.'

The woman stretched her taut lips a fraction by way of a greeting.

'Penny, I'm Chakra and this is Sèvres.'

I glanced down at the small girl standing next to her. She was pale, with very long, loose hair which could do with a brush running through it. She wore wide-legged trousers in a fabric that looked rather like hessian, with an embroidered tunic top, far too thin for the chilly December day. I smiled at her, but she didn't react at all, just stared glassily back at me. I turned back to her mother.

'What an unusual name.'

'Like the porcelain? Do you know?'

I had a stern word with my eyebrows, which wanted to flick upwards in irritation. I had dealt with enough patronising mothers in my time not to let this latest one get to me.

'Yes, the porcelain, itself named after the town. It's a very pretty name.'

She glared at me now, as if I had suggested popping to the deed poll office and changing it to – oh, I don't know, something sensible and unremarkable that other children were called and everyone could both pronounce and spell.

'Anyway,' she went on icily. 'Sèvres has a very specific diet – she doesn't eat any gluten...'

'Oh dear,' I said, genuinely concerned. I have had some children in my classes with horrendous allergies. 'Is she coeliac?'

'No, there is nothing *wrong* with my daughter. She doesn't eat gluten, or sugar of any description, and all her food must be organic.'

Oh. One of those. My heart went out even further to the little waif drooping next to her hideous mother.

'I see. Well, I haven't organised the food, but I can find out about the organic thing and help her avoid gluten and sugar.'

She glared at me as if I had suggested cutting little Sèvres a few lines of coke to enjoy during the party.

'Oh no, she won't be eating *your* food. I'm giving you everything she will eat; please see to it that she is given it.'

She reached into the voluminous bag and produced two
glass boxes with bamboo lids, which she pushed towards me.

I took the boxes.

'Aren't you staying?'

She looked surprised.

'Yes, of course I'm staying.'

And before I could hand her the boxes back and suggest she
policed her own child's party food, she marched off towards the
bar. I smiled down at Sèvres and she gazed back at me wanly.

'Come on, sweetheart, let's go and join the fun, shall we?'

I took her limp little hand in mine and led her off, without
much hope of her suddenly discovering her inner party animal.
As we went back into the living room, I spotted two children on
the cusp of a big punch up behind the sofa, dropped Sèvres'
hand, chucked the boxes on a handy sideboard and dived in.
When I emerged, I made a beeline for Miss Magick, who was
leading a group of children in a wafty dance with silk scarves
which, to her credit, they seemed to love, and asked her to get
the show going. Lavinia and I rounded everyone up and soon
there was blessed peace as – magically indeed – twenty-five
children sat transfixed as Miss Magick ran through a remark-
ably good repertoire of tricks, keeping up a patter in her
hypnotic monotone. I could easily have sunk into a chair to
watch the whole thing, but it was time to put out the food.
Xander was still busy in the other room, Lavinia was sitting
with Toby, and Bunny was nowhere to be seen, so I started
transporting platters of sandwiches and cucumber sticks from
the kitchen by myself, while Pilar filled jugs with juice and
water.

'Oh dear, oh *dear*,' I muttered to myself on my third trip,
worried that I was never going to get it all ready in time, when I
heard a calm voice behind me.

'Can I help?'

Lando. I would have been pleased to see him, anyway, but I would have hugged him if it hadn't been for the somewhat precarious sausage rolls I was now transporting.

'Oh hello, yes *please*. You could get the drinks from Pilar, thank you.'

With his help, the table was groaning with food in no time, and I was standing ready at the back of the room as Miss Magick said, 'Let us finish with the magickal words we have learnt: *scyld ðū ðē nū þū ðysne nīð genesan mōte.*'

The children seemed to me to do a good job of repeating what she said, and she waved a sort of smoking bundle of herbs around as I brought some pedestrianism back to the room, clapping my hands and announcing, 'Okay, everyone, tea is ready!'

Maybe she had cast some sort of spell, because they all stood up calmly and trickled out towards the dining room to take their seats. As Lavinia had now taken over, I hung back to speak to Miss Magick.

'That was amazing, they all loved it.'

'Thank you, thank you. I like to work with small people and with our animal companions, I find them receptive and joyful. Would you like me to read your cards?'

I hesitated. I don't believe in fortune telling and crystal energy and so on, but there was something so soothing and yet beguiling about this woman, and I was so confused about what I wanted from life, that I couldn't help myself, and I agreed. She led me over to her table, clear now except for some crystals and a deck of tarot cards, and I sat down.

'Choose a crystal, whatever you're drawn to,' she said, and I took in the selection. As far as I was concerned it was nothing more than a collection of pretty stones, but I tried to get into the spirit and pick carefully. There was one I particularly liked, which was a sort of glowing, milky white, and I picked it up and handed it to Miss Magick.

'Ah, an interesting choice, the moonstone. You are considering new beginnings and looking to be calmed yet inspired.'

I gawked at her, and she smiled serenely, then reached for her tarot cards and spread them out on the table in a practised move.

'Please pick three,' she said, and I did so, handing them to her. She turned them face up on the cloth and studied them silently. I regarded them intently, too, but could glean nothing from them but their names: Knight of Wands, King of Swords and The Fool. They didn't look very auspicious to me. She continued.

'All right, so it appears to me that in your past there was a man who was cruel, manipulative, perhaps a selfish lover? There's also a sense of wastefulness there. Does that resonate?' I nodded, intrigued now. 'But here we have the present – I see adventure, perhaps more free-spiritedness?' Again, I nodded. How did she know? She tapped the third card. 'This is interesting, The Fool. He is upright, meaning new beginnings and an encouragement to be brave. He urges you to take risks, to keep trying with childlike wonder at the world, and then you will find the love you crave, even if that seems most unlikely.'

She looked up at me, and I stared at her. For a moment we didn't speak, then she said, 'Can you take something from that?'

I nodded, still dumbstruck, and she smiled that gentle smile again.

'Here, keep the moonstone. Let it soothe and remind you. Take heart.'

I managed to stutter out my thanks as I took the smooth stone from her and went to face the rising noise level in the dining room. The table had been decimated, but all the children were happy enough. It was only when I noticed Sèvres, hunched greedily over a plate of thoroughly unsuitable food, that I remembered the glass boxes, tossed aside an hour ago and then completely forgotten. My hand flew to my mouth in horror.

'Are you all right?'

'Oh, Lando, oh God, I've made an awful mistake.'

'What's happened?'

'I was meant to give Sèvres – that child over there – a special meal her mother had prepared, and I completely forgot. Now she's eaten God only knows what, and I'm going to be in awful trouble. What happens if she's ill?'

Lando took my shoulders and turned me to face him.

'Penny. You are doing an amazing job today. I know poor Sèvres' mother of old, and she's a piece of work. Her daughter doesn't need a special diet at all, she just suffers for her mother's fashion whims. Look at her, she's absolutely fine.' To be fair, the child did look perfectly happy, hoovering up iced gems. 'And anyway, her mother's here, isn't she? She should be in charge of her child, not outsourcing it to you.'

I nodded and relaxed a fraction. I did feel responsible, but knew he was right.

'Have you had anything to eat yourself?' he asked.

'Oh! No, I haven't had a thing. Goodness, I hadn't realised, and I'm hungry.'

'Right, sit down there and I'll bring you something.'

It felt funny – nice, but funny – to be cared for. I'm always the one making sure everyone else is okay, and here I was being brought a brimming plate of food and – bliss! – a glass of cold white wine by Lando. He put them on the table next to me.

'Sorry to leave you to eat alone, I have to run back to the studio for a bit. But hopefully you'll get a break.'

And with that he was gone, leaving me to eat in peace, watching as Lavinia brought in the cake and the ritual singing and blowing out of candles was performed. I looked at all the dear, happy little faces – even Sèvres was smiling – and wished with all my heart that I had a child of my own to enjoy. For a

moment, just a moment, I didn't push away the thoughts and try
to replace them with jolly visions of an adventurous future, but
allowed myself to sit with the sadness, the emptiness. It wasn't
that I was particularly broody, babies are fine, but it's not that I
long for. It's the whole family thing, the cosy, loved, safe feeling
that I wanted to have. To care and be cared for. Even though I
was in a caring profession, I still felt that I was brim-full of love,
waiting to lavish it on a husband and child, to be part of that
club which seemed to offer such easy entry to so many people,
but kept a stubborn bouncer on the door where I was
concerned. I know that not all families are happy, and not every
moment of family life is joyful, but that didn't stop me aching
for it. I felt so very alone and so sick of being brave and independent and pretending not to mind. Tears of self-pity threatened
to well up, so I downed my wine and abandoned my empty
plate.

'Lavinia! Shall we do the Pass the Parcel now?'

Party games exhausted, it was time to go home, but none of the
children or parents looked as if they were going to leave any
time soon. Seraphina and three newfound little friends were
huddled over Hungry Hippos, pounding away at the plastic
levers with the vigour and intensity of seasoned teenage gamers.
Caspian was high on sugar and tearing around the hall, chasing
Lavinia's son, Toby, who was screeching with joyous, ear-splitting laughter as he skilfully slid past a table bearing a beautiful
vase which could have been Meissen or M&S to my ignorant
eye but was more likely to be expensive. Lavinia had been
starting to clear up, but was now on the phone in the corner,
talking to her husband about new carpet, which was, I had to
admit, a pressing issue this close to Christmas and considering
the disaster they had suffered. As a teacher, I know better than
to let children have too much fun as it inevitably gets out of

hand, but it's so much easier in the classroom; this party had descended into chaos around me before I could call time on it, and now I wasn't sure what to do. No amount of rhythmical handclapping was going to get this lot in order.

I decided to divide and conquer, by roping in Xander, who I had noticed sloping off with a bottle of Pinot Noir and the parents of a particularly noxious pair of boys, who had taken advantage of their absence by hoovering up the remainder of the cake. I was particularly irritated by this because I had been looking forward to having some later, whilst also enjoying some peace: nothing like some thick, luridly coloured icing to soothe frayed nerves. For now, I comforted myself with the thought that they would probably be sick all over the car on the way home, so their parents would get their comeuppance. Bunny had vanished upstairs to her room, claiming a headache and rubbing her bump in a way that looked distinctly fraudulent, but I couldn't blame her for using her 'get out of jail free' card in these circumstances. I was going for reinforcements when a loud voice from the sitting room stopped me:

'It's a fish finger, a *bloody* fish finger. It doesn't matter.'

I rushed in to find a tall man nose to nose with Sèvres' mother, who had gone a shade of puce I wouldn't have thought possible with her porcelain skin. He was waving the foodstuff in question in her face, bits of breadcrumb flying off to make minute greasy stains wherever they lit.

'It is *not* just a fish finger,' she replied, through teeth clenched so tightly I feared they might all shatter and tinkle to the floor like something out of Tom and Jerry. 'It is *gluten*, which will wreak *havoc* with her digestion, and it is probably also palm oil, which will do God knows what damage. I doubt there's any actual *fish* in it either – it's probably the scrapings from the floor of the factory. *Everyone* knows about fish fingers.'

My eyes slid over to where Sèvres sat, expecting to find her pinched little face even more wan after the discovery of the unexpected introduction of gluten and fish scrapings to her diet, but instead saw that she was still gobbling iced gems while her mother held her phone screen up to the man's face saying, 'See? See? Poison.'

'No Chakra, more *poisson*, I think. Come on, time to go home.'

Lando's voice cut through the noise even more effectively than my teacher tones could have done and everyone leapt to attention. I could see several of the mothers automatically smoothing their clothes and tidying their hair at the arrival of such a handsome man. The local eligible bachelor, I thought. All the more reason not to go near him. I didn't want to be joining some pathetic queue for his attentions. But I was grateful for his intervention and ran with it, starting to herd children and parents towards their coats and mouthing 'party bags' at Lavinia, who understood the severity of the situation and got off the phone pronto. It took a good half an hour for everyone to go, as they arranged taxis, rang sober spouses to come and pick them up and thoroughly messed up my careful arrangement of coats. I helped Lavinia pack her car with the ball pool and sleepy child and returned to face the remaining detritus, realising I would have to tackle most of it alone. Pilar had returned the kitchen to its usual spotless state and left dinner for us all with reheating instructions. Bunny was lying down and Xander had shut the study door, apparently to focus on cleaning up. I was sure, at least, that the bottles would be empty, but fair enough.

'Come on, you two,' I said to the twins, who had collapsed glassy eyed in front of the TV. 'Help me get some of this into bags.'

'Do we *have* to?' they complained, not moving, and I took pity on them. Such serious partying can take it out of a person.

'All right, you've got half an hour and then absolutely no fuss about bath and bed.'

They agreed readily, and probably untruthfully, and I set off to find some black bags and rubber gloves. I had started on the dining room when in through the door came Lando.

'Need some help?'

'Are you sure? I mean, I can do it, if you're busy...'

'Let me help, I'd like to.'

So, in companionable silence we scooped plates, cups and crumbs into bags and put the room straight.

'Wonderful,' I said when it was done. 'Now just the living room to go.' I glanced at my watch. 'Oh no, it's past the twins' bedtime already, I'd better get them. Look, you go, I'll sort it all out.'

I suddenly felt dreadfully weary but took a deep breath to steel myself for the tasks ahead. I called for the children who, to my surprise, came willingly and submitted to a quick shower and only two stories with no resistance. I tucked them in and gave them a kiss, passing Bunny on the way out of their room.

'You'd better be quick,' I said, 'they're nearly asleep. Are you coming down for supper?'

'Actually, Xander has asked me to go out with him for a siblings' catch up and I'm feeling much more up to it. So enjoy a peaceful evening, Pixie darling, you deserve it.'

As I went downstairs, I did feel relieved, even knowing that I had the rest of the clearing up to do. There was a new episode of my favourite murder mystery on that night, and knowing Pilar had prepared dinner was a luxury. When I pushed open the living room door, a surprise awaited me, for the room was restored to its usual pristine state, and there was Lando, stuffing the rest of the torn wrapping paper into a sack, like some sort of reverse Santa.

'I can't believe you've done all this, thank you so much.'

He grinned, managing to look gorgeous despite the Marigolds.

'My pleasure. You've been run ragged today, but the children loved the party, and you did Lavinia a really good turn.'

'I'm going to have something to eat now, Pilar's left supper. Do you want some?'

He agreed, and ten minutes later, we were sitting down at the now clear and gleaming dining room table to eat. A tiny – only very tiny, I promise – part of me was slightly missing that detective series, but that ebbed away as Lando and I chatted about everything and nothing. He made me choke with laughter over his descriptions of Chakra's previous behaviour, which seemed to veer wildly between high heels and champagne to hessian and gathering her own mushrooms.

'You seem to know a lot of people in the village,' I said. 'Won't you miss it when you move to Greece?'

There was a pause. Lando held my eyes in his and my heart quickened. Eventually he spoke.

'Greece. Hmm, yes, we'll see about Greece.'

What was that supposed to mean? I'd obviously overstepped the mark with my question – he probably even thought that I was fishing for information, pathetically and pointlessly. I had a big drink of wine.

'Well, it's full steam ahead for India,' I said with a tinny brightness. 'Can't wait. In fact, I must email my mother back, she needs some details.'

He smiled thinly.

'You're definitely going?'

'Yes, yes, *yes*! Of course! Just what I want, an Indian adventure. Can't wait. We'll have to send each other postcards.'

I trailed off feeling miserable, but keeping a big smile pasted to my face. Lando took his plate and stood up.

'Postcards, right. Well, I've got some more work to do, so I'll head back over to the studio. I was going to ask if you wanted to come over for a drink, but I guess you'll be too busy with your email.'

Every atom of my body screamed to go with him, but my brain took over firmly. Tempting though Lando's offer undoubtedly was, it would only lead to disappointment, whether by a short route – being dismissed after one quick, polite drink – or a long one – something happening between us, me getting my sorry little hopes up and ultimately ending up humiliated.

'Yes, that's right. Lots to do! Can't wait!'

That was the third time I had claimed not to be able to wait, and it was beginning to ring untrue even to my ears. I scooped up my plate and grabbed his from him.

'I'll deal with these, don't worry. See you in the morning.'

He replied with a grunt, and I headed for the kitchen, trying to congratulate myself on swerving a disaster, especially now he seemed to have reverted to his former grumpy, monosyllabic self. I kept up the jolly self-talk all the way to bed, but as I turned out the light, exhausted from the party and the pretence, the tears slid into my pillow.

FIFTEEN

I awoke the next morning feeling utterly unrefreshed, and groaned when I looked at the clock and saw how early it was. Nobody else would be up for at least an hour, even the twins, but I was wide awake. Some of the previous day's party adrenaline was still coursing around my veins, but of course I also couldn't stop thinking about Lando. What *was* that invitation for a drink? Had he really wanted me to go over? And what might have happened if I had? Oh well, no point in lying around agonising over the whole thing, and at least it had pushed the niggling worry over my text to Timothy out of the way. I swung out of bed, grabbed my laptop and hopped back in again. It was too early for the heating to have kicked in, and distinctly chilly. I opened up the email from my mum that I had ignored the day before, resolving to give it my best attention.

Dearest Pen,

How are you? It's been a little while since I heard from you, so I do hope that you aren't moping over Timothy. I know it was a nasty shock, I know you had hoped for a different outcome, but it's time to move on. I know one isn't meant to say these things, but your father and I are glad he's gone. We're sorry you've been hurt, of course, but he wasn't for you, darling. Well, I suppose what we think doesn't really matter, but maybe it will give you some encouragement. Anyway, the important thing now is *ad astra per aspera*…"

I did wish my mother wouldn't pepper her correspondence with Latin. I Googled it quickly: 'through adversity to the stars'. Well, at least it was encouraging. I carried on reading.

"… so don't waste a second longer thinking about what's-his-name and certainly don't let your mind wander to what might have been. As Yazz said: 'The Only Way Is Up'."

My mother spends too much time sharing dated social media memes with her friends. It'd be a Bonnie Tyler quote next urging me to hold out for a hero. On I read.

So, in case you've been too low to do it yourself, here are some links to job adverts around here and some lovely flats for rent – assuming, that is, you don't want to move in with us. To be honest, I'm not sure our current lifestyle would be wholly compatible with that of a working girl.

I shuddered and prayed she wouldn't go into further detail – there was too much danger that they had discovered tantric sex and were practising it day and night.

Do have a look at them, Pen, and let me know what you think. They may help you to envisage your fresh start. I want to help, you know that, and I don't want you wasting another moment of your beautiful life. Gather ye rosebuds, darling, in abundance.

Lots of love,

Mum (and Dad) xxx

A list of links followed, and I scrolled down them deject-edly. Mum meant the very best, but somehow always had the effect of making me feel even more low. She always seemed so vigorous, decisive... sorted, and her pep talks imbued in me a sort of babyish lethargy, as if I could never reach her heights, so why even bother trying? I knew, of course, that we are very different people, with different ambitions, but nevertheless I found her crushing. I clicked on a few of the links, trying to work up some enthusiasm for what should have been exciting prospects: flats with shiny tiled floors and stone balconies, chil-dren playing in dusty yards, smiling and laughing like the chil-dren I taught, but with a hot sun lighting them up, views of onion domes against modern cityscapes. I clicked the pictures shut almost angrily and let them be replaced in my mind's eye by images of Lando working quietly at his bench, of the dense greens of the Dorset countryside, of myself holding a baby. I drew in a sharp breath, as if I had been punched, and realised that I was about to be overwhelmed by emotion, yet again. Although there was no residual sadness about Timothy himself, my mother was right: I was wasting precious moments on 'what if' and 'if only' rather than pushing forward into reality. It was time to start taking charge of my life, making some choices, moving things along. I wouldn't spend any more time moping. I returned to Mum's email and clicked on the links again, trying to look at them this time as if they were friends. Ten minutes later, I hit 'reply':

Dear Mum,
Thank you for your email. Don't worry, I've been busy, not remotely sad. I can't wait to join you and Dad for my big adventure. I've read some of the links you sent...

Despite my research and email, I was still first down to breakfast, so was firmly established in my chair and magazine as the others trickled in. Bunny was first, swiftly followed by Xander. William and Daphne were next to appear, carried on a cloud of love that was for me both heart-warming and devastating. Seraphina and Caspian were next, far more excited and rowdy than I had expected after their busy day yesterday. I went to help them settle, as I could see Bunny looked drawn and could do without being jumped all over by them, but Xander was quicker.

'Come on, rabble, I'm going to beat you to the cornflakes!'

He swept them out to the kitchen as Lando came in, hair messy and with shadows under his eyes. The smile of the previous few mornings had been replaced with the original scowl, and he stamped over to his chair, spilling his coffee as he went.

'Damn. And why does Xander have to make so much noise? He shouldn't be allowed to wind those children up.'

Bunny looked up in surprise.

'Lando darling, are you all right, has something happened? It's not the Nativity, is it?'

'No, it's not. I'm fine. It would just be nice to have a peaceful breakfast in my own house for once.'

I put down my empty bowl.

'I'll go and have a word with them...' But I was interrupted by the twins and Xander erupting back into the room, waving their spoons and trying not to spill their breakfast, followed by Pilar with a cloth and an exasperated but amused expression on her face.

'No more raisins, no more raisins,' pleaded Xander, falling to his knees in surrender as the children pushed them into his mouth, almost helpless with laughter.

'It's fine, Uncle Xander, look!' said Caspy, shoving a whole handful in and chewing ecstatically, laughing as he did so. It's difficult to explain how quickly everything then changed. From silly giggles to calamity as Caspian's merry face suddenly contorted with fear and shock and he clutched at his throat, making a horrible, strangulated wheezing sound that will echo in my mind until the day I die. Although I was later told that I had leapt out of my chair in an instant, in my memory everything moved in slow motion. I saw his face, heard the noises, took in everyone else – and no one was concerned. Xander was still pretending to hate raisins, Bunny was smiling indulgently, Lando was scowling, Pilar was putting coasters under mugs and William and Daphne were gazing at one another in an adoration that made them blind to everything else. Only I seemed to realise that Caspian was choking. Choking is the biggest fear of anyone looking after a child, and thankfully I have been rigorously trained in how to deal with it.

I darted over to him, grabbed him, leant him forward and whacked him on the back. In the training they describe them as 'blows', and that came back to me, helped me: it is so counterintuitive to hit a child hard, but I knew it was what was needed. I looked at his face, oblivious to the chaos that was erupting around me as panic and horror took over everyone else in the room, and saw that he was still attempting to draw breath, but was starting to turn blue. My own fear was still deeply compressed, and I was completely focused on my job. I administered the back blows again, but to no avail, so next I grabbed him around the waist, from behind, and drew my clenched fist firmly in and up, under the solar plexus. To my relief, on the second thrust a raisin shot out of his mouth and he gave a terrifying, rasping intake of breath before collapsing into my arms. Now I heard the cacophony of voices:

'Oh my God, oh my God, Penny, is he okay?'

Bunny was screaming and crying, being held by Daphne, Xander had tears pouring down his cheeks, William was comforting Seraphina and Lando was grey with shock.

'He's all right,' I said, hearing the shakiness in my own voice. 'He's all right, but we should call an ambulance, he'll need checking over.'

I shifted the limp but breathing child over to Bunny, now on the floor beside us, and took the mobile phone that Lando was offering me, to dial 999 and explain what had happened.

'The ambulance will be here in about ten minutes, they said to keep him warm and calm until they arrive.'

It was clear that nobody really knew what to do with themselves, but seeing Seraphina's stricken face, I knew that she would be our priority once Caspian was safely in medical hands. To help myself as much as her, I started organising everyone.

'Okay, Phina darling, why don't you help Grandpa and Uncle Xander take the breakfast things into the kitchen. I *think* I heard Pilar saying she was going to make chocolate-dipped magdalenas, and there's a good chance there will be a bowl to be licked.'

I looked at her desperately, and she nodded.

'Sí, that is right, come along with me.'

Phina's wan little face lifted a little and the two men took their cue, jollying her along and getting her out of the room and thoroughly distracted.

'Daphne, please could you take Bunny to get changed to go to the hospital with Caspy? Don't worry,' I added, squeezing Bunny's hand. 'I'll look after him while you're gone. Grab the things you need; you may be there a little while.'

She nodded, kissed her son's head, and let Daphne lead her upstairs.

'Lando, could you please phone Ben and let him know what's happened? I don't think he needs to come, though.'

'Of course.'

I rocked Caspian gently as they sorted everything out,

holding back the torrent of tears I wanted to release, but that must wait for later.

When the ambulance had pulled away, with the reassurance from the paramedics that Caspy should make a full recovery, we all walked slowly back into the house.

'Thank God you were here, Penny,' said Xander, putting his arm around my shoulder and giving me a big squeeze. 'None of us had a clue what to do.'

I didn't want praise, I wanted everything to be normal again.

'I'm glad I've had the training, although it's not something you ever want to use. Come on, Phina my love, your brother is going to be fine, so how about we find something lovely to do while we wait for him to get back? I did wonder if you would like to collect some stones to paint and make presents for everyone?'

Subdued, but far from broken, Seraphina's beautiful smile appeared.

'Oh, yes *please*, Pixie, I've been wanting to do that for *ages*. Oh! We could make a really special one for Caspy.'

'Good idea. Go on, upstairs and find some clothes, I'm right behind you.'

I turned to follow her as she scampered off, but was stopped by a hand on my arm. Lando.

'Penny, what you did today, it was... it was very special.'

His skin was still an alarming shade of grey, and he had aged twenty years in the past half an hour.

'Well, like I said, it is just training. But Lando, are *you* all right? You look terrible.'

'Penny, he nearly died.'

His voice broke on the last word and, instinctively, I reached out and pulled him to me. I was surprised when he clung to me as if he were drowning. The others tactfully left the hallway, and we stood there for some time, his heart hammering in his chest. Eventually he pulled away and held my shoulders, looking into my eyes. Despite the circumstances, I'm afraid to say that the old longing to reach up and kiss him came flooding back, and I might have done, had Daphne not reappeared through the living room door, wafting ostrich feathers.

'I'm so sorry to interrupt, my dears, but I was wondering if I could join you and Phina in collecting some stones. I do feel I would like to do something *useful*.'

I smiled at her.

'That would be lovely. We can go as soon as we're all dressed.'

'I'll go and help her now then.'

She disappeared up the stairs, and I dragged my eyes back to Lando's.

'You're a very special person, Penny,' said Lando. 'India will be lucky to have you.'

'Thank you,' I mumbled. It wasn't what I wanted to say, but what else was there? 'Do you want to come and collect stones?'

'I do, but I have to work. I'm nearly there. And today... well, I need to think as well.' He lifted his hand briefly to my cheek. 'I'll see you later.'

Twenty minutes later, Phina, Daphne and I were wrapped up warm and ready to go. It was a subdued little group that left the house, still in shock from what had happened, but then around the side of the house bounded Garbo and Hepburn, tongues lolling and leads trailing.

'Look, Pixie, Hepburn has a note,' said Seraphina, and indeed she did, tucked into her collar. We pulled it out and found a sweet little sketch of the two dogs wearing Santa hats, and some writing underneath:

Dear Feenee,

Please take us for a walk with you. We would like to help you find stones and maybe some fox poo too (don't tell Daddy).

Lots of love,

Garbo and Hepburn xxx

The little girl screamed with laughter when we read her the note, and when she saw how 'the dogs' had written her name (which she could barely write herself) and I sent a silent message of thanks to Lando for his kindness. His gesture lifted all our spirits and we continued with a renewed spring in our step, Phina running on ahead with the dogs while Daphne and I got chatting.

'I'm glad things are going so well with William,' I said. 'He is absolutely besotted with you.'

'And I with him. What a wonderful thing to find each other the way we have. Wonderful for anyone, but when you are – shall we say – a *certain* age, these things become less likely. We're very lucky. But what about you, Penny? Don't think me nosy, and please tell me to mind my own business, but is there anyone special in your life? Have I noticed something of a *frisson* between you and Lando, or am I imagining things?'

I sighed heavily, puffing out a great cloud of white into the cold air.

'Oh Daphne, I don't know. I've thought the same myself, maybe, but he's about to leave the country, and I'm planning to as well... I've wasted so much time on a relationship that wasn't going anywhere, I can't bear the thought of wasting any more. And Lando...'

'Yes?'

'Lando is a very attractive man, very eligible, I suppose. He must have women throwing themselves at him all the time. It feels a bit embarrassing. I mean, what would he see in me?'

'What on *earth* are you talking about?' I was rather surprised by Daphne's vehemence. 'What would he see in you? My dear girl, he should be grovelling with gratitude that a lovely girl like you would show the slightest interest. And that's not to say a thing against Lando – in the brief time I have known him, he seems to me like rather a special man with a very special father, of course – but what I mean is that you are something of a prize yourself.'

'Me?' I barked out a laugh. 'I don't think so.'

'Why on earth *not*? You're caring, clever, wonderful with children, lovely-looking – the complete package.'

I stooped to pick up a perfect stone for Seraphina to paint.

'Well, that's very kind of you, Daphne, but I'm ordinary – and nearly forty.'

'What's being nearly forty got to do with it? It's an advantage if you ask me. Lando doesn't want someone ten years younger than him with nothing in common.'

'Plenty of men do.' I tried to sound jokey, but I could hear the edge of bitterness in my voice. 'Forty-year-old men don't want forty-year-old women, they want someone younger. Everyone knows that.'

'Well, *I* don't,' said Daphne stubbornly. 'I suppose you mean babies?'

I shrugged.

She continued, 'You're not too old to have a baby, or two if you get a move on. And someone like Lando – he strikes me as having a bit more to him than looking for someone for nothing more than their ability to pop out children. I know it's what you want, Penny darling, but there honestly is more to life.'

'I know.' I scuffed my toe into the frosty ground. 'I know. But it's not nothing. And look at the glamorous life that Lando has led and the stunning ex everyone talks about. I'm just a

frumpy, middle-aged primary school teacher and I won't be
seen to be mooning over him.'

Daphne stopped walking, took my arm and turned me
towards her. To my surprise, she looked annoyed. I had been
expecting sympathy maybe, or agreement.

'Penny. I know that your boyfriend left you, and he sounds
like a particularly nasty specimen. But you mustn't waste a
second longer in self-pity.'

My mouth dropped open. Self-pity? How dare she! She
continued, 'You are not washed up, on the shelf, a dried-up old
spinster or any of those other vile, misogynistic lies. You're
gorgeous and warm and completely perfect for Lando. Why do
you think those other things – the fabulous lifestyle and glossy
girlfriend – are in his past? Because that's not what he wants
anymore. That's my understanding, anyway, given what
William has said of it.'

'But he's moving to Greece to be an artistic hermit.'

'Well, that might be what he *says*, or even what he thinks he
wants, but from what I've seen of him, I think it's very unlikely.
He obviously adores his family, even if they do drive him mad.
William has told me how much Lando loves his niece and
nephew and looks forward to seeing them – they come down
quite often, you know, not just at Christmas.'

Hope sprang in my heart, then rapidly sank back down.

'Maybe he won't leave, but I'm planning on going to India,
you know.'

'I do know. Please forgive me if I'm speaking out of turn
here – after all, I barely know you – but are you *really* going to
India, or is it just a comforting image of escape? From everything I've seen of you, you'd be far happier tucked up in Dorset
with Lando.'

I blinked at her.

'Sorry to be hard on you, darling, but you must not give up.
Look at me – seventy-two and still giddy. You're still young,

don't waste yourself. There's plenty of passion there still, admit it! It's your confidence and self-belief which have been knocked, and there's only one person who can build them back up – you!'

I seized her hands.

'Daphne, I think you might be right. What have I been thinking? I've let bloody Timothy make me feel like crap.' I felt inspired by this amazing woman, but then some of the old fears instantly started tugging at my brain and I tempered my enthusiasm. 'I do need to resurface, but I'm still not sure that Lando is the way to do it. I don't think another romantic knock-back will do me much good. Oh, I need to think.'

She gave me a small smile.

'Good idea. But please, whatever you do, don't let age or fear of being hurt or even humiliated come into your decision-making. These things... they don't matter. I promise.'

'Thank you, Daphne. You've made me feel all sort of – fresh. I'll peep through a couple of doors, even I'm not guaranteeing I'll open them all the way.'

'That's all I'm asking – give yourself a chance.'

We had nearly reached the village, and Seraphina came running back towards us, her mittened hands full of stones.

'Look at these, Pixie, we can make some *super* presents. But first... I know you'll say no, but *please* say yes...'

I grinned.

'Try me.'

'Can we go to the pub for a hot chocolate? Pleeeeeease?'

'Ooh, what do you think, Daphne? Do we all need a hot chocolate?'

Daphne adopted a grave expression.

'I think that is an eminently sensible suggestion, young Phina, we've all had a shock and a chilly walk. In fact, maybe Penny and I should have an Uncle Xander special? Goodness knows I've heard enough about them from him. Positively medicinal, he says.'

I nodded.

'Any doctor would agree with you. We should definitely do this.'

Phina whooped with joy, and we picked up our pace as we headed towards The Curious Badger.

Ten minutes after we got back to the house, Bunny and Caspian returned, having been picked up from the hospital by Lando. Caspy had been given a thorough check-up and was declared fit and well, other than a slightly hoarse voice and some minor bruising where I had hit him.

'Gosh, Bunny, I'm so sorry, I feel terrible about leaving marks.'

'Pixie, my darling, please don't apologise for one second. If it hadn't been for you, for your quick thinking...' Her eyes filled with tears and mine rushed to match them. 'Well, Caspy could have died. I am forever in your debt.'

I hugged her tightly.

'You're not in my debt. I'm so relieved I could help. Come on, let's hear no more about it. Caspian, what would you like to do now?'

'Well, do you remember that gingerbread house kit? I'd like to do that please. All of us.'

'Of course, the one you won at the party. Great idea. Come on then, everyone to the kitchen!'

And everyone came. For a festive scene you couldn't beat it. All of us squashed around the table, decorating and constructing a fiendishly difficult gingerbread cottage. There was William, laughing with Daphne as she added an icing boa to her figure. There was Xander, swearing under his breath as the walls refused to stay stuck together for the fourth time. The twins and Bunny, snuggled close against each other, gluing on jelly sweets in abundance. Pilar, slipping a skilled hand in every so often to correct our clumsy mistakes. And Lando, piping meticulous and beautiful designs on the roof in white icing. I smiled as I mixed up some green buttercream for the grass. Thanks to the talk with Daphne, for the first time in weeks I felt a proper sense of peace as I relaxed into Christmas with this wonderful family.

SIXTEEN

When the house was finished, I gave the children their tea, then handed them over to Bunny, who wanted to put them to bed.

'I so nearly lost him, Pixie darling, it's making me think about all sorts of things.' She put her hand on her tummy thoughtfully, but I couldn't ask her right then what was going through her head; I hoped she was finding peace with the pregnancy.

Pilar and I cleaned up the kitchen, and I had decided to go and once more look through those links that my mother had sent when Lando came in.

'Uh, Penny, hi.'

'Hello. The gingerbread house looks good, doesn't it? I'm not sure how we're going to eat it, though.'

'I'm sure those twins will find a way. Er, look, I was wondering if you'd like to pop over to the studio later for a spot of supper – to say thank you for posing as Mary?'

It felt like something of a 'now or never' moment, and Daphne's beautiful, encouraging face floated through my mind. I pushed down the Greek chorus of worries that piped up and took a breath.

'Thank you, that sounds lovely.'

Despite my attempt at a serene demeanour, my body and mind put on a fireworks show as I went upstairs to get ready. He was expecting me in an hour, which, on the one hand, was not long enough to get my thoughts and feelings under control, but, on the other hand, was far too long to be fretting.

'I'd rather get it over with as quickly as possible,' I muttered, as I flicked through my scant wardrobe. Then I laughed as I realised that 'getting it over with' was *not* the right approach to a potential romantic encounter. It was more what I had used to feel when Timothy started to get amorous and I would rather read another chapter of my book. No, tonight my impatience was more linked to the desire to quell my racing heartbeat and churning stomach, to flip to the end of the story because the anticipation of calamity was too unpleasant. 'Come on,' I said, 'try to enjoy it. What's the worst that could happen?' Rallying, I picked out a pretty chiffon top and paired it with my smartest jeans, jumped in a quick shower, topped up my makeup and spritzed on some perfume I thought was sexy, but Timothy claimed made him sneeze. He preferred me wafting Devon Violets, like his grandmother.

'Hello?'

I pushed open the studio door and was immediately greeted by Garbo and Hepburn bounding over to me, closely followed by Lando. I fussed over the dogs for a moment before entering the studio.

'Oh, wow, this looks amazing!'

The room had been tidied up and there was a small table covered with a white cloth, gleaming glasses and cutlery, candles and a little vase of winter berries.

'Thank you. I really am most grateful to you for posing for me.'

That's right, I told myself firmly. *You shouldn't have got so worked up. This is a thank-you supper, nothing else.*

'It was my pleasure. Is the Nativity finished?'

'All but. I hope the church likes it. Now, my cooking facilities here are limited and I've left a couple of things up at the house. Do you mind waiting while I fetch them? Here, have a drink.'

I accepted a glass of champagne, happy to wait in the warm studio while he dashed back up to the house. I looked idly at his workbench, touched to see the star I had made looking very smart for its coat of varnish and with a golden string run through a neatly drilled hole. I ran my eyes over the Nativity figures, each one exquisite and unique, from the lovely Mary to a solemn King, characterful sheep and an utterly adorable baby Jesus. A glossy brochure with bright photographs caught my eye, and without really meaning to, I took in what it was. Properties in Greece, and didn't they look tempting? I bit my lip as I noticed a letter lying next to it, an estate agent's logo and yesterday's date at the top. I turned away quickly, unwilling both to violate Lando's privacy by reading his letter, but also, unsuccessfully, to try to erase what I had seen. If the estate agent had written only yesterday, it must mean that Lando was still planning to go. His apparent prevarication the day before, and Daphne's assertion that it would never happen were red herrings. How could I be so pathetic, to let my heart and mind wander over a man I barely knew? How could I keep blaming Timothy when my desperation was evident, and I was willing to overlook so much in my quest for a happy ending? Funny, for such a seemingly sensible woman I'm so hopelessly romantic. I walked over to the pretty table and sat down to wait, pulling out my phone as I did so, and opening my email. Mum had been so pleased I'd read her links and liked them, and had responded with even more, including a flat that a friend of hers was renting out and which looked gorgeous.

Hi Mum, thank you for these links. The apartment looks great, can't wait to get moving. I'll put in applications for some of the jobs and hand in my resignation on the first day of next term come what may.

Love, Penny

'Right, I think that's everything, sorry to keep you waiting.'

'No problem.' I tucked my phone back in my pocket. 'I was just emailing Mum about India.'

'Oh. Right. Great.'

He could sound a bit more enthusiastic, given that he was also off on a foreign adventure. Maybe he wished he'd chosen India rather than Greece.

'Anyway, shall we eat?'

He put down a steaming plate in front of me, and I inhaled the rich aroma greedily.

'This smells wonderful. Mushroom risotto, how gorgeous. But it has something extra – what's that lovely earthy smell?'

He sat down.

'Truffle oil, and a particularly good one I get from a woman in the village who makes her own. I hope you like it.'

As I tucked into the savoury, creamy dish and sipped the glass of wine that had replaced the champagne, I began to relax. Lando was excellent company, back on the good form I had seen at the Winter Wonderland. He made me cry laughing with scurrilous stories of his City days. He also showed himself to be a good listener, asking me about teaching and even drawing out a little about what had happened with Timothy. I was initially reluctant to talk about it, but his kind demeanour tempered my shame.

'I felt so... discarded. We'd been together for such a long

time; it wasn't like going on a first date when someone doesn't want to see you again and you know it's only that you're not into each other. It was more like I'd been a place marker – good enough until he wanted a proper life.'

'You must have felt cheated.'

I stared at him. How could he understand that, so instantly?

'That's it exactly. But admitting that – it makes me feel foolish. Why didn't I realise sooner? He strung me along, gave me just enough to make me keep believing that there was something solid to expect from him.' A raw laugh escaped my throat. 'The biggest joke is that I never even thought he was some grand passion myself. I loved him, but I accepted too much compromise. I thought that is what you did.'

'Is that what you saw in your parents' relationship?'

'Oh no, quite the opposite. They adore each other, get on like a house on fire. I suppose what they have, it seems unobtainable, so rare. The truth is that I decided to settle. I didn't have the guts to hold out for something better and risk not finding it.'

'Well, you're not alone in that. Isn't that the sort of relationship many people are in?'

'Probably. Anyway, all I can do now is move on and take some lessons from it.'

'Move on to India?'

'Yes, that's right. It's time I shook things up. I'm not running away, you know.'

'I wouldn't suggest that for a moment. Although people have said the same to me about the Greece plan.'

'Are you? Running away?'

'Maybe. But you can never get away from yourself, can you? And that's more terrifying than anything. I'm not so lacking in self-awareness that I don't know I'll still be *me* in a charming little rustic cottage in Greece, as much as I'm me here in Dorset and was me in a sticky-floored bar in London.'

He slumped back in his chair and stared at his empty plate.

'Lando? If you don't mind me saying...'

He raised a small smile.

'Go ahead.'

'The *you* I've seen, well, there's nothing wrong with him. And he sounds very different from the *you* that lived it up in London. Not different so much as a character maybe, but different in his choices. And isn't that what *makes* the difference in life? Our choices? I'm not sure you need to force yourself into such a severe lifestyle to protect yourself anymore. Are you so worried that you'll relapse?'

'Not really. I feel more confident now than I ever felt then. That was all bravado and front. But I'm so... wrecked. I don't have anything to offer – other, maybe, than the art I produce. I had a nervous breakdown, for God's sake, so I clearly can't cope. Who needs that in their life? My father has found Daphne, for which I am truly grateful, and I don't want to inflict myself on anyone else.'

Listening to him, my eyes filled with tears.

'What's wrong? You see, I've upset you, brought you down. I'm sorry, I shouldn't have invited you here tonight.'

He stood up abruptly and cleared away our plates, then disappeared into the room at the back of the studio again. I was glad of the breathing space to think over my answer, and when he reappeared, I felt more composed. Mind you, that was put in severe jeopardy when he placed a bowl of chocolate mousse decorated with crystallised orange pieces in front of me and poured some dessert wine from a tiny bottle.

'You haven't brought me down at all. I'm just so sorry to hear you speaking like this. You've got so much to offer – your wonderful talent, your generosity as a host – and you're brilliant with the twins.'

'No,' he said stubbornly, 'I don't bring anyone any good.

Look at you, saving Caspian's life today. I couldn't have done that.'

'But I could only do that because I'm trained to. That's luck, not some innate skill or talent. Take a first-aid course if it would make you feel better.'

Thank goodness that made him laugh, because I was beginning to feel worried about how to answer this complicated man, when all I really wanted to do was put my arms around him and tell him everything would be all right. A ringing noise sounded across the room, and I looked up.

'Sorry,' said Lando. 'That's mine, ignore it. Look, Penny, I'm sorry for being so morose. Thank you for listening to me...'

The mobile rang again, and again Lando made no move to answer it, but continued speaking.

'Are you sure I haven't brought you down? This was meant to be a nice supper, not a therapy session.'

'It is nice. It's really lovely, thank you. And please don't worry, I don't mind these big conversations. Better out than in.'

'That's exactly the sort of thing primary school teachers should say. Do you find yourself saying it every day?'

It was good to see that the cloud had lifted and Lando was back to a more cheerful, teasing frame of mind.

'Yes, that's right, it's my go-to phrase in myriad contexts, most of which I'm sure you don't want to know about.'

The phone rang yet again.

'Sorry, I think I'd better answer that – someone's obviously keen to get hold of me and it's unusual.'

'Of course.'

He snatched it up.

'Hello? Oh, hello.'

I was trying not to listen, but it was difficult in the small studio. He sounded rather annoyed with whoever it was.

'Look, I can't talk now. Do we really need to talk at all? All right, I'll ring tomorrow.'

He came back to sit down, and I studied my spoon with fascination, desperate not to look nosy but, of course, desperately nosy.

'Sorry about that,' said Lando, finishing his coffee. 'That was my ex, Zara.'

My heart skipped a beat.

'I've no idea what she wants and don't really want to know, but she seems to think it's pressing. I haven't seen her for months and months.'

I didn't reply. I didn't know what to say. Surely, there was only one reason that Zara was calling: that she wanted Lando back. And I could never compete with this goddess I had heard about.

'Look, Penny.' To my surprise, Lando took my hand. I lifted my eyes to meet his. 'Are you really going to go to India? Is that what you want?'

A million replies, thoughts, images raced through my head. No, came the answer, clear and loud, that is *not* what I want. I want to hunker down here with you in this beautiful house in Dorset and have a baby. *That's* what I want. But how could I say that?

'Are you really going to Greece? Is that what *you* want?'

We stared at each other in silence. Lando was the first to speak.

'I want... I do want... Penny, I like you so much. I think I want...'

Warning bells rang loudly, frantically in my head, with a helpful, protective voice shrieking: *he doesn't know what he wants, Penny. If he wanted you, he'd be sure about it. Danger! Danger! Don't waste your time on this one.*

I pulled my hand away gently.

'I certainly know what I *need*, Lando. I need to be the architect of my own life, not waiting around for other people to make decisions for me. Right now, yes, that means going to India. I have to feel that I am actively doing something for myself. I've been passively waiting around for too long.'

'But is it what you *want*?'

I shrugged.

'We can't always have what we want, and maybe that's often for the best. I wanted Timothy to propose to me, but now I'm bloody glad he didn't. There are things I want, of course there are, but I can't wait and hope for them anymore.'

He nodded.

'I hear you. I'm not sure I should have what I want, because there's too much chance I'll screw it up. Wise words of yours, Penny. I should focus on what I need.'

I gave him a small smile and stood up.

'Thank you for a delicious supper. I can't wait to see the Nativity finished and all set up in the church.'

He pushed back his chair and stood up too.

'Maybe you would help me take it down?'

'I'd love to, thank you.'

He whistled to the dogs.

'I'll give these two a run and walk you back up to the house.'

Back in my room I undressed slowly and took a long shower, as the events of the evening swirled around in my head. It was funny, I reflected, that Lando's concern – that his mental health history made him unsuitable for a relationship – was the least of my worries. What concerned me more was his seeming uncertainty about how he wanted to move forward with his life. It was obvious he was vacillating over the Greece plan and leaning towards more of a family set-up in Dorset, which should have encouraged me. But I had been seriously thrown by the phone call from Zara. He may have dismissed it as unimportant, but here was a woman from his past who clearly wanted to see him again, presumably to make amends. Who was to say she hadn't changed, realised her mistake in leaving him? She was not only beautiful, if reports were to be believed, but *familiar*, and that could be very tempting to any one of us, let alone someone who struggled to let down his guard with new people. He had taken my hand, I knew he was reaching out to me, but it seemed too much of a risk, however tempting. I had known him for just a couple of weeks. We had undoubtedly connected and God knows I thought he was absolutely gorgeous, but there was too much scope there for heartbreak. Wasn't there? When I had put my pyjamas on, I went over to the window and saw the familiar light burning away in his studio. I felt a powerful tug in my stomach, urging me to throw on a coat and some shoes and run to him, to say 'let's give it a try', but the careful, sensible voice won out. Go to bed, Penny. Stay safe. And with a heavy heart, that is what I did.

SEVENTEEN

I felt tired and drained the next day, wracked with indecision, and was relieved that I hadn't planned to take the children out. I pulled on a comfy pair of tracksuit trousers and a flannel shirt soft from repeated washing, and we sat down in front of a Christmas film about naughty elves whilst making paper chains. The twins were entranced by the ease and relative speed with which they could make reams of the decorations, and soon we were surrounded by a sea of colourful rings.

'We'll run out of paper soon, then what?' I asked, smiling.

'Then we can use Mummy's magazines and Uncle Lando's newspapers...'

'And Uncle Xander's newspapers – they're the best because they're orangey pink.'

I grinned and felt grateful for the fact that the Lords still favoured real, print newspapers over the digital version.

'Good idea, we might have to.'

As we beavered away, I started to relax and feel better and was going to suggest a pause for some gingerbread when the doorbell rang. I jumped up and went to answer it. Outside on the doorstep stood a woman. She was tall and slender with glossy, wavy dark brown hair that fell almost to her waist. It was so lush that I found myself wondering if it could possibly be real, then berated myself for my bitchiness. Some people were just naturally blessed with stunning looks, and she was one of them. She had smooth, olive skin, huge dark eyes and full lips which, were, unfortunately, forming a very slight sneer, as if she had something unpleasant smelling under her perfect nose. It rather spoiled the effect: she must have been ravishing when she smiled.

'Hello!' I said chirpily, hoping a big grin would detract from my scruffy clothes, scrubbed face and pulled back hair. She stared at me stonily.

'Lando?'

'No, Penny,' I replied, hoping to raise a smile. I might as well have hoped to raise Elvis. Her face didn't flicker.

'I mean, where *is* Lando?' Her foot tapped and I was reminded of Cruella De Vil. Better lock up Garbo and Hepburn.

'Oh, er, probably in his studio, working.'

'Very well, I'll wait for him in his office.'

She moved towards me, and I stepped aside hurriedly as she swept past in a cloud of heavy perfume. Although she hadn't deigned to tell me her name, it was a pretty sensible guess that this must be Zara, the gorgeous ex. I shrugged and went back to check on the children. They were still engrossed in their film and paper chains, so I popped into the kitchen.

'*Hola*, Pilar.'

'*Hola, Penélope*, who was at the door?'

'Well, she didn't tell me her name, but she was stunning and rather rude and here to see Lando. She's gone to wait in his office.'

'Beautiful? Long, dark hair?'

'That's right, do you know her?'

Pilar let out a wonderfully derisive snort. I wondered if she'd teach me that rather than more Spanish.

'*Sí*. What is she doing back here? She does not do Lando any good.'

'I suppose I'd better go and find him.'

'No, Penélope, you do not have to scurry around after her. *Se puede cuezar en su propia salsa.*'

'What does that mean?'

'That she must cook for a while in her own sauce. Let her sit.'

'Oh! Leave her to stew in her own juices. All right, I will. In the meantime, can I take some gingerbread for the children?'

I was duly issued with enough gingerbread shapes to see us from here to the new year, and a promise of hot chocolate to follow. I returned to the living room and was halfway through a large, pillowy gingerbread star when the door opened and in stalked Zara, a peeved expression on her lovely face.

Without preamble, she demanded, 'Why haven't you gone to find Lando? I've been waiting for ages.'

I finished my mouthful before replying.

'I don't recall you asking me to, you said you'd wait. Would you like some gingerbread?'

'No, I would *not* like some gingerbread.' Her mouth twisted and, taking another bite of the delicious biscuit, I wondered if she'd ever even tried it. It was probably all kale and macrobiotics round her way; she'd get on well with Chakra. She continued, 'Any idiot would have realised that finding Lando for me was what I intended. I assume that you *are* here working for the Lords' – she raked her eyes up and down my scruffy ensemble as if to confirm my serfdom – 'so you should have gone immedi-ately. Oh, I'll go myself, I know where that blasted studio is.'

I am a mild-mannered person, but even I took exception to being accused of idiocy by this unpleasant woman. I opened my mouth to reply, but stopped when Bunny wandered in.

'Oh, Zara. I didn't know you were here. Did Lando invite you?'

Zara did not answer the question.

'I have been here for at least twenty minutes, waiting for The Help' – she gesticulated sharply towards me – 'to go and get him, but she seems either stubborn or incapable in some way.'

'Zara, please don't talk about Pixie like that. She is here to help me with the children, which is exactly what she is doing right now, as wonderfully as ever by the looks of things. Lando will probably be back up to the house for lunch.'

I could have cheered. Who knew Bunny had such a steely core? Zara was undaunted.

'I can't sit around till *lunch*time waiting for him. I shall go and find him myself.'

I stood up. Somehow, I wanted to take control of this situation, and I hated the thought of her bursting into that beautiful studio, breaking its peace and possibly Lando's at the same time.

'Look, I'll go. The children are fine here for a few minutes. I won't be long.'

Before anyone could object, I nipped out of the door, shedding gingerbread crumbs in my wake. I shoved my feet into my boots and pulled on my coat; even though the studio was only across the garden, it was freezing cold outside, to the point where surely it was only a matter of time before the snow started falling. A white Christmas in this setting would, I reflected, be almost ridiculously idyllic – but maybe not if the icing over was caused by one glance from Zara. I shivered for reasons other than the cold as I opened the back door and hurried across the frosty grass, my breath billowing out behind me in great clouds. I pushed open the studio door and allowed myself a moment to enjoy the slightly fuggy, wood-scented warmth as it draped itself around my body like a velvet robe.

'Hi there.' I felt rather nervous, seeing Lando sitting there in front of the window, his back to me as he leant over a piece of work. At least I had a legitimate reason for turning up, so there could be no confusion about my motives. He turned around and smiled when he saw me.

'Penny! I – I didn't think you'd come today. I'm glad to see you. I didn't explain myself well last night. Please, sit down. Would you like a tea, coffee – something stronger?'

The pull inside me to curl up in a chair with a cup of tea in my hand and a dachshund on my lap was powerful, but I squashed it down firmly.

'Oh, no, I'm sorry, Lando, I came to tell you that you have a visitor. Up at the house.'

'Right, I see. Who is it?'

'Um, it's Zara.'

'Zara? What on earth is she doing here?'

'I don't know, she didn't confide in me, I'm afraid.'

He must have heard the edge in my voice.

'Was she *very* rude? I'm sorry, Penny, she's not very good with attractive women.'

'What?' I let out a shout of laughter. 'I don't think *that* was her problem.'

'What do you mean?'

'Lando! Look at me.' I gazed down at my comfortable clothing and tugged at my ponytail. 'I hardly think I constitute a threat. I'm not sure who you're being kinder to – me, by suggesting she might think I'm a looker, or her, for suggesting she might have a reason better than being supercilious to 'The Help' as she called me.'

'She didn't, did she? Penny, I'm sorry, she is rude. But I meant what I said. A tracksuit and tied-up hair doesn't disguise your looks. You're beautiful. I meant it when I said it before. And she can see that. It's no excuse for her rudeness, but she's got no self-confidence beneath the surface.'

'I— I—' I stammered, confused. 'I think you'd better go up and see her, she was getting pretty impatient.'

And with that, I turned and scuttled out of the door and back across the lawn. He had called me beautiful. Again! What was going on? Once inside I threw off my outdoor clothes and dived back in to the children, to their world of gingerbread and paper chains and safety, pretending not to notice when the back door opened a few minutes later and Lando went to the office and shut the door behind him.

About twenty minutes later, I was drawing the curtains against the lowering sky as Pilar bustled around straightening up the room, when Lando and Zara came in. His expression was impossible to read, but he looked tired and stressed. She finally had a smile on her face, and I tried not to wonder what had put it there.

'Pilar, Zara is going to be staying tonight. I wonder if you would be kind enough to make up the yellow bedroom, when you have a moment?'

'Actually, Pilar,' said Zara, her smile stretching a fraction wider, 'could you do it as soon as possible? I've had a *terribly* tiring time and I'd be *so* grateful. I simply *must* have a lie-down before lunch. Unless I can use our – I mean *your* – room, Lando darling?'

Grateful to have a job to busy my hands, whilst also transfixed by this little soap opera unfolding, I fussed for longer than was strictly necessary over hanging the tie backs.

'I'm sure that won't be necessary,' said Lando, supplication in his voice. 'Will it, Pilar?'

'Of course not, I'll go and do it now. It will only take me five minutes.'

'I'll give you a hand,' said Lando, darting out after her.

I wasn't sure what Zara's agenda was, exactly, but it didn't seem as if Lando was glad to see her.

'And maybe *you*' – the hardness had returned to Zara's voice, and I realised she was talking to me – 'would bring me up some hot water and lemon juice?'

I left the curtains and walked over to the twins, reaching out my hands which they immediately took.

'I'm sorry, I'm busy looking after these two, they're having something different from us for lunch. But I can show you where the kettle is if you like?'

'I *know* where the kettle is,' she hissed. 'This was *my* house once, and probably will be again, so don't play lady of the manor with me because you've had your feet under the table for five minutes.'

I ignored her.

'Come on, you two, let's see if those toaster waffles actually work. Waffles in under five minutes do seem too good to be true.'

We scurried out and were soon assembling lunch together, me silently praying that the venomous Zara wouldn't come in to boil the kettle for her drink. Somehow, I thought it was unlikely; she'd probably make Pilar do it for her. There was a woman who was used to having people running around after her.

'Who is that lady?' asked Seraphina, squeezing ketchup into a perfectly placed dimple on her moulded woodland creatures plate. 'She's very pretty, but I don't think she's kind.'

'She used to be a friend of your Uncle Lando's,' I said carefully.

'Do *you* think she's kind, Pixie?'

I hesitated. I believe in being honest with children, but I wasn't sure what the situation was with Zara, and I didn't want to tell the whole, unvarnished truth – that I thought she was a class A bitch with the soul of a vampire.

'Um, well, this is the first time I've met her, and although she wasn't super friendly, maybe she was just tired. It's always a good idea to give new people a chance.'

'Well, I've known her for a lot longer than that and I agree with you, Phina darling – not at all kind. Pixie is being exceedingly charitable.'

'Mummy!' The children rushed to hug her, and she held them tightly, looking at me over their heads and rolling her eyes. I wondered how Zara's reappearance would go down with the rest of the family.

Lunch was casual, but everyone was there, so it didn't take me long to find out. Zara, of course, made her entrance after everyone else was already in the living room having a drink. The time she claimed to need to rest must have been almost wholly used on her appearance: her hair had been washed and blow-dried into glossy ringlets, punctuated by little crystal clips and her makeup was immaculate, giving her skin the appearance of flawless velvet, while her lips were full and shiny. She was wearing a skin-tight pale gold dress with a high neck and while it came down to her knees and should have been demure, it managed to give the impression of being virtually see-through. It was wholly inappropriate for the time of day, but you couldn't deny that she looked amazing. I thought that I had put in a little extra effort, with my gauzy blouse and freshly washed hair, but I felt like Little Jimmy Krankie next to this vision of feminine perfection. She stood for a moment in the doorway to make and then assess her impact, and I wondered how pleased she would be. If it was reaction she was going for, she certainly got it, but there wasn't much admiration shown. William – lovely, warm William – stared at her expressionlessly, then turned and murmured something to Daphne, who squeezed his hand, looking worried. Bunny didn't glance over at all, but busied herself fussing over Caspian's juice, probably for the first time ever. Lando, who had been talking to his father, stood up and went over to the drinks cabinet, where he merely added more soda to his glass. It was Xander who gave the gratifying response she was presumably looking for.

'Zara! Stunning! Far too glamorous for this little corner of Dorset. Come and sit down – *can* you sit down in that dress? And let me get you a drink.'

'Thank you, Xander,' she purred. 'It's been *ages* since I've seen you. I'll have champagne – this *does* feel like a celebration, after all.'

'Great idea, you don't mind if I open a bottle, do you, Lando? Anyone else?'

You would have thought it was a room full of strict Methodists, the way we all shook our heads. It seemed that no one else felt like celebrating. Undeterred, Xander and Zara soon held sparkling glassfuls and their loudly flirtatious conversation dominated the room. It was a relief when the time came to go through to the dining room. Grateful, I took my usual spot between the children, then grinned when Bunny sidled up and shifted Phina along so that she could squeeze in too.

'It does feel a bit *safer* tucked in here, Pixie,' she whispered. 'Zara always makes me feel like she's going to put something nasty in my food.'

I giggled. It made the whole thing less awful to know that Bunny detested the woman too. But my grin faded when Zara took the seat directly opposite me and fixed me with a gimlet glare.

'I must say, Lando, I'm rather surprised that the children and their Help are dining with us.'

Way to go to make me feel a foot tall. But Lando snapped back at her.

'The children are part of the family and so is Penny, while she's living with us. And this family *dines* together.'

I smiled gratefully at him, and he held my eyes and smiled back.

Zara suddenly gave a little scream and, of course, everyone's heads immediately swivelled towards her.

'Oh, I'm *dreadfully* sorry, I've knocked over my water glass.'

Once the water was cleared up, lunch continued apace. Zara managed to find fault with all the food and nearly made Caspian cry when she suggested he and Seraphina were too little to have real glasses and should surely still be drinking out of plastic beakers. Bunny and I turned into paragons of child-care virtue, lavishing the twins with completely unnecessary attention in our attempts to avoid having to make conversation – or even eye contact – with Zara. William and Daphne kept themselves to themselves at one end of the table and Xander enjoyed the whole thing enormously. He made no secret of how attractive he found Zara and roared with laughter at her bitchy comments. Lando seemed to have turned into one of his wooden sculptures: polite but stiff and showing no emotion. I longed to reach out and squeeze his hand to try to reassure him but couldn't do anything of the sort. I smiled at him once or twice, but he gazed back at me with troubled eyes, which then slid back to Zara. I couldn't read him at all. He didn't seem glad that she was there, but then again, he *had* let her stay the night – albeit in her own room. Maybe the talk we had had yesterday was having some impact. Perhaps he had decided that a hermit's life wasn't for him, after all, and to give it another go in the beautiful house they had bought and decorated together. She may well have let him down, but she was a known quantity, and given Lando's insecurities, maybe that was exactly what he found comfort in. Unsurprisingly, my mood dipped further and further as the meal proceeded. I ate pudding – a delicious clementine cake with brandy cream – but when coffee was offered, I took my cue.

'Thank you, I won't. I think it's time the children got busy elsewhere.'

The twins mounted the usual token protests, but I had noticed that they were getting bored and twitchy, so when I gently insisted, they soon let me herd them from the room. As we left, I heard Zara's tart little voice:

'Finally. Now it's the proper grown-ups, we can relax and have some fun.'

I didn't wait to hear how anyone responded, but pulled the door shut gently behind me and steered the children towards some magazines I brought with me, full of pictures of their favourite TV characters to colour in, and with pages of stickers. Watching their earnest little faces as they pored over their work, I felt weary with fighting the truth. This was all I wanted, all I dreamed of, and I was soon going to have to confront my grief over the fact it was unlikely ever to happen for me.

I left them colouring for a moment and popped upstairs to find a cosier jumper, glad at the thought of the blessed peace of my room, if only for a few minutes, when a figure came up the shadowy stairs.

'Oh, Penny?'

'Hello, Zara.'

'Just a quick word.'

I lifted my eyes resignedly to meet hers, hard little chips of diamond for me, not melting and helpless like when she turned them on Lando, or flirty and flashing for Xander's sake.

'I can tell from those rather unsubtle cow eyes of yours gazing at Lando that you have clearly developed something of a *crush* on him. Maybe you even think you *love* him.' She gave a little laugh, as if the mere idea of my daring to love Lando was mirthful. She cocked her head on one side, but I said nothing, just stared at her. I wasn't willing to show any emotion for this succubus to feed off; I'd rather be the dumb serf she had me pegged as. She continued, 'Anyway, I *hate* to be the one to dash your romantic hopes, but you should probably know that Lando and I were only driven apart by circumstance, and now that things have changed, it's only a matter of time before we're as deeply in love and inseparable as we once were.'

I wondered how long she had taken to prepare this little speech, to make sure that each and every word and inflexion were as nasty and as patronising as she could possibly make it. My continued silence was beginning to annoy her. She clicked her tongue and flicked her hair over her shoulder. But what could I say? She decided to stop toying with me and finish me off once and for all.

'He's asked me to stay for Christmas and then – it's off to Greece. So, a word to the wise – concentrate your affections elsewhere. I'm sure you've got plenty to keep you busy with those children, but if you feel like getting out on your evening off, there's probably a village dance or something you might enjoy.'

She afforded me a final withering glance and turned on her heel to march back down the stairs. I went to my room and shut the door gently behind me. Maybe I should be in some sort of servants' garret, I thought, rather than this beautiful suite. But then I rallied. No. That was how *she* wanted me to feel, like I should be doffing my cap to her and filling coal scuttles. What a bitch. Well, she didn't matter. And if Lando really wanted her, which he presumably did if he had invited her to stay for Christmas, then he didn't matter either.

That evening, I opened my laptop and found the resignation letter, made a few tweaks and dated it for the first day of next term, then emailed it to myself to print off and to Mum and Dad to read over. Next, I pulled up some of the job applications in India and spent the next hour and a half completing forms and submitting them, before I lost my nerve. My original plan had been the right one, I thought. I needed to dig deep and find 'exciting Penny', who seeks adventure and relishes freedom. That was the way to protect myself, to move forward in life – not being such an obvious doormat that men trample over me again and again on their way to something better. I switched off the computer with a feeling of a job well done and didn't even glance across at the studio as I drew my curtains for the night.

EIGHTEEN

The next day Bunny wanted to take the children to visit a friend of hers in the next village.

'Do take the morning, Pixie darling. Maybe you could help Lando again?'

'I'm sure he's got quite enough to do with Zara here. It's fine, I'm sure there's plenty to keep me busy. What about the wrapping?'

Bunny clapped her hands in delight.

'Oh, Pixie, you *wouldn't*. It's an absolutely loathsome job, I always end up awake until about three o'clock on Christmas Eve, I hate it. I can't possibly drop it all on you...'

I laughed.

'Yes, you can! That's what I'm here to do – help.'

Truth be told, although I also disliked wrapping presents, I was grateful for it. I would make myself useful whilst being hidden away in my room, safe from Zara's acid tongue. Breakfast had been a rather more sombre affair than usual with her there. While the rest of us shuffled in wearing pyjamas as usual and tried to hide behind magazines and newspapers, she appeared fully – and exquisitely – dressed and sat bolt upright at a small table by the window, graciously allowing Pilar to serve her. She kept trying to make conversation with various family members (not me, of course) about pressing issues in current affairs, but everyone resented their peaceful breakfast being intruded upon and she was met with a series of noncommittal, brief responses which varied from fairly polite (Daphne: 'Mmm, I don't know anything about that, dear') to verging on rude (a grumpy 'harumph' from Lando). Eventually it was Xander who saved the day.

'Oh, do put a sock in it, Zara. You know how breakfast works in this house, and we all like it. If you want civilised conversation, I suggest you go down to The Curious Badger. Cecil's always up for a nice long chat about politics.'

I hid a smile behind my mug of tea at the collective sigh of relief that rippled around the room, but I didn't feel even a tiny bit sorry for that horrid woman, who was looking distinctly sour.

When I took my things through to the kitchen, I was surprised to find that Lando had followed me.

'Are you all right?' he asked gruffly, as we stared awkwardly into the dishwasher.

I wasn't about to tell him all the shaming things that Zara had said to me the night before; now was the moment to show I was nobody's doormat.

'Wonderful!' I said brightly. 'Quite excited, in fact. I've applied for some of those jobs in India.'

He blinked at me.

'Oh, right. I see. Well, good for you.'

'Thanks! I expect you're getting your plans finalised too? Zara said she was off to Greece with you.'

My smile was now getting so wide and so forced that it threatened to pop a muscle in my neck. Lando, on the other hand, went grey.

'She said what?'

'Oh yes, she was *dying* to share your plans with me, said

you'd invited her for Christmas and then – off to Greece you go. Marvellous, congratulations. Anyway, I'd better go, lots to do, presents to wrap, better check my inbox.'

Before he could reply, I belted out of the room and upstairs. I was quite pleased with myself for my dashing speech. Now Lando would see I wasn't someone to be pitied, to find a bit embarrassing, but an independent woman with her own life. He would probably be grateful to be released from my – what was the charming expression Zara had used? Oh yes – *cow eyes*.

Once Bunny had the children safely out of the way, I dug all their presents out from their various hiding places and took them to my room. I equipped myself with scissors, tape, ribbons, tags and pens and got to work. I was all right with the boxes, but these were woefully few and far between, and soon I was struggling with all manner of strange shapes. The year before I had watched a very together woman on breakfast TV instruct her hapless viewers on how to wrap any present elegantly, the paper floating into position from her skilful hands. Mine ended up lumpen and misshapen but cheerful enough, and I knew the twins couldn't give a hoot. Phina would be distracted by the ribbons and sticky bows and Caspy would fall in love with the first thing he opened and want to focus solely on that.

By eleven o'clock I was bored and riddled with paper cuts, so I decided to chance going downstairs to get a cup of tea and some of those delicious soft German chocolate-covered gingerbread biscuits. I had seen a few packets in the cupboard and hadn't been able to stop thinking about them. I stood at the top of the stairs for a moment but couldn't hear anyone about, so down I scuttled. I entered the kitchen slightly breathlessly and, naturally, there was Lando, sitting at the table with a coffee, eating my biscuits.

'Oh!'

'Sorry, weren't you expecting anyone to be in here?'

'Er, no, not really. I came down for a quick drink – and some of those actually. What *are* they called? I can never remember. Leprechauns or something?'

He laughed.

'Lebkuchen – but I'm not sure how you pronounce it. I've made dreadful inroads into this bag, I'm afraid. Shall we open some more?'

'Why not?'

I switched on the kettle and busied myself, working up enough courage eventually to ask in my most casual tones, 'Zara not around?'

'No, she's not, she's gone off into Dorchester to get her hair done.'

'Oh, right. It looked okay to me.'

'It was fine. She spends a lot of time being groomed, like one of Phina's My Little Ponies.'

I giggled.

'Maybe she'll come back with candy cane stripes in her hair.'

'It might be an improvement, lighten things up a bit. Look, Penny...'

I stirred my tea intently. There was a tone of voice there that set off alarm bells.

'Mmm hmm.'

'I don't know if you *want* me to explain this... well, look, I want to, okay? Zara – I didn't really invite her for Christmas. She invited herself and the way she went about it... I knew it was a pack of lies, but it was hard to say no.'

I couldn't help myself.

'What did she say?'

'Some story about not being able to stay in her flat and not having any friends she wanted to be with. More likely no one will have her; you've seen how demanding and critical she is.

She asked Pilar this morning to make everything gluten-free from now on, as she suspects she might have a slight intolerance.'

'Ouch! I can imagine the response to that.'

'Well, quite. Luckily, Pilar made it in Spanish, so we only got the gist, but her meaning was perfectly clear.'

I giggled, picturing the scene.

'I couldn't bear to miss out on a crumb of Pilar's food. You know she's going to make some special Spanish biscuits later – oh, I can't remember what they're called... she said they meant 'dusty'. Anyway, she said she'd teach me how to make them too.'

'She makes those every year, they're amazing. They're called *polvorones* – once tasted, never forgotten. They're like a sort of very crumbly shortbread. And you're learning to make them?'

I nodded.

'Then you can stay.'

My heart picked up pace, but I talked myself down and answered lightly, 'Not much point if you're gallivanting in Greece with Zara. You'll have to learn to roll your own vine leaves.'

He snorted.

'Zara may think she'd love the rural life in Greece, but she'd be bored within days and nagging me to take back my old City job. Anyway, she's not invited.' Now my poor heart skipped a beat or two. 'The whole point of going is to get away from it all, to concentrate on my wood carving, *not* to set up home.'

My heart, thwarted, thudded into my stomach. How could I have forgotten?

'Yes, of course it is. Like me and India. Look, I'd better get back to the wrapping. Thanks for the leprechauns.'

We smiled at each other, but the easy atmosphere had been deadened, and I trudged upstairs to finish the hated job.

· · ·

I was soon surrounded by a sea of wrapping paper and ribbon, so when my phone rang, it took me a moment or two to locate it. And when I did, the shock of seeing Timothy's name on the screen gave me another cause for hesitation. But curiosity got the better of me, and I tapped the green, juddering icon.

'Hello?'

'Penny?'

'Yes, hi, Timothy.'

'How are you?'

We made small talk for a moment or two. I was dying to know why he had called, but determined not to ask. New, confident me wasn't that bothered. It was odd to hear his voice: unsettling but, conversely, strangely comforting. He was so familiar.

'So, I got your text message.'

Oh goodness, that text! I'd almost forgotten I'd sent it. When he didn't reply, I'd breathed a sigh of relief and sworn myself off drunk dialling forever.

'Er, yes?'

'It was good to hear from you. I did pop round to see you, but Janice next door said you'd gone away for Christmas?'

'Yes, that's right. I got a job looking after twins down in Dorset. It's great.'

'I see. It was rather annoying going all the way over to the house only to find you gone.'

A little flame flared inside me. That was typical Timothy. He'd done something he considered noble, or self-sacrificing, but my not being there – when I had been completely unaware of what was going on – had spoiled it. And that was my fault. Not long ago I would have apologised, but I felt a little burst of pride in myself as the flame rose higher.

'Right, well, maybe you should have called first?'

'But I wanted to surprise you,' he said peevishly.

'Well, I suppose that's the risk you took. When you broke

up with me, I wasn't going to sit at home moping in the hope you might pop round.'

There was a silence, but I didn't care. The urge to apologise had now completely subsided. Eventually he spoke, a more conciliatory tone to his voice.

'Of course not. Anyway, I have something for you. I wonder if I could have the address of where you're staying so that I can send it. It's so close to Christmas now that I'll have to sort out a special courier – it's far too late to post it.'

Again, that tone of irritation at the inconvenience I had caused him.

'There's really no need. Why don't you send it to me at home after Christmas? No need to put yourself out.'

'No, I'd like to. Please, Penny, let me have the address, I think you'll really like it.'

I didn't want his present, but I couldn't think up any reason not to let him send it, so reluctantly I told him the address, and a few minutes later we said goodbye. I pushed him from my mind as I continued tackling the pile of gifts.

After supper that evening, we were all sitting in the living room playing another increasingly silly game of Charades. Even Zara joined in for a while, although her frustration at not being able to guess a film or book from her teammates' ludicrous gestures soon saw her give up and retreat to an armchair to tap away at her phone. The rest of us got noisier and more competitive the more we played, so when Daphne suggested a speed round, we were fully hyped up for it. It was my turn first, so I barely heard the doorbell ring, or registered Xander, who was on the other team, go out to answer it.

'Film!' my teammates shrieked, and I nodded vigorously. 'Er… er… er… romance, it's a romance! The!' I mimed sunbathing, throwing myself to the floor and squinting at the ceiling. 'The Beach!' *No!* I pretended to pack a suitcase and William shouted, 'The Holiday!' A thumbs-up and I was on to my next one – *Octopussy*. I screamed with laughter, signed 'book' and 'film' and was just showing eight fingers and doubling up with giggles wondering how on earth I'd do the rest of the word, when a familiar voice behind me said my name. I spun round and felt as though a large, freezing snowball had hit me in the stomach.

'*Timothy*? What on earth are you doing here?'

The rest of my team was shouting at me to carry on, as time was running out, but I was oblivious to them.

'Surprise!'

Timothy opened his arms.

What was I supposed to do – run into them?

'Aren't you pleased to see me?'

I looked around at all the faces staring at me: confused, amused, concerned, blank. And I wondered how mine appeared to them, because I had no idea how I felt. Timothy was the last person I had thought I wanted to see, but there again was that tug of familiarity, the feeling of not having to try quite so hard anymore. The sort of relief you feel when you pull on an old pair of tracksuit trousers, which is always mingled with a sort of self-disgust that you look horrible and should put in more effort. Eventually I managed to choke out some words.

'I– I'm surprised, that's all. I thought you wanted to send me a present. Why didn't you tell me you were coming?'

'I thought it would be a nice surprise for you.'

'I don't understand. You left me. Why are you here?'

'Because, Penny, when I got your text, I realised that I'd made a terrible mistake.'

There was a collective intake of breath from our audience, and I went cold all over. That *bloody* text; how I wished I'd never sent it. But how could I possibly have known that this would be the result? I glanced round at the Lords, then grabbed Timothy's arm and pulled him out into the hallway.

'I'm sorry, you think you made a mistake?'

'Yes. I've missed you, Penny.'

'You've *missed* me?' I was beginning to feel angry now. 'So you just thought you'd turn up here – at my place of work – and I should what? Drop everything?'

'Well, er, well, I thought you'd be pleased,' he said again feebly. 'You did say in your text that it would be good to see me. Anyway, now I'm here, I want to say that I am going to propose to you, Penny.'

A little gasp was audible from the living room where, I now realised, the riotous evening had gone suspiciously quiet. *Oh, who cares?* I thought. I was getting into my stride.

'Right. And is that now, or at some point in the distant and probably fictional future?'

'Oh, well, I thought you'd be delighted. I haven't actually got a ring with me, so I thought the proper proposal should wait until I do.'

'I see.'

'And I know you want babies, so we can talk about that too. When work slows down. Which I'm sure will happen soon. So, what do you think, Pen old girl, shall we give it another whirl?'

My mind was alternating uncomfortably between going completely blank and having a million thoughts and emotions whizzing around it. Here I was, being offered the words from Timothy I had waited to hear for *ten years*, and all I wanted to do was cry. Or scream. Or punch him. Certainly, burn my mobile phone so that I could never send another tragedy text in my life. Luckily, I was saved from doing any of those things by a swift string of events.

First Lando, bursting into the hallway. 'This is ridiculous. I'm going to go and do some work.' He stormed out.

Then Zara. 'Lando, darling, wait for me, I'll come and help.' With a smirk in my direction, she followed him.

Then, thankfully, Bunny. 'Well, it's frighteningly late and I, for one, am exhausted. Timothy, there's a bedroom you can use tonight, I'll get you some sheets and show you where it is. I'm afraid I need Pixie to finish off some preparations for me, so I'll be keeping her busy for the next hour or so. Pixie, wait for me in my room, please, I won't be long.'

I nodded, silently thanking her for the sudden 'strict boss' act and ran upstairs two at a time to find refuge in her beautiful room before anyone else could ask me any impossible questions.

About fifteen minutes later, Bunny came quietly into the room and shut the door. She handed me a drink and sat down, sipping from her own glass.

'Don't worry, Pixie, mine's fizzy water, but I thought you could do with a giant G&T.'

'Thank you, it is exactly what I needed.'

I took a sip and reeled slightly at the strength. Maybe Bunny thought I should be drinking for two.

'I've installed Timothy in a room nice and far away from you. I think that was what you wanted?'

'Yes, yes, it is, thank you...'

I trailed off miserably.

'It *is* what you wanted, isn't it, Pixie darling? I can tell you where he is?'

'Oh, Bunny, I don't know *what* I want, it's all so confusing. I had written Timothy off, started to move on, resolved to change my life and not let anyone waste another second of it. Then I stupidly sent him a text message when I was feeling low, saying it would be good to see him.'

'Oh yikes. And he took you seriously. So how are you feeling now?'

'Well... This is all very recent and raw. It's not as if I *can't* go back to Timothy, and he's suddenly offering me everything I have wanted for the past ten years. If I accept his proposal, then those years won't have been wasted, after all.'

Bunny nodded.

'Tempting. I can see that.'

Why wasn't she disagreeing with me? Oh God, did she think I *should* go back to Timothy? The thought that she might encourage it was bizarrely disconcerting, given what I had just said.

'What do *you* think I should do?'

'I don't want to tell you, Pixie darling, I don't know enough about it all. But I don't think that marrying Timothy is the only way to reframe all of this. If you don't, then are you sure the last ten years were wasted? Can you think of them differently?'

I paused and drank my gin. *Could I?*

'Maybe. I thought I had managed that, deciding that I would stop hankering after a husband and kids and rush off to India, but... well, exciting though that all sounds, all that has really crystalised in my mind is that I *do* still want to settle down with a family. I believe that's my kind of adventure. But it looks like that ship has sailed.'

'Nonsense,' said Bunny briskly. 'It's definitely not too late for you. And...'

I glanced at her, and she smiled.

'I don't want to pry, but I had rather thought that you and Lando seem to be getting on rather well?'

I felt my face flush and pressed the cool glass to my hot cheek. I was sick of pretending, and certainly didn't want to lie to Bunny.

'We are. We were. But he seems so set on going to Greece and sequestering himself away, and then Zara turned up...'

'Pah! Don't pay any attention to her, horrid woman.'

'She said that she and Lando were getting back together.'

'They won't do any such thing. For all his grumpiness, Lando, as I am sure you are well aware, having seen him fuss over those dogs, not to mention my children, has the softest heart of anyone. Zara turned up with some sob story, and he can't bring himself to turn her away at Christmas. But there's no way he's going to take up with her again. Besides, have you seen the way he looks at you? He adores you.'

I felt a wonderful surge of excitement course through my body, mingling pleasantly with the gin. I stared shyly into my glass.

'Do you really think so?'

'Yes, I do. And I'm glad to see that he has finally found some sense, although why he hasn't declared himself to you, I don't know.'

'I think he's tried.'

'Oh good, good, good! Then you can gently steer him to try again. Oh Pixie, hoorah, this has cheered me up no end.'

'I'm not sure it's that simple.'

'But why not?

'I do feel so drawn to him, but... I'm not sure he really knows what he wants. Greece, solitude, me, Zara... He says he doesn't want a family, that he doesn't think he would cope. How can I risk my heart again on another man who doesn't deliver?'

'Pixie, he would, I know he would. Lando may say all those silly things about being some secluded artist, but look at him with my two, he's a natural. He's had his fingers burnt, rather like you have, my darling. Zara leaving him when he was at his lowest ebb – that was hard to take.'

'And you don't think he'll take the chance to repair it?'

'Not with her. But he does need someone he can rely on.'

'But that's just it!' I exploded. 'I can't spend my life being leant on, unless I'm sure I can lean in return.' Thoughts were whirling round my head. 'I can't possibly go to India, it's a bloody ridiculous idea and I've known that all along. I'm not sure I can risk Lando, wonderful though he is. Maybe the chance I can give myself to be happy *is* Timothy. But why don't I *feel* happier about it, when it's everything I've always wanted?'

A single tear trickled down my cheek and I brushed it away impatiently.

'Pixie, my darling, you *know* all these answers. Following your heart will be brave, and terrifying, but it's all you can do. Follow it where it leads you, otherwise you'll spend the rest of your life in what ifs.'

'But what if it all goes wrong?'

'Then it all goes wrong, but at least you know you tried. But if it's truly for you, it will work out, even if it doesn't look like you imagined it would. Your safety, Pixie, will come from being in the right place for you, and that doesn't necessarily mean the place that has a big flashing sign saying, 'This Is Safety'.'

I nodded, finished my drink, went back to my room, praying that I wouldn't bump into anyone in the corridor. The only thing I needed now was time and space to think, and to hope I could make the right decision.

NINETEEN

I had arranged to take the twins over to Lavinia's house the next morning for a playdate with Toby and nearly managed to get them breakfasted and out of the house without seeing anyone other than Pilar and, fleetingly, William.

'I don't blame you for escaping,' he whispered conspiratorially, grabbing his hat. 'Daphne and I are spending the day in Dorchester, can't take any more of Zara. She always looks at me as if she's wondering how long it is until I die and get out from under her feet.'

I giggled. It did feel good to know that he liked her as little as I did.

'What will that young man who turned up yesterday spend his morning doing?'

'Timothy? I have no idea, but I didn't invite him, so I don't see why I should entertain him. My responsibility is towards the children. I did worry that it might be rather rude to you all to leave him in the house by himself, but Bunny said it was absolutely fine.'

'Quite right, quite right, well said, my dear. Well, enjoy

your day. Ah, here is Daphne, we must go now. Adieu, darling Penny!'

I thought I had avoided seeing Timothy that morning, but as I ushered the children into the car, I heard an ominous crunching on the gravel behind me.

'Pen? Where are you off to? I thought we could talk? I must say your boss was rather dictatorial last night. I hope these people are treating you well.'

I gave him a tight smile.

'Yes, they're very kind but *very* demanding.' I sighed. 'In fact, if I don't get these two off and away quickly, Mrs Lord will probably be out here wondering why not.' I clipped the children securely into their car seats and opened the driver's door. 'I'm sure you understand. Maybe we can talk later?'

'Er, yes, all right then, but...'

Unfortunately for poor Timothy, it was at this point Seraphina's patience wore out and, using her very loudest voice, she started intoning: 'We want to go! We want to go!'

Of course, Caspian immediately joined in. The effect of these rather penetrating chants, in which I have found small children specialise, is electrifyingly aggravating even for a seasoned professional like me.

'Sorry!' I shouted over the din. 'Better go!'

Timothy nodded, defeated, and hurried towards the house, while I leapt into the car.

'Ice cream for you both tonight,' I said, to cheers, and we pulled away.

We spent a very relaxing morning with Lavinia. Her stresses over the flood were over and a smart new carpet had been installed and lavish Christmas decorations put up. Toby had acres of toys and games, not to mention the run of the wonderful old house and gardens, so he and the twins were blissfully occupied while we sat down for a coffee and some dangerously moreish stollen bites. I filled Lavinia in on Timothy's reappearance last night.

'Gosh, it does sound rather romantic. A grand gesture. Nothing like that has ever happened to me. Giles and I sort of knew for years we'd end up getting married and one day he mumbled, "What about it, old girl? Time to make things official", and that was that. Mind you,' she added, taking another stollen bite, 'I've never felt any the less loved because of it. Giles has always been there for me, always, very stolid. It may not be the stuff that romantic heroes are made of, but it's meant the world to me.'

Her words gave me pause for thought. Timothy's appearance, though on the one hand unsettling, had rather impressed me. I wasn't silly enough to believe that his deep passion for me had driven him to it, and there was still no actual ring, or date, but the fact he had missed me, come all that way to find me... Surely that counted for something?

We went back to the house for lunch, an event I was not greatly looking forward to. I tried my old trick of sitting between the children and busying myself with them, but Zara was not to be put off.

'So, Penny,' she asked in ringing tones. 'Have you come up with an answer yet to Timothy's proposal? Christmas romance, *so* exciting.'

I looked up into her beautiful face; her cold fish eyes stared back at me.

'Not yet. But I'll make sure that you're the first to know.'

'I think we all know what the answer will be, though, don't we, Pen?' said Timothy smugly, helping himself to far too many potatoes. 'I'm being made to wait, but I accept my punishment.'

I didn't reply but risked a glance at Lando as I tried to force some quiche down my poor, constricted throat. He was, very unusually for him, staring intently at his phone and taking no part in the proceedings around him at all.

'I simple *adore* weddings,' continued Zara, pushing aside her half-full plate and taking a sip of sparkling water. 'I'm sure you'll make a charming bride, Penny, and you a most handsome groom, Timothy.'

He simpered. He definitely simpered. She continued, 'What sort of look will you go for? Maybe a sort of shepherdess vibe would suit you, it's been in some of the magazines.'

I burst out laughing at the thought of myself trotting down the aisle towards Timothy, clad in some lacy, frothy affair with a large bonnet, maybe with a crook and a couple of desultory sheep wandering behind. Perhaps one of them could be the ring bearer? But now I had started laughing, I found I couldn't stop, and the giggles overtook me in a way that verged on hysteria. Tears started trickling down my face and I couldn't get a grip on myself. I was aware of everyone looking on, but every time I tried to stop, I was taken over by another, increasingly uncomfortable, wave of laughter. I saw Lando get up and, as I wiped my eyes with a sodden tissue, felt his strong, gentle hands on my shoulders, turning me to face him.

'Look at me, into my eyes. Can you try and take a breath, Penny? Try breathing in for four, holding it, out for four, holding it. I'll breathe with you.'

He squeezed my shoulders gently in time with his instructions and my breath slowly became less ragged and the gasps smoothed. I felt an overwhelming urge to lean against him and close my eyes.

'Feeling better?'

I nodded, embarrassed.

'Yes, thank you. I'm sorry, I don't know what came over me. It was the thought of the shepherdess...'

Suddenly, it didn't seem at all funny. Lando returned to his chair as Xander spoke up.

'Quite the magic act there, Lando, I didn't know you had healing powers.'

'I don't. It's a technique I was taught to control panic attacks when I was ill.'

He picked up his phone again and the lunch limped along. I think everyone was grateful when pudding was finished and Bunny suggested we disperse for coffee.

'I, for one, would like to go and speak to Pilar about the party tonight. Pixie, I need your help so Xander, would you take the children? Timothy, you won't mind entertaining yourself for a while, will you?'

Her rapid questions did not invite answers and the two men nodded meekly as Bunny gently took my arm and steered me towards the kitchen. Daphne, offering to help with arrangements, came too. I was glad to have my mind taken off things by planning the party and soon we were all involved in different tasks. Bunny went to rally people to move furniture and get mismatched chairs from all corners of the house so that guests could sit if they wanted, Daphne organised glasses and napkins and Pilar soon had me totally focused on the repetitive but completely absorbing task of piping teeny little flourishes of differently flavoured cream cheese onto minuscule crackers. They looked rather like savoury iced gems when they were finished.

'How many have I got to do?' I asked, looking in dismay at the twenty I had already completed that barely filled a single plate, and then at the tin filled with a million naked little crackers.

'*Muchos*,' she replied sternly. 'Mrs Lord says you must be kept busy – and your guests, they must be fed. Do not stop, Penélope.'

I wouldn't have dared, and anyway, I was quite enjoying the

work, piping away intently as people buzzed around but didn't disturb me. When I did eventually finish, and stood back to admire my work, I was instantly given a new job of brushing egg onto puff pastry shapes before each tray was whisked away by the indomitable Pilar to go in the oven. So it was only when Daphne came in, calling my name, that I realised how late it had got.

'There you are, Penny! Come on, it's time to go and get ready. I thought it would be fun for us to get dressed together. I've brought my suitcase of glam, and look! William thought that some delicious champagne was in order.'

She brandished a bottle and two glasses.

'Oh gosh, I wasn't really expecting to go to the party, I didn't realise I was invited. What about the twins?'

'Of course you're invited. The children will be around for the first bit and then we can pop them into bed and come down again. Now, chop chop! Let's go and start zhuzhing.'

Pilar waved me away, so I followed Daphne to my room.

'Did Bunny put you up to this? She is being incredibly kind, babysitting me out of Timothy's way all the time.'

'Well, she did mention that it might be helpful for you to have some thinking space away from him, and I agree. I wouldn't presume to start giving you advice, Penny my dear, but it never does any harm to take time to consider things.'

'I would love your advice, Daphne, truly I would.'

'Good, because I really *do* enjoy imparting it – when asked, of course. But first, let's see what you are thinking of wearing.'

The problem was, I hadn't packed for a cocktail party, more for tramping through snowy woods with small children.

'I have the outfit I was going to wear for Christmas Day, but I don't know how suitable it is – and I'll have to wear it twice then. Um, what about jeans and this jumper? It's sort of sparkly.'

I held up some limp, oft-washed clothes and saw Daphne

try masterfully not to shudder. She fiddled with the champagne foil, eased out the cork and poured two glasses.

'Hmm. They are what I would call maybe 'smart-casual' – very pretty, but I think we need something with a bit more pizzazz for this evening. I have something here that I think would suit you perfectly, if you'd like to try it on?'

I nodded casually, but was secretly dying to have even a pinch of Daphne's stardust sprinkled over me, and watched with excitement as she pulled out a mid-length black tulle skirt, scattered with tiny sparkling chips of diamanté, followed by a deep pink velvet top with a ruched neckline and cap sleeves.

'Oh, Daphne, they're so beautiful. Are you sure I can borrow them?'

'My dear, I picked them specially for you from my collection, so I would be sorry if you didn't. Here, try them on.'

Wondrously, they fitted beautifully, and I twirled in front of the mirror, enchanted at my transformation. I had some decent black shoes with a heel, and I slipped those on too.

'There, you look lovely. Now, would you trust me with your hair and makeup?'

'Yes, please! I feel like Cinderella.'

I sat obediently while Daphne opened pot after jar after palette of cosmetics and started her delicate work. She chatted as she painted, and I found myself opening up to her again.

'I feel torn. I was with Timothy for such a long time, and I wanted to marry him. I can't pretend that I have no feelings towards him at all.'

'But?'

'But when I got over the shock of him leaving me, none of it was as bad as I thought it would be. I didn't feel devastated, just empty and silly – duped.'

Daphne tapped a brush gently on the side of a little pot, sending a glistening puff of powder into the air.

'So why are you tempted to accept his proposal now?

Because you wanted it for so long that you think it must still be what you want?'

'I suppose that's it. And I do feel that I can reclaim the past years, that they won't be thrown away, wasted.'

'Is there perhaps a tiny bit of pride coming into it as well?'

I paused. Was there?

'Yes. Maybe. I suppose it does make me feel less of a – well, less of a fool.'

'Oh, Penny darling, you're anything but a fool. You're open-hearted, hopeful. There's nothing wrong with that and it's far better than cynicism or hardness.'

'But what do I *do*? It feels like whatever way I turn it's a risk.'

Daphne laughed.

'Well, of course it is. That's life! You have to decide which risk is most worth taking.'

I sighed.

'Can't *you* tell me what to do?'

'Sadly, I can't. Only you know that. And you *do* know. Don't rush it, Penny, no decisions have to be made right now. Why don't you try to enjoy the evening and see what unfolds? You'd be surprised how many answers reveal themselves when they're left alone. As a young woman I pushed and pushed for resolution, I couldn't bear the suspense of loose ends, but it never helped. I eventually learnt to let life work itself out a bit more, to step back, and that has served me well. Try not to worry so much, Penny, try not to be so fixed on what you think life *should* be – or how you think *you* should be. Try letting life come to you, being open to possibility but true to yourself. I have great faith that things will work out beautifully for you, so you try to have that faith too. Now, let's take these rollers out, we're nearly done.'

I let her words sink in as her fingers moved deftly in my hair. She was wise and had seen very clearly what I tended to do: set my sights on one option, decide it was the only path and then find myself bitterly disappointed when it didn't work out. I squared my shoulders and took a breath. Tonight, I resolved, I would think no more about Timothy, Lando or India. I would enjoy the party. And when Daphne finally allowed me to see my reflection in the mirror, I felt a further surge of confidence and optimism.

'Daphne! Wow! You're my fairy godmother. I had no idea...' I reached out a hand to touch the reflected me in wonder. 'No idea that I could look so...'

'So beautiful?'

'I– I don't know.'

I didn't want to call myself beautiful, but it was true that Daphne had worked wonders and my usually rather scruffy and utilitarian self now looked soft, elegant and even a tiny bit sexy.

'Well, I think you are beautiful. Now go knock 'em dead, my dear.'

And that seemed like good advice to take.

TWENTY

I went downstairs and was glad that the first guests hadn't yet arrived. I found Bunny in the living room with the children, she putting some final touches to the winter greenery arrangements, they deeply involved in inspecting and ordering a pack of cards that depicted different breeds of dog.

'Let's put the dachshund in this pile. It is definitely one of our favourites.'

'It is our absolute favourite, so it ought to be at the very top. What about the Dalmatian?'

I went over to Bunny.

'Oh, Pixie! You look breathtaking. Oh, how wonderful! I hope this isn't... I mean, is this all for Timothy's benefit?'

'No. It's for my benefit!' I laughed. 'Daphne has given me a pep talk, so tonight I'm not worrying about anything other than having a good time. How are you feeling?'

'Well, darling, better in myself since that dreadful fatigue has passed, but I can't pretend to be *full* of Christmas cheer.' Her eyes filled with tears, and I hugged her. She continued in a low voice, glancing over at the twins to make sure they weren't listening, but by now they were involved in a very earnest discussion over which pile to put the Jack Russell in and were deaf to anything else. 'What will I do if Ben leaves and I'm left with *two sets of twins*? I won't possibly be able to cope.'

'Bunny, if that were to happen – and I'm sure it won't – but if it *were* to happen, I promise you will cope. You will find a way, and there will be so many people to help you – me amongst them, if you'd let me.'

I hadn't realised I was going to say that until the words were out of my mouth, but as soon as I uttered them, I knew they were true. I had grown to love Bunny and the children, even in the short time I had known them, and they had been such a support to me. Should the worst happen and Ben left Bunny, there was no way I would also leave them in the lurch.

'Oh Pixie, if you would – would you really?'

I nodded hard, swallowing down emotion.

'Of course, I'm here for all of you.'

'Thank you, thank you, that makes this terrible idea all much more bearable.'

We shared a warm hug and then the doorbell rang.

'Here we go, Pixie, best game faces on. Let's try and enjoy ourselves tonight.'

After those first arrivals, people came thick and fast, Lavinia and Giles among the first, along with Toby, who was chirruping with excitement and wheeling a colourful little suitcase, as he was to have a sleepover with Phina and Caspy. There must have been forty people there by the time Zara made her appearance, looking extremely gratified when the hubbub of chatter lulled as everyone took her in. She had straightened her hair so that it hung in a smooth, glossy sheet down her back, showing off her exquisite bone structure. She wore a very short, very tight gold sequinned dress which came up high on her neck but was sleeveless, demonstrating how toned and tanned her arms were.

Both wrists were stacked with several inches of thin gold bangles and her shoes, also gold, had four-inch heels. I looked down sadly at my own outfit, thinking how pretty I had felt but knowing there was no competition with this goddess. Then I felt my glass go heavy in my hand as more champagne was splashed into it.

'I may not be a fan of these parties, but I can't have empty glasses in my house.'

'Oh, hello, Lando. Thank you. I was just, er...'

'Looks amazing, doesn't she?'

I hung my head.

'Yes. Stunning.'

'Shame she's as hard through and through as the gold she seems to like so much.' I looked up at him in surprise. He was looking at me intently, unsmiling. 'I prefer something softer. You look good in velvet.'

'Th-thank you. I, er, Daphne helped me.'

'Good. I like Daphne. I'll like her as a stepmother.'

'Oh! Are she and William getting married?'

'Not that they've told me, but I think it's inevitable, don't you?'

'That would be lovely. Do you mind?'

'No. I miss my mother, of course, every day, but I'm glad that Dad has found happiness with someone so nice. God, how long has this party been going on? Is it five or six hours?'

I laughed.

'About twenty minutes. Don't you know all these people? Didn't you invite them?'

'No, I did not. Bunny comes down a few times a year and seems to manage to be bosom buddies with everyone within a five-mile radius. It's her party really, not mine. Oh look, isn't that your friend over there?'

I glanced across the room to see Timothy desperately trying to engage Zara in conversation. She was bestowing the occasional smile on him, but mostly scanning the room, presumably in the hope of finding someone more interesting to dazzle.

'Yes, that's Timothy.'

'Are you going to accept his proposal?'

I looked straight into Lando's eyes and felt a lurch of adrenaline.

'Do *you* think I should?'

He opened his mouth to reply but was interrupted by both twins suddenly barrelling past him, shrieking at the tops of their voices: 'Daddy!'

We turned to see Ben standing in the doorway, looking tired but much happier than he had the last time I had met him. He swept them both up in his arms and hugged them to him, then, as they slithered down and ran back to their card game, cast his eyes around until he saw Bunny, who was standing awkwardly by a table, putting her orange juice down then picking it up again. He strode over to her, took the glass away and gathered her into his embrace, burying his face in her neck. They stood there for a moment, seemingly oblivious to the people all around them who were watching with great interest. All except Zara, who was still yakking away to Timothy, who hung on her every word. Eventually Bunny extracted herself and looked around.

'Sorry, everyone, as you were,' she said, slightly shakily, then took Ben's hand and led him from the room.

'Gosh, I wonder what that was all about?' said Lavinia, who had appeared at my side.

'I don't know, but hopefully it means a happy Christmas for all of them,' I said, looking after Lando as he was buttonholed by one of his neighbours, and realising he wasn't going to be able to answer my question any time soon. 'Come on, let's go and get something to eat.'

We wandered over and started filling our plates with the delicious offerings. I was just pointing out my piping to

Lavinia, when a warm hand landed on my shoulder. Full of hope, I turned with a smile on my face, only to see Timothy standing there. I wanted to cry; proof enough, if I needed any more, that I should definitely *not* be marrying him, no matter how many gallons of water had flowed under that particular bridge.

'Pen.' Oh dear, I knew that pettish tone. I was definitely going to be told off. 'I think you've been avoiding me, and that makes me very sad.'

'I'm sorry, Timothy, I haven't really, but I don't think this party is really the right time to talk. Anyway, you've seemed to be keener to chat to Zara than me.' I wished the words away the moment they had come out of my mouth. Timothy smiled.

'She is very charming, and I only wanted to get to know the family you're staying with. As it seems she's about to get back together with Lando Lord, I rather thought that included her. I *am* sorry if it made you feel jealous, there's really no need, old thing. After all, you're the one I came all this way for.'

I felt an unusual rage rising in my chest, and was formulating a reply when Lavinia, who Timothy had rudely had his back to throughout this interchange, tapped him on the shoulder. He turned his head and looked up at her.

'Yes?'

'I'm *frightfully* sorry, but I've accidentally smeared something – well, actually, it's fish paste – all over the back of that *lovely* sweater. I'm sure it'll come out all right – man-made fabrics are *so* much easier to clean than wool, aren't they? But I'd probably go and change – or give it a rinse at least – before you start to pong.'

I shrugged helplessly, fighting back hysterics, as Timothy gesticulated frantically at me, his face suffused with magenta, then rushed wordlessly away.

'Oh, Lavinia! Thank you. How did you think of that? And you sounded so genuinely sorry.'

'Well, of course.' She smiled beatifically. 'Finishing school isn't just balancing books on your head, you know.'

'I don't know, but I'm very grateful. Come on, let's go and eat this before anyone else can interrupt us.'

The party wore on and, for the most part, I enjoyed it. There were plenty of interesting people to chat to, and I managed to avoid any further encounters with Timothy, who – now that he had changed out of the fishy sweater – was being challenged for Zara's attention – successfully by the looks of things – by Xander, who was looking extremely smooth and handsome in a tuxedo. I didn't get a chance to speak to Bunny again until Ben took the children up to bed and she came over and hustled me into a corner, her eyes shining.

'Oh, Pixie, I'm so happy, everything is going to be all right. Poor darling Ben, he wasn't planning to leave me for a *second*. How could I ever have thought he would? He was just dreadfully worried about a thing at work – it seemed for a moment as if we would all have to live in a garden shed or something. But it came good, it's all worked out. Oh, *Pixie*! It's all right, I'm so happy.'

'And I'm so very happy for you.'

'Thank you a million times over for all your love and support. You *will* stay in our lives, won't you?'

'Of course I will.'

We hugged and then she pulled back and looked at me seriously.

'Oh, Pixie, *please* don't go rushing off to India. I know I'm being frightfully selfish, but I don't want to lose you from our lives. And Lando...'

'Lando?'

'Darling, Lando adores you, I know he does. I've seen the way he looks at you. He's just scared. He doesn't want to be pushy, and he doesn't want to make himself vulnerable. But you're so ridiculously perfect for each other. Please don't let it slip away.'

'What about Zara?'

'Oh, her. She'll be out on her ear the minute the mince pies are finished, you mark my words. And by the looks of things, she may well be leaving with my brother.'

We glanced over to where Zara and Xander were now standing together, Timothy having drifted off. They seemed very intimate.

'He can certainly give her a run for her money,' said Bunny. 'I'm not sure either knows what they'd be getting themselves into, but at least it gets them out of our hair.'

'Won't Lando mind? It's a bit close to home.'

'This is what I've been *saying*, Pixie. He'll be bloody relieved. Please say you'll speak to him.'

I felt a little dizzy from the champagne, and Bunny's conviction was also intoxicating.

'I promise you I will think about it, no more than that.'

'Then I suppose that will have to do, but I'm keeping everything crossed. Now if you are going to be all right, I think I'll go upstairs. Ben should have the children tucked up now, ready for kissing, and I'm ready for some kissing myself.'

She floated away and I felt so glad for her as well as feeling a flicker of hope for myself.

TWENTY-ONE

The party was reaching its end now and most people had left. I collected up some glasses and took them through to the kitchen, then went to check the dining room. Although people weren't really meant to be in there, it was inevitable that some would have gone in, and would probably have left drinks behind. The lights were on low, and a figure was sitting at the end of the table, lifting a bottle to pour himself another glass of red wine.

'Timothy?'

'Penny. I knew you'd find me, knew it. Knew that you would be drawn to me. Well done, old girl, come and sit down and have a drink.'

He pulled out the chair next to him and patted it clumsily. I sighed. All I wanted to do now was go and find Lando, who had sloped off about an hour ago, but I had managed to avoid Timothy all afternoon, and I supposed that I should give him an answer to his proposal. I sat down but declined the bottle he waved in my direction.

'D'you prefer a glass? Here, have mine, I don't mind the bottle. I haven't been affected by living in this house, got all la-di-da like you have.'

'No, thank you, I don't want another drink. And I haven't got 'la-di-da' as you put it, not at all.'

'Well, you've certainly changed.' He sounded petulant.

'I haven't really,' I replied mildly. 'Not in the few days I've been here. I think that the big change for me came when you ended our relationship. Remember that? You very suddenly ended a ten-year relationship that I, quite reasonably, believed to have a future. It was that incident that caused me to rethink everything about my life, not staying here for a few days.'

I could hear the anger in my voice and fought the urge to tamp it down, to apologise for my feelings, to smooth things over. No. Not this time. I had every right to be upset. Timothy obviously didn't think so.

'If you say so. But anyway, that's all behind us now. If *you* remember, I proposed yesterday. I thought that was what you wanted, having sent me a text message.'

I reddened.

'Look, I'm sorry about that. The text was a mistake.'

'I see. A mistake. And now that I *am* here, *and* have proposed' – *Dear God, how many times was he going to remind me?* – 'you haven't even done me the courtesy of giving me an answer.'

Now I felt not only anger, but rage rising inside me. Was I supposed to be *grateful*? I looked at him and took a long, deep breath before replying.

'Is that what that was? A proposal?'

'Of course. I asked you to marry me, didn't I? Or did you expect a hot air balloon?'

'No, I didn't, but I do think a proposal should show slightly more preparation – and maybe a ring?'

'I thought you'd like to choose it yourself.'

'No, I wouldn't. I wouldn't want to take that job on as well as everything else.' As I said the words, a little lightbulb pinged on in my head. 'That's it, isn't it?'

'What?'

'It's all a question of responsibility. You have never wanted to take responsibility for anything. That's why our relationship never moved forward. I was waiting for you to do or say something, not wanting to be pushy, but you were never going to. I'm actually amazed that you got yourself together to dump me. How on earth did you find the energy?'

Now Timothy looked absolutely stunned.

'Well... it was a mistake, wasn't it? That's what I've come here to say.'

But my dander was up now, and I warmed to my theme.

'No, there's something else, I know there is. A better offer. You thought you could move seamlessly from me to someone else, or somewhere else, where you could sink back into your customary torpor, only perhaps with a bit less expectation of some action on your part. What was it, Timothy? A job offer? Another woman? And why did it fall through, sending you scuttling back to me?'

He tried to glare at me, but his eyes kept shifting away. I had known him for long enough to know that I was right. I also knew that there was absolutely no way he would tell me; I would probably never find out the truth. I continued, 'Oh, forget it. I don't need to know.'

'Fine. Although I can't believe that you are accusing me of infidelity.' He looked as wounded as he possibly could. I didn't bother replying. 'So?' he said.

'So? So what?'

'So, are you going to give me an answer to my proposal?'

I let out a shout of laughter.

'Timothy! Are you serious?'

'I am. I would appreciate the civility of a reply.'

I nodded.

'I see. You need to hear it. Well, Timothy, after careful consideration of your beautiful and deeply sincere proposal of marriage, which made me feel so special, so loved, so wanted... the answer is no. I thought the ten years we spent together were wasted, but now I see that they have been incredibly valuable, because they have shown me, in glorious technicolour, exactly what I *don't* want. So, thank you and goodnight.'

I stood up to go, but Timothy grabbed at my arm.

'But – what am *I* supposed to do?'

'I'm so sorry, but that's no longer my problem. I would suggest that you pack and leave as soon as possible. It's rather embarrassing to be an uninvited guest in any house, particularly over Christmas.'

'You've become very hard, Penny. What do you think *you're* going to do, anyway, stay as the Lords' skivvy? Go back to your teaching and your little suburban house? While away the rest of your life as a spinster in the service of others?'

Such spiteful words would once have been agonising to hear, but I felt as though I had a newly formed shield around me. What was it made from? Self-respect, perhaps. But his words bounced off it.

'Any of that would be preferable to spending another second of my life in *your* service. You're not my only viable option, you know. Maybe I will stay with Bunny and help her with the children. Maybe I'll go to India, or Peru or – or Cheam! But whatever I do, I'll do it because it's what *I* want, not because I'm running away or trying to prove anything to anyone. And certainly not because I'm so scared of getting it wrong. You know, Timothy, for a while I hated myself for being such a *sensible* person, but it has great advantages. The greatest, perhaps, being that whatever happens I know I can cope. And you've helped show me that, so *thank you*. I thought the worst thing that could possibly happen was you leaving me, and then you did. And guess what? Everything is working out beautifully.'

He spluttered away but didn't manage to articulate

anything, so I continued, 'I'm going to bed now, and I suggest you do the same. There will be trains in the morning; I'm sure Xander will give you a lift.'

And with that, exit Penny, stage left.

To my relief, none of the party stragglers stopped me to chat as I left the dining room and went upstairs to my room, still strewn with wrapping paper and ribbon. I started collecting it up, feeling surprisingly energetic, then took off Daphne's beautiful clothes, hung them carefully, and jumped into the shower. Even ready for bed, I felt restless and couldn't distract myself with the internet or my book. The surge of confidence I had felt when I was speaking to Timothy had ebbed away, and although I couldn't get Lando out of my head, some of the same old insecurities were still poking away at me. So eventually I decided there was only one thing for it: ring Mum. Goodness knows I had been given enough good counselling over the past few days, but I felt like I wanted to run the new Penny by her, to have her blessing over my next move – even if I wasn't sure yet myself what that was. I picked up my phone and dialled, listening to the long, chirruping tone and hoping she would pick up.

'Hi Mum, it's me, Penny.'

'Penny, are you all right? Why are you ringing at this time?'

Her voice sounded groggy with sleep, and I glanced at the clock – only half past ten here.

'What's the time there?'

'It's three am.'

'I'm so sorry, I never seem to get it right. Shall I call you back?'

Please don't say yes...

'No, it's all right, I'm awake now. Your father, of course, hasn't stirred. Hang on a minute, I'll go into the kitchen.'

Thank goodness. She drove me up the wall at times, but

right now I had never needed to hear her wise and confident words more.

'What can I do for you? You are all right, aren't you, darling? It's not Timothy upsetting you?'

I could hear the disgust in her voice. She had never been a fan of poor Timothy, and since the dumping, she had made no secret of how boring and pedantic she found him. She had even used the word 'icky' at one point, which I thought was going a bit far, but she had insisted.

'No, not him. Although he did turn up here, in Dorset, and propose.'

'He did *what*?'

'Don't worry, I said no.'

'Well, thank God for that. I never fancied him as a son-in-law. Turgid.'

'Yes, all right, thanks Mum. Look, forget Timothy, I have.'

'Good. So, what's up that couldn't wait until a civilised time in the morning to discuss?'

'I can ring back if you like, you can go back to bed?'

I knew this would be a sure way to get her full attention; she can't bear suspense.

'No, no, now I'm here you might as well get it out.'

'Right.' I smiled. 'Well, I'm not really ringing for advice, I just want to talk something through. Timothy is history, but now I have to decide what to do next in my life.'

'I thought you were coming out here?'

I didn't reply.

'Penny, is there another man in the picture?'

'Well, sort of... but I'm not sure it's ever going to work.'

'Who is he?'

'He's the brother-in-law of the woman I'm working for, Bunny. He owns the house we're staying in here.'

'And why is it never going to work? Oh *God*, he's not married, is he, Penny?'

I love my mother, and I value her advice, but I do wish she would let me string two sentences together without chiming in with an assumption or question. Or both. I took a steadying breath.

'No, he's not married.'

'So, what's the problem?'

'It's lots of things, really. After Timothy, after all those wasted, mocked years, I wanted change.'

'Yes, you're coming to India.'

I bit my thumbnail.

'Mmm. Well, I wanted adventure, and I said I wasn't going to fall in love again, that I was done with all that.'

'Oh yes, darling, but nobody ever really believed that, least of all you, surely? You don't have to stick to it just because you announced it in a fit of pique. Is that all that's holding you back?'

'No, it's not only that. It is partly me – I really don't want to risk any more of my time being wasted...'

'Well, *is* he a time waster? What's his name, by the way?'

'Lando.'

'Lando? What sort of name is that?'

'It's short for Orlando. His brother's called Benvolio, their parents loved Shakespeare.'

'Hmm. Anyway, so this Lando – a time waster?'

I sighed.

'I don't know. When I first met him, he was so...' What word to use? My mother didn't have a very good understanding of mental illness, being extremely robust in that department herself. '... out of sorts. He'd had a difficult time at work and a relationship breakup and was planning to go and live abroad, to focus on his craft.'

'And now? By the way, what does 'out of sorts' mean?'

I ignored the second question.

'Now he's doing better, we're getting on brilliantly...'

'But?'

'But his ex has turned up.'

'And?'

'What do you mean, "and"? His *ex* has turned up, Mum.'

'Well, so what? That doesn't tell me – or you – anything. Did he invite her? It doesn't sound like it.'

'No, he didn't, and he doesn't seem particularly pleased to see her.'

'So, forget the ex. What's stopping you?

'Oh, Mum... I don't know if I can face it. I'm so sick of being a doormat, of being laughed at. I've lost all my ability to judge how these things are going, how do I know if I'm being an idiot? What if he's not really interested, seriously, and then he ups sticks to rush off and live in Greece with his lumps of wood or, worse, sets up home here with *her*? How can I know?'

'Lumps of wood?' I didn't reply. 'Sorry, sorry, not the point. Fill me in another time. Darling, what is your intuition telling you?'

My mother sets a lot of store by things like 'intuition' and 'gut feeling', and for her it's easy. She's so sure of herself that when she thinks a thing, she believes it and then acts on it. She's not always right, of course, but that doesn't stop her sallying forth merrily, confident that her feelings must be true. I mistrust mine. I thought Timothy loved me, remember? After that embarrassing debacle how could I ever be brave enough to think such a thing again? And if Timothy didn't love me, after all those years together, how could Lando possibly love me now – a washed-up primary school teacher, her best years, whatever they were, firmly behind her? But another little voice suddenly piped up in my head, a new one, a very welcome one. It reminded me of how good I had felt when I had turned Timothy down, how strongly I had realised that I was in control of my life and confident to take risks. I had earned the right to listen and to trust in this new voice, not to run scared from it.

'Penny, are you still there?'

'Yes, I'm still here. I was thinking about what you said, about my intuition...'

'And?'

I paused. This was new territory for me.

'I think there's a chance with Lando, a good one. I think it's what I want. At least I want to find out. If it doesn't work out, it's not the end of the world. I've got this.'

It was momentous to say the words out loud. Mum obviously felt the same, as I heard a most uncharacteristic sob come down the phone, wrapping me in love across the miles.

'Penny, my darling, darling girl. There it is! There *you* are! My girl. You have *always* had it, *always*, you just had to know it for yourself. Your destiny is *yours*, no one else's. Now, I would say 'go get him', but it doesn't seem quite right. No – go and be you, that's all you have to do. Be Penny, she's amazing.'

By now we were both sobbing, and I wished we could hug each other, but knowing I had her unconditional love and support, with nothing to prove, was worth everything. We spoke for a few moments more, then said goodbye with promises to speak again soon. I switched off my phone, straightened my back and gave a nod. It was time to go and start shaping my future.

TWENTY-TWO

I looked out of my window and, sure enough, the light was burning in Lando's studio. A thought flashed across my mind: what if he was there with Zara? But as quickly as it came, another, stronger voice countered it: so what if he is? If they're locked in a passionate embrace and booking airline tickets for Greece, then at least you'll *know*, and you can ricochet off that particular situation and on to another future. This is exciting stuff! I felt a great sense of urgency, almost panic, and rushed to find some clothes. At first, I stood paralysed in front of the wardrobe, not knowing what the hell to wear. What said, 'Marry me!' but ever so casually, with a thrown in, 'And if you don't, that's cool'? My clothes were definitely letting me down as most of them said nothing more than 'meh'. But I was in no mood to be defeated. Inspiration sparked and I swept through the hangers until I found a shirt I had thrown in last minute, not expecting to wear it. It was something I had bought in a sale and never quite dared to wear out anywhere, but I loved it and somehow knew that one day it would be perfect. The epitome of 'smart-casual', it was made of a flowy, ludicrously flattering fabric, black but shot through with sparkly rose gold thread. I wriggled it over my head and flicked open the top two buttons. There. It was sexy without being desperate and, appropriately, looked as if I had just thrown it on. I pulled on my good jeans and grabbed the nearest pair of clean socks and my trainers, then was out of the door and jogging downstairs before I could change my mind.

I thought that the party was completely over by now, and the household tucked up in bed, but as I passed the living room, still in low light, I saw Zara and Xander in a very passionate clinch on the sofa. My heart lifted and did a merry Christmas jig at the sight of them. Not, I am afraid to say, because I was happy to see they had found each other, but because it meant that Zara was clearly out of the picture as far as Lando was concerned. I zipped past the kitchen, which was in darkness and towards the back door, which I flung open with fervour, then recoiled. God, it was cold. Would my flimsy shirt take me as far as the studio? It would have to. I was in no mood to put on a sensible coat. I ran across the lawn, already crisping up with frost, and arrived at the door in record time. Once there, I paused, only briefly, to take a couple of steadying breaths, feeling that the 'collapsing in a gasping heap' look wasn't exactly what I was going for on this occasion, then pushed the door open.

The scene was perfect. The warm, woody studio was as messy and cosy and welcoming as ever and there was Lando, hunched over his bench, Garbo draped on his shoulders, whittling away intensely. I drank it in. Briefly.

'What the *hell* is that cold draft? Shut the door, can't you?'

'Oh God, sorry.'

I shut the door quickly as Lando turned around.

'Penny! I didn't realise it was you.' He stumbled to his feet, clutching Garbo so she didn't slip off. 'Sorry, I didn't mean to shout.'

I smiled.

'It's okay, I'm kind of getting used to it.'

'Hmm, I'm not sure that's such a good thing. That the grumpiness is something to get used to, I mean, not that you would be getting used to me... Aargh, I'm rambling. Look, would you like a drink?'

'Actually, what I'd really like is a cup of tea, if that's all right. I've had enough champagne for one night.' I stopped to think. 'Now that's something I never thought I'd hear myself say.'

'I'll put the kettle on. A cuppa is exactly what I need too.'

'Can I see what you're making?'

'No! Er, that is, no, it's not ready, sorry. Another time.'

He pulled a cloth over whatever it was he had been working on and disappeared through the door at the back, returning a few minutes later with two steaming mugs.

'Here you go. Do sit down, you know the routine, chuck something on the floor.'

I cleared a small wicker chair of its pile of books and tools, handing him a wicked-looking chisel rather than leaving it on the floor where it might hurt one of the dogs. I eased off my shoes and tucked my feet up.

'Ah, my favourite socks,' said Lando, grinning.

I looked at my feet, which I now realised were clad in the dancing elves again.

'Oh, for goodness' sake. I should give these to the charity shop. They were a present, by the way, from one of the children at school, not a personal choice.'

'Oh, please don't give them away, they're too good. So, what can I do for you?'

I sipped my hot tea and tried to gather my thoughts. Now I was actually sitting here, Lando in front of me, it was difficult to know where to begin. Some of my new-found confidence and determination was backing down in the face of reality.

'Um, well, we had talked a bit about our plans for the future, and I suppose I wanted to say some more about that.'

Way to go to make perfect sense, Penny.

'I see. Or, rather, I don't see. Sorry, go on...'

'Well, I have decided not to go to India. Probably.'

'Right.'

He drummed his fingers on his workbench, but his face was expressionless, and I couldn't tell if he was pleased about my announcement or bored, and keen to get back to his work.

'So, er, I've realised that I do want a change in my life, but that won't involve haring off halfway across the world. I don't think. Not immediately, anyway.'

He stood up abruptly, startling Hepburn who had been lying at his feet, and strode towards the window, where he stared into the dark and frozen garden for a moment. I had obviously annoyed him, but I wasn't quite sure why. I started to make a move to leave, since coming here had obviously been a mistake. But then Lando turned around. When he spoke, his voice was thick, and dull.

'So when will the wedding be?'

My head spun. Wedding? What wedding? Was *he* proposing? It seemed an odd way to go about it, so dour, but then my idea of a proposal had already been somewhat challenged recently. I sat back down in my chair.

'Sorry, I don't think there's going to be a wedding...'

He turned to resume his gaze out of the window.

'Oh. Well, congratulations, anyway. I assume you will both stay on here for Christmas?'

'Both? I'm sorry, Lando, I haven't got the faintest idea what you're talking about.'

He sat down at his workbench again and stared at me intently.

'I thought you said you weren't going to India.'

'Yes, that's right.'

'I assumed that meant that you had accepted Timothy's rather watery proposal and you were off with him to live happily ever after.'

I gasped.

'Oh! No! Gosh, sorry, no, that's not what I meant at all.'

Now I started giggling, the nerves and adrenaline getting the better of me. Lando was marginally less stony, slightly more confused. I managed to pull myself together and continued.

'Sorry, it's so completely the opposite of what I was trying to say. I spoke to Timothy earlier this evening, told him that I wasn't going to accept his proposal – if that's really what it was, because I'm still not convinced it was entirely genuine – and that he should leave in the morning. I'm still rather embarrassed that he gate-crashed at all.'

Lando waved his hand in the air.

'Oh, don't worry about that, I'm used to people coming and going at this time of year. The family seems to think my house is some sort of B&B for waifs and strays. Last year Bunny invited some lunatic she'd met at a bus stop, and we spent the whole of Christmas lunch hiding the sherry and defending our decision not to have a turkey.'

'How funny. Do you think she really expected them to turn up?'

'Oh, who knows with Bunny? Actually, I think she forgot all about it, but when this woman arrived at the door, asking for her new best friend, Bunny threw her arms around her and professed her delight at seeing her. Then she spent the next half an hour trying to get us all to find out this dear friend's name.'

I doubled up in my chair with laughter. I could easily picture the scene, Bunny breezing about without a care in the world as everybody else recoiled in horror from the oddball invitee who had the nerve to complain about the lunch she was given. How could I ever leave this warm, bonkers family? I would miss them all too much.

'So why don't you think Timothy's proposal was serious?' asked Lando. 'From where I was standing, it looked as though coming all this way and then popping the question must be the real thing.'

'Oh, I think he's serious, but about himself, not me. I don't think he missed *me,* I think that whatever he was moving on to, that he thought was going to be vastly superior to being with me, either didn't work out or didn't live up to his expectations and he realised that he'd actually had a rather comfortable time of it with boring Penny. To be honest, that 'proposal' made me feel angrier than I've felt in a long time. And I felt – *shamed,* somehow, at being thrown this scrap and expected to snatch at it gratefully. For all that he was suddenly, apparently, offering me exactly what I wanted, I found that it wasn't so compelling, after all.'

'And what is it that you want?'

I swallowed. It was time.

'Look, Lando, that's what I came here to say. I do want what I have always wanted, that is to say – to be blunt – a family. A husband and children. I'm not going to try and be cool about it anymore, to pretend I can take it or leave it or that I would be one hundred per cent satisfied with my life if those things didn't happen for me. But I also now know that I don't want those things at the expense of other areas of my life. I don't want those things with Timothy, it wouldn't be fair to either of us or, ultimately, make either of us happy.'

He nodded.

'Quite right.'

'I know that I want change, and adventure, but I understand now that those things take many forms and can't be forced by, for example, belting off to India. I think, for me, the adventure takes the form of a risk. Of choosing to try things that I never would have dared to before, preferring to stay home safely in a nice, controlled way and hope for a happy ending.'

Lando leant forward in his chair and looked at me intently.

'So what risk is it you're preparing to take?'

My heart started beating horribly fast and I felt dizzy. Why should this feel so scary? What was the worst thing that could happen? Why was it so awful? Then we both spoke at the same time:

'Because I'm rather hoping—'

'Well, Lando, the thing is—'

'Sorry, go on.'

'No! You go on.'

We both stopped and giggled, and all those frightening feelings ebbed away. I carried on.

'The thing is, Lando, and maybe I'm horribly wrong and about to bring a load of embarrassment and awkwardness down on everything just before Christmas, but the thing *is* that I think we – that is, you and I – that we've been getting on well, and I sort of thought that there might be a possibility that you could have some part in my new adventure. If you get my drift?'

He nodded and looked pleased, I thought. I rattled on before he could say anything.

'I don't want to pressure you, I know I've said everything I've said about Timothy and babies and settling down, and that stuff *is* true. I'm not going to pretend to be cool about it anymore. If – I mean *if* – we were to, maybe, give things a go, I wouldn't want you to feel obliged, I know what you've been through, but I also don't want to risk us passing each other by completely and I *must* be honest. Look, maybe this won't happen, maybe it will happen for a bit, but, well, there are my cards, on the table.'

I petered out, suddenly feeling foolish and wondering if I

had made even a modicum of sense. Lando was looking at me with a serious expression and opened his mouth to reply when the door flung open, letting in an appropriately chilling blast of air. There stood Zara, framed in the doorway like some beautiful, wicked pixie.

TWENTY-THREE

For a moment, we all remained frozen, like a scene from some nineteenth-century melodrama. Zara was the first to move, stepping into the studio and pulling the door shut behind her. She shivered elaborately.

'God, it's cold out there.'

She stared accusingly at us as if we were somehow responsible for controlling nature's thermostat. Lando was the first to recover himself.

'Look, Zara, I don't know why you're here. I thought I made it clear...'

'Oh yes, *darling*, as crystal. I could hardly believe you would make such a stupid mistake as to turn down *me* as well as a life that you know holds everything you always wanted.'

I wondered if I should be taking notes. Vile though this woman was, she certainly had plenty of self-confidence. My stuttering speech was nothing on this – not once had I suggested that Lando would be stupid for turning me down.

'Everything I always wanted,' repeated Lando. 'That's right – want*ed*, but don't want anymore. I have told you repeatedly, Zara, I don't want that life anymore.'

She started to speak, but he continued, 'No. Not the money, the cars, the holidays, the expensive watches – any of it. I have everything I want right here.'

He swept his hand around him, and I desperately tried to work out if the gesture included me or not. By the sneer Zara cast in my direction, I could see she was wondering the same thing. Luckily, she wasn't one to hide her feelings.

'I suppose you include *her* in that?'

'I don't think that's any of your business anymore, do you?' replied Lando quietly.

Zara snorted and I stared at my feet, wishing once again that there weren't elves cavorting around on my socks.

'Anyway,' she continued. 'I only ever came to this godforsaken hole to give you one last opportunity to repair your life, but it is *very* obvious to me that it would never have worked. So I have come here tonight to tell you that I'm leaving, and nothing you can do or say will stop me.'

For a moment, nobody spoke, although I was impressed with myself for suppressing the cheer that wanted to erupt and glancing at Lando's face, which had relaxed considerably, I guessed that he felt much the same. He spoke.

'I wouldn't dream of trying to stop you, but it's very late.' He glanced at his watch. 'Nearly Christmas Eve, in fact. How on earth are you going to get back to London? You'd be lucky to get a taxi to the station, and even then, there won't be any trains.'

'It's all sorted,' she announced triumphantly. 'Poor Timothy, feeling very wounded by *you*' – she glared accusingly in my direction – 'is far too distraught to stay, and darling Xander has managed to rustle us all up a car.'

'Sorry, are all *three* of you leaving?'

'Yes, that's right. And we shall have the most marvellous Christmas as far away from this dump as possible. Goodbye, Lando.'

And with one last withering look in my direction, she

turned and left, her dramatic departure only slightly hindered by having to wait for Hepburn to wake up and move away from the door so she could fling it open and slam it behind her. Lando and I looked at each other and burst out laughing. Once we'd started, we couldn't stop and soon we were clutching our sides as the tears rolled down our faces, gasping out Zara's choicest words, which each time set us off again.

'The most *marvellous* Christmas...!'

'Poor, distraught Timothy!'

'You can't stop me so please don't try!'

Eventually our mirth subsided and the dogs, who had slunk away at the unaccustomed hysterics, bounded back joyfully to join us.

'Sorry, Garbo,' said Lando, picking her up and draping her around his neck. 'I didn't mean to frighten you, but some humans are just extraordinary.'

'I've rarely seen such a performance,' I said, 'other than from a five-year-old, of course. I wanted to give her a round of applause. Quite spectacular.'

'Spectacularly self-absorbed,' said Lando. 'Poor old Xander, finally being sucked in. He used to loathe Zara. I wonder how long that will last.'

'I saw them snogging like mad after the party. Do you really not mind?'

'Not remotely. They'll be good for each other, I expect, although there might be a few arguments over who gets to stand in front of the mirror the longest.'

'Do you think Bunny will mind that her brother has gone off?'

'I shouldn't have thought so, no. She's so besotted now Ben is back that she probably won't even notice.'

'Yes, that's true. Isn't it wonderful? I'm so happy for them.'

'Indeed.'

A silence fell, friendly but thick with atmosphere. It looked like the small talk had dried up and my nerves returned as I remembered where we had left off before Zara came bursting in. Maybe I should cut my losses and go now, pretend I had never said any of it. But then Lando spoke.

'So, where were we? Yes – your cards were on the table. I'd like to add mine.'

TWENTY-FOUR

I nodded, but Lando didn't say anything else. Instead, he lifted the cloth on the workbench in front of him and picked up a small carving, about twenty centimetres tall. He cradled it in his hands for a moment, then handed it to me. I looked down, then gave a sharp intake of breath, for there were Lando and me, exquisitely carved, holding hands, looking at each other and laughing at some unknown joke. By our feet were Garbo and Hepburn, so perfectly done that you could see their doggy personalities immediately. I turned the piece over in my hands, wondering at all the little details: Lando's shoelace undone, my hair messily escaping its bun, Garbo's smooth furry body so appealingly wrinkled that I stroked it gently with my finger.

'You can see that it's not finished,' said Lando, 'but it seemed like the right time to show you.'

'It's so beautiful, a real work of art. But...'

I trailed off, wanting to ask what it meant, why he had carved it, but these were questions I knew the answer to in my heart. I didn't need to hear him explain, this little piece of carved wood said it all. Lando continued, 'Look, you know by now that I do find it difficult to *say* stuff, to express myself with words, but I did want to show you, Penny, how I felt. So I let my fingers do the talking and this is what emerged from the wood. A family. A happy family. I– I hope that's all right?'

I looked up into his dear, worried face and smiled.

'It is wonderful.'

In two strides he was across to my chair and lifting me to my feet, holding me in those strong arms and I was half sobbing, half laughing into his shoulder.

'Penny, I know I can be difficult, bad-tempered, and I truly don't mean to be. Since you've been here – you've made me laugh, I've felt some sort of darkness lift from me, as if there's a new dawn, new possibilities. I got so worried when I thought you were determined to go to India, and when Xander was moving in on you...'

'I don't think he was ever serious,' I interrupted. 'I'm hardly his type.'

'Don't be so sure. But even if that *was* true, it wouldn't have stopped him messing around with you.'

'Look, forget Xander. I was never interested in him.'

'I know, I remember how horrible I felt – and how rude I was – when he was flirting with you. I'm sorry.'

'It's fine. I was quite flattered, if you must know, but then you didn't give me any other reason to think you might be interested.'

'I was so sure you were going off to India, I didn't want to look like a fool when you reminded me of your plans. But there was something else, something that still worries me.'

He fell silent, and I pulled back from his embrace and looked at him in concern. What on earth was left? He continued, 'All the – issues I've had, Penny. The mental health problems. The breakdown was the big feature, and had clear catalysts, things I have removed from my life now, and I think I understand how to protect myself, although I can't guarantee it will never happen again.'

I nodded, not wanting to speak and interrupt him. He went on, 'But it's not as if, now that is over, I am completely fine. I have learnt that, although very strong in some ways, in others my mental health is vulnerable. I have tools to help me, and I'm good at using them, but there are still times when I struggle. I don't want to inflict that on you, Penny, or on anyone. It's the main reason I wanted to go to Greece. Yes, I felt that the solitude would be safe for me, but I also felt that I would stop being a bother to others. My father is moving on in his life, with Daphne, and that's wonderful. I don't want him having to nurse his grown son. I don't want anybody to feel responsible for me, worried about me.'

I gazed up into his troubled eyes and felt tears come to my own.

'Oh, Lando, I'm so sorry you've been through all of this. I'm not an expert on any of it, but there *are* things in life I *do* know. One is that we all suffer illness of one sort or another, throughout our lives, whether mental or physical. And we couldn't possibly stop that. But we also can't assume that other people can't or don't want to live with it. Dear God, nobody's perfect. All I can say is that it doesn't frighten me, that I will try to understand it and support it as best I can, and I won't always do that perfectly. And in the same way, I know that you will do the same for me when I need extra help, which I will, one way or another, because we all do. We're adults, we enter into relationships knowing that this will be part of it and understanding that that only makes the relationship – and life – deeper and more valuable. I know – I *know* – that your troubles don't turn you on other people; the rest of it we can work on.'

He pulled me back into his arms and his voice was muffled as he spoke into my hair.

'Penny. Penny. I never thought, never dreamed, that this might be possible.'

We stood for a while, holding one another, then he pulled away and led me to sit down on my usual chair, pulling his stool over next to me so that he could hold my hand while he spoke.

'I do believe that it can be okay. This Christmas, well, I was dreading it, I always do, and I usually hide myself away as much as possible. The noise, the chaos, the seeming hundreds of people that Bunny troops into the house. But this year I've found it different. Not just bearable, but enjoyable. The children – they're such a joy, and my bonkers father with marvellous Daphne... It's been invigorating and shown me that family life isn't quite as terrifying as I had thought.'

I laughed.

'And for me, it's shown me that I was right all along, that for me the biggest adventure won't be haring off halfway around the world but going after what I really want in life. India was only ever an escape from myself, not what I actually wanted. Oh, and my mother was convinced it was the perfect answer, but that meant that she had given up on me ever finding what I really wanted, whereas I hadn't. I got so muddled between what I wanted and what I *thought* I wanted that for a while I didn't know which way was up. But now I can see that contentment and fulfilment, well, they come in all different shapes and sizes and that pushing yourself towards something only because it looks good on paper isn't going to work.'

'But that's exactly it!' exclaimed Lando, his face lighting up. 'That's what I was doing during all those years in the city – bashing away at trying to enjoy something that simply wasn't right for me. It looked good, it could be great fun, it filled up the bank account – and everyone around me was telling me that I was doing the right thing. But it wasn't right for *me*, and that's what Zara could never understand – still doesn't. Life isn't a 'one size fits all' thing, is it?'

'Absolutely not. Timothy and I staying together all those years was doing us *both* a disservice. We were square pegs in round holes and probably shouldn't have got any further than dating for a month or two. But it all *looked* so good. I've been very upset because of those wasted years, but I can see now that they weren't wasted at all – just a very long and thorough learning experience.'

I pulled a face and Lando laughed.

'You know what I've heard it called? An AFGO.'

'What does that mean?'

'Well, the A is 'another' and the GO stand for 'growth opportunity'. You can fill in the F.'

I thought for a second, then gasped and giggled.

'Oh! I see! That's brilliant. Well, I think you and I have been through enough of those for a while, don't you?'

'I do.'

We fell silent as we contemplated the growth we had both experienced in the past. For a moment, my mind wandered to Timothy as I wondered what he would do next, but I pushed the thought away firmly. He was not my responsibility, not my problem to solve, my damsel in distress who needed rescuing. I had far more pressing things to pay attention to, primarily the intense – I might even say smouldering – look that Lando was now directing at me.

'Penny, all this is very interesting, and we could probably set ourselves up as self-help gurus on the back of it, but there is something much more important to me right now.'

Oh dear, maybe he had forgotten to feed the dogs?

'What is it?'

'Well, we've done an awful lot of talking but absolutely no kissing. What do you think?'

A jolt of electricity shot through my stomach, but I kept my voice casual.

'Oh, yes, I suppose you're right. Well, maybe it's about time that was remedied.'

Lando took my hands and we both stood. Then, infinitely slowly, he slipped one hand up to my neck, pushing his fingers into my hair and, eventually, his lips met mine. As far as adventures go, the next couple of hours rivalled any exotic relocation or city bonus.

TWENTY-FIVE

As we had drifted off to sleep in the early hours of the morning, the snow had started falling, and when I woke up that Christmas Eve morning, I saw immediately through the huge window that the entire garden was carpeted with white. The sun was shining bravely and the resulting light that suffused the studio was bright and clear. Lando was sitting at his workbench, a position that was becoming wonderfully familiar to me, with the Nativity figures all standing in front of him as he worked on one. They glowed in the pale sunlight, and I saw now that he was rubbing some sort of wax into them with a cloth.

'Good morning,' I said, pulling the duvet up a little shyly around my chin. How *did* one segue elegantly from being naked in bed to some sort of morning normality? Lando turned around and beamed at me, washing away my awkwardness.

'Good morning, Penny,' he said, coming over, sitting on the side of the bed and taking my hand. 'How are you?'

I beamed back at him.

'Wonderful, actually. You?'

'Very, very happy.'

For a moment, we grinned giddily at each other, then he

leant forward to kiss me. It was some little while before either of us spoke again, and then it was a very welcome question from Lando.

'Would you like a coffee?'

'Oh yes, please, I'd love one. What time is it?'

'Horribly early, I'm afraid. That's the one problem with sleeping in the studio; these windows don't let you sleep past the very first hint of sunlight.'

I snuggled back under the duvet as he pottered around with cups and a cafetiere.

'What are you doing to the Nativity? I thought it was finished?'

'I'm putting on a final layer of olive wax – it should protect it for a good few years before it needs doing again, as long as no one puts it in the dishwasher or any other such sacrilege.'

I laughed.

'Surely, no one would do that.'

'Don't be so sure. They needed a whole new set because someone took it upon themselves to refresh the paint on the other one, and they all ended up looking like Beano characters.'

My hand flew to my mouth.

'Oh no, how awful.'

'It was awful, I saw them. But I'm glad because it gave me this wonderful commission. Come over and see. Here, you can put this on.'

He threw me a shirt, which I grabbed gratefully and pulled on over my underwear, swiftly located, then I climbed out of bed and went to see his work.

'Oh Lando, it's so beautiful. The church will be thrilled with what you've done. Although that radiant figure of Mary is in direct contrast to its model this morning.' I struck a vampish pose, and we giggled.

'Yes, well, maybe we won't mention that you're a bit more

Magdalene than Virgin, although the church is no stranger to scandal.'

We drank our coffee looking out into the glittering garden, the dogs draped over us. I didn't think I had ever felt so purely content in my entire life. It would have been nice to have stayed like that forever, but my tummy suddenly emitted a loud rumble.

'Ooh, sorry, but I am actually very hungry.'

'I don't have anything here, I'm afraid,' said Lando, 'other than coffee and champagne, so we'll have to go up to the house for something to eat.' He checked his watch. 'People should just about be surfacing now.'

Driven by my suddenly ravenous hunger, I started pulling on my clothes, then, halfway through tugging up an elf sock, stopped.

'Oh dear, it's going to be rather obvious, isn't it, if we both turn up fully dressed? Shall we nip in and put our pyjamas on?'

Lando grinned and ran a hand through his hair, succeeding not a jot in making it any more groomed.

'Well, I'm usually a very private person, but for once I couldn't care less *who* knows.'

I grinned back at him and soon we were in danger of being *very* late for breakfast, if it hadn't been for my traitorous stomach putting in another complaint.

'Come on,' said Lando, 'let's go.'

As we wandered up to the house leaving four sets of footprints – two human and two doggy – in the pristine snow behind us, I felt saturated with bliss. Lando's warm hand in mine, the cold, bright morning air fresh in my face, Garbo and Hepburn cavorting around us. Well, Garbo attempting to cavort, but struggling with her short legs in the snow. Eventually Lando scooped her up and plopped her around his neck.

'There you go, in your happy place,' he said, stroking her silky head as she gave his cheek an appreciative lick. I could relate to that.

As we slipped through the back door, the house seemed quiet, just the odd snippet of conversation drifting from behind the closed living room door. I suddenly felt shy.

'Look, I'm not interested in keeping secrets either,' I said, 'but I do feel a bit funny walking in together like this. I think I will pop upstairs for a moment, if you don't mind?'

'Penny, I don't mind anything. Please do what makes you comfortable. I'll see you in a minute.'

He kissed me and then we went our separate ways. I was glad for a few moments alone to gather my thoughts after the events of the past hours. I pulled on my cosy pyjamas and looked at myself in the mirror, wondering at the subtle yet definite change that showed in my face. I was flushed from the cold, and slightly tousled, but it was my eyes I noticed. Their new sparkle gave away the fact that my mojo, or va va voom, or whatever you want to call it, had definitely returned from exile.

When I wandered into the living room a few moments later, as nonchalantly as I could, I knew that the jig was up. Although no one said anything, the faces that swivelled towards me all wore big smiles, with Lando's the biggest of all. I felt a blush seep across my face, then Bunny came to my rescue.

'Don't worry, darling, no one is going to embarrass you by saying a thing. Other than I'm afraid we spotted the pair of you walking across the lawn looking ever so slightly starry-eyed, and that we are all delighted. Now, come in and have some breakfast.'

I sat down gratefully and let the rituals of cups and spoons and bowls and milk return the atmosphere to something a little closer to normality, helped on its way by the twins. They were, of course, completely oblivious to Lando and me, but thrilled by the return of their father and dying to tell me all about it.

'Daddy says it's going to be the happiest Christmas ever and that we are *definitely* on the nice list, so we had better watch out for lots of presents.'

'But Daddy is on the naughty list because he keeps kissing Mummy *all the time* and that is a bit yucky.'

'Yes, *and* he said that our best present this year is going to be two babies, but not yet. And we don't think that's much of a present at all, do we, Caspy?'

'Not really, because I wanted a penknife, not babies.'

I nearly choked on my tea; I was laughing so hard.

'But don't you think baby brothers or sisters – or one of each – will be fun?'

Four brown eyes regarded me seriously.

'Only if they don't cry,' ventured Cas.

'Babies *always* cry,' said Phina scornfully. 'They will be fun when they are four like us.'

And that seemed to be the final word on the subject.

'Would you two like to take a walk with Penny and me this morning?' asked Lando. 'We're going to take the Nativity over to the church and we could do with some help – if that's okay with you two?' This last question was directed to Bunny and Ben, who nodded slightly *too* enthusiastically. Phina piped up.

'Yes, *please*, Uncle Lando. We haven't been in the snow yet and we want to build a snowman and have a snowball fight and make snow angels.'

'Well then,' I said, 'if we're going to fit all of that in, we'd better get moving.'

Half an hour later, the four of us were standing in the studio looking at the figures.

'There are an awful lot of them,' I said. 'Do you think we can carry them all?'

'How many are there, Uncle Lando? About a hundred?'

'Not that many! Shall we count them together?'

With all the various people and animals, the final tally was eighteen, and although they weren't huge, the wood was heavy.

'Hmm,' said Lando, 'what to do? Well, I suppose I do have *one* idea... but it means you two having an early Christmas present. Do you think you could bear it?'

'Yes, yes, oh yes, please! Can we really? What is it?'

Lando took a cloth off a large, wrapped present and beckoned the twins over to open it. They needed little encouragement to rip off the coloured paper and screamed with delight when they saw what it concealed.

'A sledge, oh, it's a sledge!'

'That's amazing,' I said, going over to look at the beautiful wooden sledge with its elegantly scrolled runners and padded velvet seats. It was painted bright red, with glittery green holly leaf details. 'You didn't – did you *make* it?'

Lando tried and failed to look modest.

'I did. It's my first attempt at something like this, so I hope it works okay. If it does, I'm thinking about making them to sell next year. We usually get enough snow round here to make it worthwhile.'

We lifted the sledge carefully out into the snow and loaded it up with the wrapped wooden figures, then gave it a tug. It slid along joyfully, as if it were pleased finally to be fulfilling its purpose in life. Looking across at Lando chatting and laughing with the children, I knew exactly how it felt.

The vicar, Richard was waiting with his wife, Molly, at the church.

'Welcome, all of you,' he said, ushering us inside. 'Come on in, it's beautiful out there but freezing, and we can't wait to see the Nativity.'

'We've put the old one away,' said Molly, giving the twins a hug and letting them have a peep at the sleeping baby snug in a sling on her front. 'Apart from the regrettable paint job, it had been rather nibbled by woodworm and mice, so it was definitely time to retire it.'

'I have put protectant on these,' said Lando, as Richard gave him a hand to carry the laden sleigh into the church, 'but it'll need doing again every so often. I've written down instructions.'

'Good job,' said the vicar, 'with you moving away to Greece. You won't be here to advise us.'

'Well, actually,' said Lando, 'I've decided to stick around for a bit longer, so maybe I can do it for you.'

Richard's experienced eyes didn't miss Lando and me beaming goofily at each other and he squeezed my shoulder and patted Lando heartily on the back.

'Wonderful, wonderful. I'm glad to see a bit of Christmas magic still doing its work. Now, here's the stable, that's okay as you know. Shall we start setting it up?'

The six of us carefully unwrapped each beautiful figure and set it in place, then stood back to admire our work. Tears sprang to my eyes, and as I glanced around, I saw that everyone was looking rather misty as we gazed upon the lovely, moving art that Lando had produced. He reached for my hand and squeezed it, but I also felt like pinching myself, so impossible was it to take in the fact that my dreams had come true.

TWENTY-SIX

NINE MONTHS LATER

It was the most glorious day for a wedding, clear and bright with that slight autumnal nip in the air that gives you an excuse to wrap up in a warm but still glamorous pashmina. Mine was a rich emerald green, which sat beautifully against the coppery russet of my silk dress. As Lando and I walked into the church, I remembered the Christmas before, gathered around the Nativity with the twins and thinking how purely happy I was. The time in between then and now had only cemented that happiness. I had handed my notice in but decided to see out the school year rather than doing anything in a rush. It had taken Lando and I so long to find one another, and now that everything was so perfect between us, what was the point in hurrying? I had finally learnt not to push for my happy ending, but to let it come to me. We had split our time between my little house and Lando's not-so-little house and found ourselves equally happy in both, but since the end of term in July, I had put mine on the market and moved down to Dorset permanently. For now, anyway. Who knew where life might blow us in the future?

'I'll see you later, darling,' said Lando, kissing me. 'I'd better

make sure Xander has got the orders of service properly in hand
before I go back to the house to collect Dad.'

'Perfect. I only wanted to check that the flowers were all in
place, so I'm going straight to the Curious Badger. I'm sure
Daphne is as cool as a cucumber about everything, but I said
we'd walk to the church together, along with her sister.'

Daphne made the most stunning bride. Having shunned white
('I really don't think anyone's going to believe that, do you?') she
had chosen to wear an elegant ensemble of a deep cream, knee-
length dress with a long, hot pink jacket over the top, embroidered with colourful birds and flowers.

'William won't know what to do with himself,' I said, as we
walked the short distance from the pub to the church.

'Oh, I shouldn't worry about *that*, dear girl,' said Daphne,
her eyes twinkling. 'You know as well as I do that these Lord
men aren't half as clueless as they'd like to make out.'

She had chosen to walk down the aisle alone, so her sister
and I left her at the door for a few final words with Richard, the
vicar, and went to find our seats. I squeezed on to the end of a
pew with Bunny and her now very large family. I kissed and
hugged them all warmly, delighted to see everyone but maybe
in particular my new little god-twins Cressida and Aurelius,
now three months old and as golden as the meaning of their
names.

'Cress did a poop in her nappy just as we were coming into
the church,' giggled Phina, snuggling up to me and slipping her
little hand into mine. 'Daddy had to go and change it in the
vesty.'

'Do you mean the vestry?'

'I don't know, but it sounded like somewhere the vicar puts
his vest on.' She giggled again, and I couldn't help joining in. I
was so firmly part of the family now and loving every second of

it. She was about to whisper something else to me, doubtless another tale of the babies' misdemeanours, when the organ struck up with 'The Entry of the Queen of Sheba' and we all stood and turned to watch. Daphne was wonderful walking down the aisle, radiating happiness, and I sneaked a look at William watching her, his face a picture of joy and wonder. Lando and Ben, standing on either side of him, looked as pleased and proud as if it were their own son getting married.

As the service started, I sneaked a look around at the other members of the congregation, many of them quite familiar to me now I was living in the village, including dear Lavinia, who gave me a grin and a little wave. And there was Xander, who had come to the wedding without a date and without even the expectation of a clinch with a bridesmaid at the reception, as there were no bridesmaids.

'Is he still a reformed character?' I muttered to Bunny, as we shuffled to our feet for the first hymn.

'Pixie, it's remarkable. If Zara wasn't so ghastly, and hadn't upset darling Lando so much, I'd be tempted to write and thank her.'

'I suppose so,' I replied, unwilling to give her any credit. 'It wasn't deliberate on her part, though. She broke his heart without any compunction.'

'I know.' She looked over sadly at her brother, stumbling his way through the words of the hymn she and I had given up on. 'Poor darling Xander was so utterly besotted with her, goodness knows why, and I think he surprised himself more than the rest of us by actually planning a proposal. He really thought she was the one.'

Until, I thought, *she decided that his boss, twenty years her senior and about ten times as rich as him, was more likely to be The One for her.*

I did feel sorry for him, drooping slightly in his pew as all around him we celebrated love, but I had a feeling that he wouldn't be down for long.

After the service was over, most of the guests started wandering back to the house for the reception, whilst some of us stayed behind for the photos. The babies were fast asleep in their pram, tucked into each other like baby mice, while Phina and Caspy were collecting up as many little pieces of confetti as they could stuff in their pockets. I watched with Bunny while the photographer organised various shots.

'I'm so glad you made me their godmother,' I said, gazing into the pram. 'They're so beautiful.'

'Especially when they're asleep,' she replied, but smiled down on them adoringly.

'Actually,' I said, my heart picking up pace a bit, 'there was something I wanted to ask you... if, in about six months' time, you might return the favour?'

Her scream of joy caused everyone to stare at us as she threw her arms around me, and we hugged tightly. I grinned at Lando over her shoulder, and he laughed.

'I'll tell Dad and Daphne as well, shall I?' he called over, and I nodded as we shared the happy news of our next big adventure with the family.

A LETTER FROM THE AUTHOR

Dear Reader,

Huge thanks for reading *Christmas with the Lords*. I hope you loved going on Penny's journey with her as much as I loved writing about it. If you want to join other readers in hearing all about my new releases and bonus content, you can sign up here:

www.stormpublishing.co/hannah-langdon

If you enjoyed this book and could spare a few moments to leave a review that would be hugely appreciated. Even a short review can make all the difference in encouraging a reader to discover my books for the first time. Thank you so much!

I wrote this book during the Covid pandemic, and it offered me a welcome respite from everything that was happening. I could leave behind the daily news bulletins, the stresses of teaching and all the other associated worries and disappear off with Penny to Lando's idyllic country house. Although the world has opened up again for many of us, I do hope that you get the same pleasure from leafing through *Vogue* with Bunny, breathing in the woody air of Lando's workshop and sharing a drink or two with William.

Thanks again for being part of this amazing journey with me and I hope you'll stay in touch – I have so many more stories, characters and ideas to share with you.

HANNAH LANGDON

- facebook.com/hannahlangdonwrites
- x.com/hmvlangdon
- instagram.com/hannahlangdonwrites

ACKNOWLEDGEMENTS

When you write a book, it is a solitary process for many months: just you and your characters happy inside your head. Then comes the scary part: showing people. At first this is probably friends and family, followed by – if you're lucky – helpful professional eyes. The next stage is the most terrifying, and the most demoralising, as you start sending out to editors and agents, praying that your precious story finds its way into the hands of someone who loves it and 'gets' it. Which *Christmas with the Lords* eventually did. So, from sitting on my own typing away during what was for me as a teacher and mum a very busy pandemic, to the book you are holding today, there are many people to whom I am grateful for helping me realise this very long held dream.

I must go back fifteen years for my first thank yous, to an adult education class in Richmond where, we were assured, if we followed the rules, we could produce a novel in a month. There I met my dear friend Lisa, who has always been an encourager and cheerleader for me, as well as the tutor and author Sara Bailey who led the course and taught me the technique which has been my go-to ever since: put your fingers on your keyboard and just *write*. You can agonise over the details when you have a finished novel in front of you. I did indeed finish that novel in a month, and although it wasn't publication standard, I now had the tools and the confidence to keep trying.

Fast forward a decade and a half and my next thank you, to Kathryn Taussig, my wonderful editor. She has both championed my book and steered it gently to make it the best version it could be. I have learnt so much from her and am so lucky to benefit from her professionalism, experience and encouragement.

Everyone at Storm Publishing has been so helpful and supportive which, for someone brand-new to the industry, has been invaluable. Oliver Rhodes personally ensured that I understood every step of the process and contract, for which I was extremely grateful. Sincere thanks also to Alexandra Holmes, Naomi Knox, Amanda Rutter and Catherine Lenderi for their meticulous work during the editing process; Anna McKerrow, Chris Lucraft and Elke Desanghere for their marketing and digital expertise; Tamsin Kennard for her wonderful narration of the audiobook and all at Audio Factory for helping my words come off the page. Finally, thank to Eileen Carey for her utterly gorgeous cover design. I want to spend Christmas there myself! What a lovely publishing 'family' to be part of.

I joined the New Writers' Scheme of the Romantic Novelists' Association three years ago, and it is through this that I was given the feedback, advice and confidence to keep writing and submitting. The RNA is unique in its offer of support, education and community and I am proud now to be a full member. I look forward to the time when I can give something in return for everything they have done for me.

Asking someone else to read your book for the first time is daunting, and my thanks go to my early readers – Sarah, Kathy, Cynthia, Gwen and Emily – for their overwhelming positivity and kind, constructive criticism. You are all busy women and the time you gave me was greatly appreciated.

Although my dad is no longer with us, his unstinting belief in me has lived on. He would have been so pleased to see me published, and I know he is beaming with pride from some

Elysian field which is as idyllic as any setting in a romantic novel.

And thank you, Mum – although where do I start? If there was ever an embodiment of a 'can do' attitude, it is you. Through all the noise, work and exhaustion, I always hear your voice telling me to keep going, that I *always* have a choice and that there's always a way. And thank you for the hours of child-care, the practical aspect of making things possible.

My final thanks go to John and Rose, who are everything. You have given me a true understanding of Happy Ever After.